W9-ANJ-390

WILDERNESS

WILDERNESS

BY

ROGER ZELAZNY

AND

GERALD HAUSMAN

A TOM DOHERTY ASSOCIATES BOOK

NEW YORK

WILDERNESS

A Forge Book
Published by Tom Doherty Associates, Inc.
175 Fifth Avenue
New York, N.Y. 10010

Interior illustrations by Mariah Fox Hausman

Designed by Ann Gold

Library of Congress Cataloging-in-Publication Data
Hausman, Gerald.
Wilderness / Gerald Hausman and Roger Zelazny.
    p.   cm.
ISBN 0-312-85654-7 (hardcover) : $21.95
1. Frontier and pioneer life—West (U.S.)—Fiction.   2. Wilderness survival—West (U.S.)—Fiction.   3. Colter, John, ca. 1775–1813—Fiction.   4. Glass, Hugh, ca. 1780–1833—Fiction.   5. Trappers—West (U.S.)—Fiction.   6. Hunters—West (U.S.)—Fiction.
        I. Zelazny, Roger.   II. Title.
        PS3558.A76W55   1994
    813'.54—dc20   93-43247
                CIP

First edition: February 1994

Printed in the United States of America

0 9 8 7 6 5 4 3 2 1

Grateful acknowledgment
is made to John G. Neihardt,
Burton Harris, and Fred Maas

"... the wilderness gave it to me
and the wilderness will not let it go."

—Carl Sandberg

ONE

COLTER

In 1808 a mountain man named John Colter ran one hundred and fifty miles, half-naked, while pursued by several hundred Blackfoot warriors.

Three Forks, Autumn 1808

John Colter, the man the Crows had nicknamed Seek-heeda, White Eyebrows, knew that he was in a tight spot. Why else would the little hairs at the back of his neck stand straight?

He craned his neck, listened. Downstream, the wren that only moments before had been trilling in the choke-cherries, stopped in midsong.

Perhaps, he thought, I have gone too far.

This was saying a lot for John Colter, the man who had hunted and blazed trails for Lewis and Clark. The man, who, it was said, had gone farther into the unexplored mountains of the Western Rockies than any man alive. He had single-handedly discovered the stinking springs of Yellowstone, the place the old-timers were now calling Colter's Hell and the year before, along with a small band of Flatheads and Crows, he'd almost been killed in these dark thickets. The Blackfeet had pinned them down and pummeled them. Colter took a lead ball in his right leg and had to limp back to camp. But he was alive—though, now, he wasn't exactly sure why.

Just behind Colter, in the river where the two men had set their beaver traps, was his friend, John Potts. He could hear him, clunking around. Far off in the hazy depths of the firs, he heard a magpie's comic shriek, but it was suddenly cut off. Potts didn't hear it, or if he did, wasn't much impressed, for he continued clunking.

Colter, sensing danger, came out of the copse of willow where he had been listening.

It came like muffled thunder from the ridge above the fir tops.

"Buffler?" Potts called dreamily from the stream.

Colter didn't bother to answer.

He saw them pouring down the ravine, maybe a thousand Blackfoot runners—perhaps the whole tribe. In a couple minutes, he and Potts were surrounded.

"Will ye look how many warriors come t'fetch ol' Seekheeda's head?" Potts remarked, dismally.

Then, as a hundred bows were raised at him, Potts stubbornly reached for his rifle. There was a singing of feathers, Potts sagged to his knees, stumbled, said: "John, I'm dead," and dropped into the stream without another word.

Colter knew what would come next. He surveyed the faces, the hawk-feathers dancing in the sunlight, the black rivers of loose hair, the old, the tired and the new men cleanly arrayed in deerskin and trader's cloth, blanketed and banded and breech-clouted. There were, indeed, a lot of them. Not as many as he had first feared, but what did it matter. There were certainly enough to torture him to death, which was what he knew they were going to do.

The man who stepped forward looked like a shaman. His hair was pulled into a topknot on his head. On the crest of the topknot was a raven's head that bobbed when the man moved. He had the usual scarification—loops and ridges across his naked chest, whorls of knife-point artistry.

Colter held perfectly still as the shaman's knife played upon his own deer pants and shirt. A few simple swipes of the blade and Colter felt the cool autumn air on his skin. The shaman had shorn him of clothes, but left him a semblance of breech-clout at the groin: the shortened remains of his pants. To Colter this was a clue to his survival. Leaving him his dignity meant that something out of the ordinary was about to happen.

In the Crow tongue, the shaman asked Colter if he could run.

Colter shook his head.

Then the man took a slice of Colter's breast muscle. A small flap of skin came loose, and with it a gush of blood. There was an astonished sound, the release of many breaths, among the gathered men. Then voices raised in wonder.

"I have blood," Colter said in Crow, "just like you."

"I see," the shaman said, but his eyes made no reference to it.

"You will run," he said.

"When?" Colter asked.

"Now," the man said, "go, now!"

The feather-haired men, knowing the race was about

to begin, fanned back, making room, as Colter leaned forward and began to sprint. His speed, even at the outset, surprised him. He dashed like a yellow deer out into the white meadow beside the river where his friend lay dead.

Colter was eighty yards out when he heard the simultaneous thud of blankets being thrown to the ground and the flapping of buckskin as the runners removed their leggings. He was two hundred yards out when the ground seemed to tremble with the footfalls of the warriors. He dared not turn, for it would slow him down. Instead, he opened his stride so much that, in effect, he was running to keep up with his feet. Colter knew the foolishness of it all: The longer he ran, the longer the Blackfeet would torture him once they caught him. This was a principle of honor, not a gesture of evil.

But surely, he thought, I cannot hope to keep up such a pace.

Yet a part of him thought that he could; the wild man, who on a dare, had traveled five hundred miles, alone, in the middle of winter. Hustling through the jumbled and tumbled, snow-riven peaks carrying a pack of awls, beads, vermilion, needles, knives and tobacco to trade with the tribes. Running against the Mandan, Hidatsa and Absarokas, he'd often come out the winner. The previous winter, however, his friend Edward Rose had not been so lucky: He'd lost most of his nose, bitten off in a brawl, and his forehead bore the ugly brand where a warrior had burned him with a flaming pine knot. It was Rose who had shown Colter how to run barefoot, how to feign a limp like a hurt rabbit, and then, when the other runner sought to pass, break his spirit with a long, powerful stride.

Colter's passion for privation was already legend. A scribe with Lewis and Clark called him "the double of Daniel Boone." Colter snorted at the thought of it. If double to anyone, it was Micajah, his Scotch grandfather from Ireland, who, back in Stuart's Draft, Virginia, had given the faith that when you salted a bird's tail, you could always catch him. The birds, Micajah said, were no less his own kind than the bears, the wolves, or the native Indians.

He felt it rising higher in his chest, the burn. The first sign of exhaustion. His feet were covered with the silver fur of prickly pear spines, which lay about the dry meadow grass. The thunder behind him had begun to soften, so that he heard the rivers of feet resounding far away, punctuated, every so often, by the runners nearest him. These were the fastest. He chanced a quick over-the-shoulder glance, saw three lean men just behind. Then, back of them, a tawny cloud of sun-smoke, the seven hundred. He had, anyway, put some space between himself and the greater number of the tribe. But, as he well knew, even this could be a trick. Sometimes they sent the sprinters out first. This way, like wolves on a hunt, when the fastest fell back, the deer was too tired to outrun the rest of the pack.

Colter knew that to outlast the pain, he must drive the leanest, hard-muscled men into the ground, must make them think, always, that he had more in him than they had. Usually in a race, he'd come behind the front runner, taking advantage of his wind drag. Then, when the time came, he took him out, smoking past him like a brush fire from Hell. Once in the lead, Colter augmented his hellish pace, upgrading it into a vicious sprint. This would go on for half a mile or more, as long as it took to grind down the bones of his pursuer. As long as he'd lived, he'd won. Meriwether Lewis once said of him, "Colter's never had to draw a second wind. Maybe he hasn't got one."

But here on the Jefferson Fork, running for his life, John Colter had no choice. It was the second wind, or the wind of death. He was a mile into it, keeping his lead of about a hundred yards. The three were not going to break, Colter knew that now. They were elbow to elbow, running like antelope. He saw them, or imagined he did, in back of his head: the sinewy grace, the Indian stride that knows no end.

He, on the other hand, was well ahead—but not by the margin he required to break their pursuit, or their spirit. They were coming on hard, and they knew it, but they would wait for the right time to press him. Right now, they were studying his shoulders and back, searching his legs for any weakness, any small faltering move. Colter, desperately in need of a trick, felt his fading stamina, the metal taste in his mouth, the bell of his heart, the burn boiling up in his chest. He was, he knew, going much too fast. Yet he could not slow down and still hope to live. If anything, he had to work the runners harder, push them out of that long-legged Indian lope, make them know he wasn't going to tire.

From a Mandan runner he once learned the trick of fixing the eye on a distant ridge, keeping it there until all else shrank from view. The fusion of leafy gold, the great cottonwoods by the river juncture, now became Colter's compass. On these huge overarching trees, he merged his mind, and the fire of their October leaves became the sole content of his brain. Thus focused, he forged on with renewed speed.

The warriors noticed Colter's fresh-seeming gait. From where they ran, their bodies shining with sweat, they saw the tall white man beginning to gain ground. A moment before, the lead man thought they were going to close the distance: Colter looked tired, his shoulders were starting to sag. But now this one saw there was more fight in him than he supposed. Colter had stepped up into a second-winded sprint of madness. He was actually pulling ahead.

The lead man, so as not to lose him, opened his stride. And his companions, hanging doggedly at his elbow, started to fade.

No man can run that way for long, the lead told himself.

Colter, five hundred yards in front, heard weapons clatter to the ground. Lances, bows, long rifles were now being discarded as the runners lightened their load.

Good, he thought, I am hurting them.

His own pain was turning into nausea, but it gave Colter satisfaction to know that he was forcing them to throw down the very weapons they would require to kill him.

Far into the second mile, Colter felt something quake down in his right ankle. He remembered the old, telltale bone-break, the crashing bullet—gift of the same tribesmen who intended to catch him today. The twice-fractured bone had not fully mended; it sent a sudden warning through his whole system. Slow down. But that wasn't what Colter had in mind. The gold fusion of leaves was a fire in his brain, and his body—poor broken thing—was not his anymore. The feet, silver-furred in bristles of cactus, were not his. Neither was the cracked ankle, nor the nose that was beginning to bleed, nor the throat turning to dust of chalk. His failing limbs were not his. Only the golden bower of leaves belonged to him. To him and him alone.

Suddenly, he stumbled and fell. Dive-rolled off his right shoulder, pivoted, caught his balance, faltered clumsily to his feet. The yardage he'd gained was now lost. He saw the blurred form of the lead man coming on him, strong and fast. Cursing the musket ball that had shattered his ankle, Colter got back into his old gait. But it was not the same. There was a hobble to it, a painful unevenness, which would spread out like rings in a pool to his entire body. The new stride was short and ragged, and punished the hurt foot.

Behind him the wolf-eyed men took notice of the limp—the long-gaited one in front, the two slightly to his right, increased their speed. The big elk had gone down, they'd seen it, the blood-song rang loud in their ears: He was theirs.

But Colter still held something of a sprint, only now he ran softer in the knees, cushioning the old bone-break, flat in the feet, leaning forward as the Mandans had taught him, with the wind between his shoulder blades. Urging his body beyond the boundary of pain, he now came to that isolate spot, that other country, that sanctuary where time stopped and things took on a different light.

Perhaps he was not aware of the lightning bolt that cracked in his cranium, the gout of blood that came from his nose. Fountaining down his face, across his chest. The sudden drumming in his ears was now worse than the agony around his heart, the anvil sitting on his breastbone.

The blood coursed, and so did Colter, trailing rags of red spit in the wind. The Blackfeet saw it, wondered at it, threw themselves into the run. Soon, soon, said their feet. Colter tasted the sweet salt of his own blood, and maybe it gave him courage and maybe it did not, for now he was coming deep into that other country where the mind knows no master. The gold trees gone, the sun gone—the winter bare trees opened upon him like frozen skeletons, encircling him. And although his stride dwindled in the sapping sun of autumn, he danced the skeleton dance of death with winter trees, flew up and over his captors, a cawing raven with black-silver wings.

He imagined himself flying. His legs, insensate, rolling futilely under him, were the great Missouri, unmindful of the man that rode above them. Then he was with Clark and Drouillard, pulling a monster catfish out of the river. Big enough to swallow a child, the thing was better than six feet long with whiskers like buggy-whips. Colter was swimming now in the deep clear stream of his own consciousness, awake, but somehow, unalive. He could feel the river and the Missouri cat flowing under him. Then he heard the bright cackles of laughter of the Mandan devil children. The little reddish bastards that lived in the mount of an ant-hill outside the village. He'd seen them, after hearing the winter stories of what they would do to a man, and he knew they had it in for him. Giggling in his ear, they nipped him with their pointy little fangs, banging the back of his head with their war clubs.

He chuckled. He knew why the devils had come. That

place, that foul place, they'd named after him. Colter's Hell. That purple place for dying. Gut-spilling, earth-entrail, steam factory, hellhole nightmare—he wished he'd never discovered it, gone into it. Only one tribe of mad Indians lived there, the dog Indians, squatting raggedly in the dim and steamy shadows, pounding roots and cooking them on hot stones. Colter had reached into the anthill when the Mandans told him not to, and, against the wishes of the Crow, he'd gone into the purple dying place to meet the dog Indians, to share their bitter tubers, steep himself in their boiling baths.

He woke then, found himself stretched out on his back, rolling around crazily. His captors, all three of them, had caught up to him, were standing amazed, watching. For a moment, he floated out of his dream and saw follies of purplish steam, phantoms of crimson mist. Then the cold clarity of reason struck him. His groping fingers clawed free of the dream of death, his elbows propped him upright. Under his palms Colter felt the grassy flanks of the Jefferson Fork. Looking up, a flock of redwing blackbirds, clicking and chucking to one another in the sun-struck parapet of cottonwood leaves over his head.

—Good God, he thought, I've made it.

Then the fuzzy edges of the death-dream vanished and he was solidly there, back in the world. And the warrior wolves who'd come for him were there, surrounding him, watching, waiting. Their knives glinted in the sun, the air was full of their panting. Colter fumbled in the dead grass for something with which to defend himself. A stick, a stone, anything. But there was nothing. He took up two handfuls of dry, gray grass. The warriors, thinking he was going to throw something at them, took a step back. But Colter roared with laughter, spat a mouthful of blood on the lead wolf, threw the sprinkling of snowy grass at the sky, and danced as the devils had told him to, a groggy little pirouette, brittle and barely human, the antic twirl of a lunatic. The blood rained the air as he spat and the Blackfeet jumped back, shearing the air with their knives.

As he came out of the last enfeebled curve, Colter suddenly stood up straight. A small smile crept across his blood-caked lips. He put his feet together, turned his palms out, gave the Crow sign of greeting.

The Blackfeet shared glances, stepped back again, hesitant. This was not for them, they seemed to be saying. This was for the medicine man, for clearly, this one was mad. He had run himself out, killed his own head. The crazy runner was now a crazy ghost, a dead man standing tall.

Again, they backed up.

Colter came forward, giving the greeting sign.

The ground trembled with the coming thunder of the tribe. The sky was yellow with dust from their feet. They were but three hundred yards off, a furious cauldron of footwork and dust.

Like a dancer Colter wheeled into the air, kicked his feet like a mountain ram. The three Blackfeet threw themselves backward, tripping over themselves to get out of his way. As he came out of the dervish-twirl, Colter hooked his feet into the earth and sprang forward, running for the sandy rivershore. It was only a few feet away from them and when he struck it, diving cleanly into the molten tapestry of fallen leaves, his body cleaved the surface and disappeared.

He streaked through the greenish gloom. The icy autumn water was fire on his skin, but he didn't feel it, he flashed through it, kicking powerfully.

By the time he had broken the surface of the Fork, the three Blackfeet had run to the riverbank. Within a few minutes, while they splashed around looking for Colter, the others began to draw up, one after another, breathless. Heavy breathing and hoarse shouts followed, and one by one, the tribe materialized by the bank of the slow-moving stream.

Meanwhile, a hundred yards downstream, Colter took a gulp of air, and dived again. He knew the river well, knew where it lay flat, knew where the current built into falls, spilled down to sawyers and beaver dams. He streaked, shadowlike, over the sand. Silver-bellies, fast as darts, shot away at his approach, while the big drowsy mudcats woggled out of his way, wondering what he was.

The river was an open book. Here, the current altered, dozing on a snag. There, it whipped up into a maze of fast-moving marbles. Here, the bottom was brown, there, gray or tan with smooth granulated seepage sand. Then out into the big-banked, open-rivered run where the underwater weeds lay flat like a woman's hair in the wind.

I am nearing, thought Colter, the place where the big sawyers are lodged. The place where whole, bark-stripped cottonwoods lie jammed and sunken. Clogged into an elbow of the Fork, he remembered.

And remembered well. The river, in an otter's game of chasing its own tail, made a deep, blue-green pool. The sawyers, the things most feared by exploring rivermen on their barge-rafts, made a tumbled-up prison of logs, which,

with no warning, would spring free, booming to the surface, crushing a raft like a matchstick. The sawyers. Colter
knew them from his river days with Meriwether Lewis. The
very devils of disaster. Walk on one, like a sprung trap, it
would come out of the depths like a whale and roll, until,
its fury spent, the thing sank down of its own water-logged
weight, down into the depths.

Colter once watched a sawyer pitch a man fifteen feet
into the air. As the man came down between two rolling
logs, his leg was bitten off at the knee. So intertwined were
the sawyers that they depended upon each other, as well as
the river, for equilibrium. And he came now into this place
of the big logs, while just behind him the Blackfeet runners
appeared, pouring over and into the riverbank, some swimming, some running, all of them swarming the river. Those
who still carried lances used them to plumb the river, shaft-
ing them into the mud along the banks, hoping to find soft
flesh.

But in the trigger-sprung trap of the sawyers, hunter
and hunted were equal prey. Colter knew this, and dived
for the bottom. Working his way down a slippery log, he
found what he wanted. A large burl. Sometimes, when the
giant trees were alive and rooted to the earth, these bulges
were home to the carpenter ant. The ants bore secret tun-
nels through the heart of the tree, nearly from tip to taproot.
If such were the case, Colter might find a breathing hole.
Taking a chance, he forced the last of his air out of his lungs
into the mouth of the burl, and took a great trusting draft of
whatever was in there—

—Air, life-giving air, came into his lungs!

He could breathe, ten feet down in the dark green of the river, arms hugging a barkless log, he could draw oxygen into his lungs, and while the Blackfeet looked for him, remain, for the moment, unseen.

T W O

GLASS

In 1823 an injured hunter named Hugh Glass crawled over one hundred miles through the wilderness from the Grand Valley to the Missouri River.

Grand River, Autumn 1823

Hugh Glass had one chance to kill the bear, and whether his shot struck it or went completely astray, he never knew. It charged him, brushing aside the rifle before he could club with it as its paw fell upon his face, smashing his nose, tearing through the skin of his brow. Then its great fore-limbs came about him, its breath awful, fetid with ripe flesh and the musky smell of skunk, overlaid with a sweetness of berries and honey that made him think of a waiting, per-fumed corpse, too long above ground while distant mourn-ers hurried for the viewing.

His spirit seemed to turn slowly within his head and breast, a white and gray eddy of dissolving perceptions, as his blood ran into his eyes and traced trails down his seamed face into his frosted beard. A large man, bearlike himself in the eyes of his fellows, he did not cry out, did not know fear; a great gasp had wrung much of the air from him, leaving him voiceless, and the attack had come so quickly that there had been no time to be afraid. Now, what he felt seemed familiar, for he was a hunter, providing game for eighty men, dealing daily death as a business of life. And it was suddenly his turn. It would have been good to say farewell to Jamie, but there are always things undone. The cracking of his ribs was not such a terrible thing through the failing white and the gray; the sound from his thigh might have been a snapping branch in some distant forest. He was no longer there to feel the ground as he crashed against it.

Riding, echoes of his mount's hoofbeats off the hills about him, Jamie saw the shadows flow and merge as he sought downhill for his friend, sky of blood and flame and roses to his left whenever he topped a rise. He could smell the Grand River ahead and to his right. The old man hunted these breaks, was probably camping near here tonight.

"Hugh?" he called. "Hugh?" And a part of his voice rolled back to him.

He continued into the northwest toward the fork, calling periodically.

At the top of another hill the horse stopped short, neighing briefly. For a great distance toward evening the flatlands stretched before him. Below, on either hand, the Grand forked, sparkling, crooked, through haze. He rose in the stirrups, staring, brushed a hand through his sun-gilt hair.

Nothing stirred but the river, and then a rising as of

ashes far ahead, with a cawing. A single star was lit above the sunset. A faint breeze came to him from the direction of the water. He called again.

The horse made another sound, took a little prancing step. Jamie touched his mount's sides lightly and headed down the hill, the horse's hoofs clattering in the shale. Level again, on firmer ground, he hurried.

"Camping . . ." he said softly, and after a time he called again.

There came the boom of a rifle from somewhere ahead, and he smiled.

". . . Heard me," he said, and he shook the reins, laughing. His mount hurried and Jamie hummed a tune to the sound of the hoofbeats.

And there, in the grassy area ahead, a figure rose, arms spread. Waving . . . ? The horse snorted and reared, tried to turn. It wasn't a man. Too big, too. . . .

His mount wheeled, but not before Jamie had spied the broken heap upon the ground, recognized the shaggy totem shape—beast that walks like a man—that swayed above it. His hand fell to the rifle boot even as the horse bolted. Cursing, he drew back hard upon the reins but there was no response. At his back, he heard a crashing of brush as the great beast fell to pursuit.

Then he drew again upon the bit and sank his spur into the horse's side. This time it swerved, obedient, to the right. The bear rushed by, passing behind him, and Jamie headed for the water, striking sand, then raising a shower of spray as he entered.

The stream was not wide here. Scrambling, scrabbling, the horse protested the rocky bottom, but a growl from the rear seemed to add impetus to its flight. Shortly, they were rising, dripping, from the water, mounting the farther bank.

Looking back, Jamie saw that the bear had halted at the water's edge. His hand went to the buckle on the rifle case, and he turned his mount as he drew the weapon. Still dry.

He swung it through an arc, cross-body, rested it a moment on his forearm, squeezed the trigger.

Through the smoke-spume, he saw the bear lurch forward, fall into the stream, tossing. He watched its death throes, recalling Hugh's instruction on the placing of shots. Immediately, his eyes were clouded for the man who'd raised him like a son.

Shortly, he was back in the water, crossing. He rode to the fallen man and dismounted.

"Hugh," he said, "I'm sorry," and he knelt beside him. He turned his friend's head then to look upon his face, and he gasped at the mass of blood and torn flesh he beheld, nose smashed flat, brows shredded. "Hugh. . . ."

How long he watched he was not certain. Then there came a soft moan.

He leaned forward, not sure of what he had heard. There followed a terrible stillness. Then came a catching of breath, another moan, a slow movement.

"Hugh? It's Jamie here," he said. "Can you hear me?"

The man made a small noise deep in his throat, lay still again. Jamie looked about. Hugh had made his camp near a spring, its trickling sounds half-noticed till now. A pile of sticks and branches lay near at hand.

"I'm going to make you a fire, Hugh. Got to keep you warm. You just rest easy now. I'll go do that."

Drawing his knife, he split wood. He built a heap of shavings and twigs near the still form, brought it to a flame, fed it, dragged over the larger branches, added more fuel. The sun had fallen over the world's edge by then, and the stars came on like a city in the sky. Jamie hunkered by his fallen companion, the older man's face even more ghastly and masklike by firelight.

"Oh my," he said. "Next thing we'd better do is get you cleaned up some."

He made his way to the spring, dipped his kerchief into the water, wrung it out. Returning, he sponged and blotted Hugh's face.

"I remember the day you saved my ass in that fight with the Ree," he muttered. "What was I—fourteen? Folks dead, I rode right out into it. You came after. Killed a few and brought me back. Whaled me later for not knowing enough to be afraid. God—Hugh! Don't die on me!"

Hugh Glass lay very still.

"It's me—Jamie!" he cried, catching up a still hand and clasping it to his breast.

But he felt no life in the hand and he laid it back down gently. He returned to the spring and rinsed his kerchief. He tried trickling water into Hugh's mouth, but it just ran down his face into his beard.

"... Jamie," he said, listening for a heartbeat. Was that it? Soft as an underground stream? He washed the face again. He added kindling to the fire.

Later, the moon came up. In the distance, a wolf howled. Hugh gasped and moaned. Jamie touched his hand again, began speaking softly, of their days on the trail, places they'd been, things they'd seen and done. After a time, his eyes closed. Shortly, his words ceased and he moved in dreams.

. . . Riding the keelboats with Major Henry's men, trading for horses in the Ree villages. He saw again the Leavenworth campaign amid flashes of fire. . . . Spring thaws and winter freezes. . . . Dressing game with Hugh. . . . Sleeping on the trail, smell of horses, smell of earth. . . . And storms, and the passing of bison. . . . In the distance, his parents' faces. . . .

The neighing of a horse. His head jerked and he realized that his back and shoulders were sore, his neck. . . . He sprawled, dozing again, dreaming of the vast prairie in its moods.

. . . And Hugh's dreams were pain-shot archipelagos of darkness and fire, though it seemed he was not alone in his hurting. He felt he had talked to another, though he was not certain his tongue and lips had really worked. It seemed he had grown roots, extending deep down into the earth, and like a stubborn shrub he held himself to it against a turmoil of weathers, drawing nourishment up into his damaged limbs.

. . . And a horse neighed, and the ground shook. Jamie opened his eyes and the world was full of morning light. His horse stood nearby. In the earth, he felt the vibrations of horses' hoofs. He shook his head, rubbed his eyes with the heels of his hands, sat up. Memories returned as he ran his fingers through his hair. He regarded Hugh, whose head now lolled to one side and whose chest moved very slowly.

The hoofbeats were audible now. Hoping it was not a party of Rickaree, he rose to his feet, turning in the direction of the sound.

No, it wasn't the Ree, but rather Major Henry and his men, come riding into the valley from out of the east. They called and waved when they saw him there, grew still as they approached and looked upon the fallen form of Hugh.

"Jamie, what happened?" Major Henry called out, dismounting and coming near.

"Hugh got mauled by a bear," Jamie replied. "He's in poor shape."

"Damn!" the major said, kneeling and placing his hand on Hugh's chest. "Looks a sight, too."

The others came down from their mounts and moved near.

"We should take him back to the camp, get him more comfortable," one of the scouts said.

". . . And get some medicine into him," said another.

"Bring up that bay pack horse," the major called out.

"I'm not sure Hugh should be moved," Jamie said.

"We owe the man every chance we can give him," came the reply.

As the bay was brought up and its pack removed, Frank and Will—the red-haired brothers from St. Louis—stooped at Hugh's head and feet, taking hold of his shoulders and ankles. They commenced raising him, slowly, from the earth.

Hugh moaned then—awful, bleating, animal-like sound. Frank and Will lowered him again.

"Ain't no way we're going to move that man 'thout killing him," Frank stated.

"I think he's bound to die, anyway," Will said. "No reason to add to his misery."

"Poor Hugh ain't got long," Frank agreed. "Let's let him be."

Major Henry shook his head and put his arm around Jamie's shoulders.

"I think the men are right," he said softly.

Jamie nodded.

"We'll wait a time," the major told him. "In case it happens soon."

And Hugh lay like a corpse, save for a periodic sigh, a groan, as the day warmed. The men made tea, and, seated in circles on the ground, conversed more softly than was their custom, of the trails they followed toward the Big Horn, of the recent campaign against the Ree, of Indian activity in the area. Some went off to seek the remains of the bear, to butcher it for its meat.

And Hugh's face darkened and lightened, in token of the struggle in which there can be no ally. His hands twitched as if seeking to grapple; and for a time he breathed deeply, a glassy mask of sweat upon his features. Jamie bathed his face again.

"Soon, lad. Soon, I fear," the major told him; and Jamie nodded, sat, and watched.

And birds sang, and the day continued to warm as the sun rose higher in the heavens. Still Hugh gasped, and saliva trickled from the corner of his mouth; his fingers dug furrows in the earth.

When the sun stood in high heaven, Major Henry moved to study the fallen man. He stared for a long while, then turned to Jamie.

"It could take longer'n we figured," he said. "He's a tough one, Jamie."

"I know," Jamie replied.

"The men are getting a little restless, what with the Ree on a war trail just now."

"I understand," Jamie said.

"So we'd be better off heading to the camp west of here, before moving on. You know the trail we were going to take."

"I do."

"So what I figure is to get a man to stay here with you and help keep the wolves away till it's—over. The rest of us'd move on, and you'd catch up with us farther along.

Jamie nodded.

Major Henry clasped his shoulder.

"I'm sorry about Hugh, Jamie. I know what he meant to you," he said. "I'll call for a volunteer now, and we'll be about it."

"Very good, sir."

• • • The bear approached Hugh again, and he could not run from it. It was as if his feet had grown roots. The bear walked upright, its face flowing like dark water. He saw his father there, and the faces of men he had had to kill. Dark birds flew out of the bear, flapping their wings in his face. He smelled the cloying sweetness and the fetor, the rottenness. . . . Then it clasped him and squeezed him again, and he was coughing. He tasted blood with each aching spasm. It seemed that there were voices—many of them—talking softly in the dark distance. The sounds of hoofbeats came and went. He saw the bear dead, skinned, its hide somehow wrapping about him, its face become his own, bleeding, smiling without humor. Closer was it wrapped, becoming part of him, his arms and aching legs shaggy, his mouth foul. Still was he rooted; still the power came up into him out of the earth. Almost a dark, flowing song. . . .

The hat went 'round and coins clicked in it, one by one, till Jules Le Bon felt the stirring of compassion and volunteered to sit with Jamie by his friend. A short, wiry man, missing a tooth leftside of his grin, he bade the others good day, stood waiting till they had ridden off. Then he moved to sit by Jamie, clinking as he walked, sighed, and stared at Hugh.

"Amazing strong, that man," he said, after a time.

Jamie nodded.

"Where'd he come from?"

Jamie shrugged.

"So there's nobody you know about—anywhere—to write to?"

Jamie shook his head.

"Shame," said Le Bon. "He was a hell of a hunter. Still, I suppose this is the way he'd want to go—while he was about his business, out on the trail. . . . Buried in one of the places he'd hunted."

Jamie looked away. Le Bon grew still. After a while Le Bon rose and made his way to a fire the men had left where a tin of water was still warm.

"Want a cup of tea?" he called.

"No, thanks."

He made himself a cup and returned with it. Later, he

smoked his pipe, drank more tea. The day wore on. Hugh muttered occasionally, grew still again. Le Bon shook his head and looked into the distance.

As shadows slid eastward Le Bon cocked his head.

"Do you hear hoofbeats?" he asked.

"No," Jamie answered.

Le Bon lowered himself to the ground, placed an ear against it. For a long time, he was still.

"Hear anything?" Jamie said.

"No. I was mistaken."

He rose again.

"Little worried about the Ree," he said. "Had me hearing things." He laughed and seized a handful of his hair and tugged it about. "Hate to part company with this stuff, is all."

Later, as they made their dinner of the supplies the major had left them, Le Bon relived his part in the recent campaign. Jamie nodded periodically, watching Hugh. Later still, as the night came on, he covered Hugh with a blanket.

"Amazing strong," Le Bon repeated. "Sad, to have your strength working against you. When there's no hope."

Jamie's dreams were a jumble, of Hugh and the bear and the Indians, of Major Henry and the men, riding, riding, into the distance. He woke unrested in the morning, letting Le Bon sleep as he broke his fast on crackers and tea. Hugh's condition seemed unchanged. Still he struggled— perhaps as Le Bon had said, against his own strength— moving occasionally, but never speaking, face drawn, gray, fingers at times still ascrabble. How long did it take a man to die?

Later, Le Bon shook his head.

"Looks a lot worse," he said. "Today or tonight will do for him."

"You're probably right," Jamie responded.

"I hope so," Le Bon said. "Not just for our sake—though Lord knows I've seen what those Ree can do to a man—but for him, struggling on that way to no account. It's indecent what dying does to a man, by way of suffering. How old are you, anyhow, Jamie?"

"Sixteen," Jamie said. "Pretty near."

"So you've got your whole life to go yet, lessen it's cut short. Just hope your end doesn't drag out like poor Hugh's."

"Yes," Jamie said, and sipped his tea gone cold.

By afternoon's light, Hugh looked as if he were made of wax, face half-melted. There were times when Jamie thought it was over for him. But always there came a small twitch, a low noise, a bit of bubbling breath. Le Bon raised ladders of smoke, puffing, and watched. Birds passed, to and from the river, uttering shrill notes and bits of softer music. The sky clouded over and there came a rumbling from within it, but no rain fell. A wind rose up and the day grew cooler.

"Wonder how far along the major and the men have gotten?" Le Bon said.

"Hard to say."

"They must feel a lot safer to be on the trail now, heading away from the Ree."

"I suppose."

"We couldn't even hear their hoofbeats for all that thunder, if they were coming up on us now."

Jamie shivered against the cold.

"Guess so."

Le Bon rose and stretched and went off to relieve himself in the bushes. Hugh did not move.

They raised a lean-to of branches for themselves and Hugh, hung a sheet of canvas over it. The rainfall was light, drumming. The sound became war drums in Jamie's sleep, and hoofbeats of mounted parties. . . .

The morning came gray and damp, and still Hugh lingered.

"I dreamed a party of them passed us in the night," Le Bon observed. "Maybe they did."

"Then we're lucky."

"So far. My! He looks poorly."

"Same as yesterday, I'd judge."

"Still breathing, though. Who'd've thought any man could hold on so long?"

"Hugh ain't like other folks," Jamie said. "He always knew what to do. He was always strong enough to do it."

Le Bon shook his head.

"I believe you," he told him. "It ain't natural to keep living when you've been tore up the way he has. I've seen a lot of folks adying, but none of 'em to hold on like this. You know it's got to be soon, don't you?"

"Seems so."

"Be a shame, the two of us to die for someone who could go any minute."

Jamie went to the spring to rinse the kerchief to wash Hugh's face again.

As they rolled into their blankets that evening, Le Bon said, "This'll be it, boy. I know it. I'm sorry, 'cause I know you're all the family each other's got. Say some prayers, if you know any. I'll do the same, before I sleep."

And the sun shone upon him in the morning. And Jamie's first thoughts were of Hugh. Turning, rising, he stared. Had it happened during the night? No. The pallor remained, but now a small fluttering breath had begun, unlike the man's earlier gasps and long silent spells. His chest moved slightly, with a more rapid, shallow breathing.

"I've seen men like this before," he heard Le Bon say. "Soon it will be over, lad. Likely with God's blessing."

Jamie wept silently. It was wrong to want it to happen, he knew.

"I just want him to stop hurting," he finally said.

"And soon he will, Jamie. Soon he will." Le Bon sounded sad. "There's few as could fight it the way he did. But soon his trials will be over. You can see it."

Jamie nodded, rubbing his cheeks dry against his shoulders.

After breakfast, Le Bon stared for perhaps an hour at the man who lay before him. Finally, he spoke:

"I've been thinking," he said, "about the Ree again. You know I'm scared. I know you are, too. Now, meaning no disrespect, and knowing Hugh'll be gone soon, it takes a time to bury a man—especially when we've only our knives to dig with. All that extra time we'll be running risk they'll find us, when we could be riding away."

"That's true."

"Being practical now—and like I said, with no disrespect—I thought we might dig it now and have it ready. We're just sitting here, anyhow, and whether it gets dug before or after won't mean a thing to him. It's the spirit that counts, that his friends mean to do right by him. It can't hurt him none to make it ready. But it could make a difference for our safety—afterwards."

"Yes," Jamie said. "I guess he'd understand that."

So, drawing his knife, Le Bon rose and moved about to Hugh's far side. He traced long lines in the earth with its point, measuring the man's great length and width with his eye as he did so. Then he plunged the blade into the ground and outlined the first piece of sod to be removed.

" 'Dust to dust,' " he said, "like the Good Book tells us. We'll do fair by him, Jamie. Proper size and deep enough to protect him from weather and the critters. We'll do it right. I know how much you care about him."

After a time, Jamie rose and moved to the plot's farther end. He hesitated a moment, and then began to cut.

They dug all that day, using their hands where it was soft, their blades where the earth resisted intrusion. They removed stones, roots, and a goodly amount of soil. They excavated to a considerable depth, then cleaned their blades in the grass and washed themselves at the spring, before they returned to Hugh's side.

Still that fluttering breath continued.

They ate their meal and the day's last light touched Hugh's face with color. They watched him till the stars came out, then muttered good nights and found their blankets.

In all their dreams, Hugh was a part of the earth.

T H R E E

COLTER

The Blackfeet knew the treachery of river jams and the first young warriors who ran out on the big logs were called back by their elders. Impatient, the youths crouched on the river bank, and waited restlessly for a word of encouragement. But the elders stared disconsolately into the water. The man they were after, White Eyebrows, was here. There was no doubt of it. Nor was there any doubt, now, that this was not just any man—he could run like a deer, and disappear like one too. Somewhere, the river said, the man was hiding. Somewhere, it teased, perhaps where they least expected . . . somewhere right under their nose. They notched bows with arrows and stared into the green, cold, fast-moving current.

Was the river his ally?

Did he breathe like a fish?

Where had he gone?

Silence hung upon the men. They cast their eyes along the banks searching for a clue. The young pups broke the silence, whispering among themselves, edging out of the circle of waiting. The scent of their prey was too near for them to wait any longer. When they fired their arrows into

the pool, no elder raised a hand to stop them. The feathered shafts came bubbling back up; the boys went to re-
trieve them. This gave way to the more precarious game of
straddling the sawyers, peering down into the green water,
loosing arrows into the shadows.

Still the elders made no move to stop them. The ruse of
stepping foxlike along the barkless logs, balancing, jump-
ing out and landing on another log, made the boys yip with
pleasure. Suddenly there came a groan from under the
water, as if a sleeping leviathan had come awake. Then a
swift, sickening, sucking sound. One upended log, as big
around as a boat, went down into the river, while another
of the same size went up, the two changing position.

John Colter, still embracing the mud-lodged log at the
bottom of the pool, felt the disturbance. All round him
there was a whining and groaning of logs, as if the riverbottom were about to become the top of the river, the
whole thing turning upside down. Although he couldn't
see anything, he could feel a tremor in the waterlogged tree
to which he was holding fast, praying that it would not
break loose in the din.

On the surface a seesawing log pitched one of the
Blackfoot youths against the top of Colter's tree, pinning his
leg at the knee, crushing it like an insect's. The boy let out a
piteous scream and his blood reddened the water above
Colter's head. Of course, he saw none of this, but some part
of him felt it, knew it was happening. The river pool was a
place of havoc now, the logs all astir, cannonball bubbles
bowling up from the muddy bottom, the logs singing out
like spiked whales.

Grappling with the thought of being suddenly exposed, Colter forced his mind away from his predicament. He knew that, any second, the log that was his savior would send him to the surface. But he tricked his mind, made it go to another place. Once, two years earlier while on a hunt with Meriwether Lewis, he had ridden down a steep ravine on horseback. His horse, wearing the elkskin hoof-guards that eased passage over rough terrain, slipped on a mossy stone, toppled, head over rump. Colter did not have time to kick free. Meriwether Lewis watched helplessly from the other side of the river as his best hunter and finest mount rolled into the rapids, where, permanently fixed one to the other, they vanished beneath the froth of Hungry Creek.

The same day Colter made a joke of it. For he had come to the surface some fifteen yards downstream, still mounted, still holding the hickory stock of his rifle in his right hand.

"A lucky one, y'are, John Colter," Potts had said, shaking his head, wondering how it was possible for one man to have all the luck of the Irish but none of the curse of the Scot.

"Not luck by any man's measure," Lewis had said judiciously, sucking upon his briar, "the man's got God sewed up in his leather jerkin."

Do I still?—Colter wondered, sucking air from the burl. He wondered. He was not a praying man, yet he prayed like any man when he had to. Thus far he had not troubled the Lord with his foolishness, feeling somehow he could get out of it himself. But sucking air for dear life, his body frozen in every limb, his head pounding, he thought that he could not last much longer. Perhaps he should give himself up and follow Potts' example: be a pincushion rather than a torture victim.

Along the riverbank the Blackfeet made a wedge of alder poles to pry free the trapped youth, who, mortally wounded, was staring blankly at his helpers. Up and down, the boys and men pried the poles, but the log that pinned the crushed youth to John Colter's tree refused to budge.

Then it happened—a tremendous heaving. As the men on shore put their shoulders into the poles, a growl ripped the sun-warm afternoon, and the log came away from the boy. At the same time, John Colter's tree pivoted completely around, spinning on its axis. Then, as if airborne, it heaved itself straight up at the sky.

In retreat from the hurling tree, the Blackfeet scooped the wounded youth out of the water and scattered like leaves. They turned and ran into the windbreak of trees at the same time John Colter was sent into the sky like a rocketeer. The old sunken cottonwood pirouetted on the surface like a breaching whale and crashed into the water.

As the Indians fled, Colter was secretly rocketed into a cottonwood that overhung the bank. Stunned, he now found himself sitting in an abandoned raven's nest. Below him the grumbling sawyers did battle in the froth, spewing whitish geysers of spray along the willowline of the bank.

Moments later, the tribe returned to watch the last fitful logroll—quite certain, now the upheaval was over, that the crushed body of John Colter would float to the surface. When after several minutes this didn't happen, they searched the river bank all over again. The elders shook their heads and sent swift young runners east, west, north and south. The rest of the hunting party made a temporary camp along the river. There was nothing to do but wait for a sign or for the runners to return with news. Every bit of ground was covered. White Eyebrows was somewhere near, he could not get away. The river tricked them. There was a legend that told of this, how the river had a forked tongue which spoke two ways.

When the runners returned empty-handed and without having picked up a single track, it was decided the men would camp there for the night and in the morning use the best trackers to hunt the swamp. There, the elders agreed, was the only place Colter could be. The day which had begun with the promise of a good run and a fine capture had settled into a deep meditation on the man they had named White Eyebrows. Was he a two-legged like themselves? Or was he, perhaps, some other order of creature, seeming to be manlike but inside something quite different? They pondered on this, each man holding thoughts not shared with the rest.

The God or gods that watched over John Colter had plucked him from the river and put him in a tree, hiding him in a raven's nest of cottonwood and willow sticks. Now, thus pocketed out of sight and surrounded by the unfallen leaves of cottonwood, he was all but invisible. Yet, from his vantage point he could peer between the flash of leaves and see what was going on below him.

Once he realized that he was hidden, Colter began to inspect his feet, which were covered with prickly pear spines. He knew from the years with Lewis how to work out the painful barbs, one at a time. The sun cresting the firs on the western ridge told him how much daylight was left before the autumn shadows would fill the valley. Then he fell to the task of saving his hurt feet.

The calluses of previous years had stood him well. "Where'd such feet as yours come from, John?" Potts once asked him as they sat around a campfire.

"These has danced," John Colter replied, "on the Mandan anthills and the Crow snows and burnt hills of the Blackfeet—"

They both laughed at Colter's love of poetry, of conjured phrasing.

"I've seen them little fire ants," Potts chuckled, "and the Crow snows when you took on that passel of fellers, running loco, barefoot, as I recollect, but nary a white man run the Blackfoot courses I know of. Them's the fastest buck runners in the Rockies."

" 'Twas on the lower Gallatin, runnin' for my life. One boot on, one boot off and the blood tricklin' down my leg bone where a Blackfoot musket ball was lodged—and still is, point of fact," Colter remarked.

He told Potts the legend of how the Blackfeet got their name, walking across burnt hills. The immemorial tale of a people walking far on scorched earth that ate away their moccasins, scarring the soles of their feet and, according to the legend, leaving black tracks on green grass.

Now his own feet looked like the hind end of a frightened porcupine. But no worse, he reasoned, than the year before, when, one-legged, he'd dragged himself five hundred miles without a firing-piece, carrying only a small bag of awls, beads, vermilion, some needles, a knife and a plug of tobacco left over from trading with the Crow. He remembered the camp where the Crows had wintered that year of 1806. They'd fed their horses cottonwood bark and when that got scarce and the temperatures dropped to forty below, the Indians had dug up a small evergreen herb that smelled like sage, and fed this to their starving animals. Colter had eaten it himself and found it horsey and dry but quite palatable.

Living with the Crows he'd learned, as he told Potts, to run barefoot in the snow, a practice for which he had al-most—but not quite—acquired a personal liking. What he actually enjoyed was his own fool's tolerance for lengthening the threshold of pain. But now, sitting in the slapdash stick nest of a raven, Colter began to size up his chances. Thus far what had happened to him was nothing short of fantastic—one miracle after another. It made him wonder if Lewis was right. Yet the hunter in him knew his luck would have to stop somewhere.

The Blackfeet were all around him now, setting up cooking fires and laying down their blankets for the night. The smell of drifting smoke and cooking meat wandered absently up to his nostrils and reminded him that he hadn't eaten since daybreak. His belly turned on him, groaning. He took some cottonwood bark to ease the pain of his cramping stomach. He did not want the bark but the sweet middle layer of tissue that lay between the bark and the flesh of the tree. Coaxing this off with his fingernail, he began to nourish himself, a little at a time, chewing long and slow to make a meal of it.

In the Blackfoot camp there were strips of elk, smoking on sticks close to the fire. The night came on cold with a first hint of winter, of snow drifting into the high mountains. Most of the warriors had gone back to the village. The fun was over, the chase, now the rigors of the hunt—and only those who were trained for this stayed on, the rest wandered back to the warmth of wives and home fires and buffalo stew. The boy trapped in the wake of the sawyers had died of blood loss; there was mourning back in the village, cries of death and disfigurement as the women of the family slashed their forearms to prove their sorrow.

The fastest runner of the Blackfeet was elder brother to the boy who had died. This was the one who had seen Colter writhing in the grass like a snake. He had hesitated to kill the man because he had believed that he was crazy. There was a certain unnamable fear of madness among the tribes and crazy people, thought often in touch with the gods, were given plenty of elbow room. But now, sitting with his uncle around their small campfire, the warrior knew that Colter was not mad, or if he was it was the madness of a magpie, the kind that will trick you to your death.

White Eyebrows was certainly not crazy. . . .

"Such a man," said the uncle whose name was Long Arm, "is watched-over. The white man has his gods, just as we have ours. They are not the same as our gods, but they have power. White Eyebrows has gods that look over him at all times."

The warrior nephew of Long Arm was not satisfied with this. His name was Flint In The Face. He had never lost a race, never lost a fight, he owned many stolen Crow ponies and already had two wives. He was young and strong and he hated the white man since the first day he saw him.

"The Great Mystery One does not favor the whites,"

Flint In The Face said, chewing on a strip of smoked elk. "That is all that matters."

Long Arm sighed. The evening star was out, he checked it and turned his own meat on the stick, then gave a penetrating look at his nephew. He saw the vengeance trail in his eyes, and shook his head.

"It is said the Mystery One made three kinds of men, my nephew. The first was pale and white. The Mystery One was not satisfied with this. He made a second man which was darker, but still He was not satisfied. Then he made a man of our color, and He was satisfied because good things would come of His creation."

Here Long Arm paused and pulled the blanket around his shoulders. "There are other stories that other men tell," he went on, "and some of these say other things."

Flint In The Face waited for him to continue. He valued his uncle's word. If it were said, he admired him more than any other man and it was his shadow that he purposely stood under.

"They say," Long Arm said, tearing at the elk strip with his teeth, "there was once a pool of water. Long, long ago a white man came to this pool and cleaned himself there. He used up most of the water and when he was finished he left it dirtied. Then he went away. Then came one of our people. He cleaned himself in the water that was left from the white man, and they say that when he came out, his skin was not clean the way the white man's skin was clean. It was brown and dirty. And the water of the fresh pool was no longer a good thing."

Long Arm laughed and looked to the evening star again. Then, chewing his meat, he smiled. "Do not be so angry, Nephew. It is only a story made for the campfire. I do not know if it is true. It came to me from a tribe, far to the south."

Flint In The Face looked darkly into the flames. "I am told they are a people without gods. And without dignity. You will remember what these men did to the beaver. They killed them so that other men might wear them as hats—for this foolishness they cleared the beaver out of our country."

"It does not mean they are without gods. They have their ways and we have ours. That is the way it is."

"No, Uncle. Their ways are not ways. They do what they wish, when they wish, and always it is for themselves. For them alone. Do you remember when their leader, the man they called Many Weathers, was shot in the backside by one of his own men? This happened because white men were shooting wildly, killing more elk than necessary. And what have they given back to us? They call the wicked water that burns the heart and brain out of a man the Milk of the Great Father. If this Father is so great why does he drink milk that burns? He has given us the thing they call the Jefferson Face. A piece of worthless metal. I have seen one hanging from the neck of a skeleton."

"Nephew, are you having a dream? Our chief wears such a medal, he got it from a Crow killed in battle. They say it is the face of the Great Father who lives in the East."

"It is a bad omen. The skeleton that I saw was also a Crow. I believe the metal killed him, or the Great Father's Milk, for they are the same."

By now darkness had closed upon the two men and they were less inclined to speak, and more inclined to listen. The call of a barred owl echoed in the firs. Five notes with a descending scale ending in a cough, which made the silence of the camp more silent.

"I am going to rest now," Long Arm said softly. "In the morning we will again hunt White Eyebrows." Then he chuckled, "but I do not think we will find him. I feel him near us, even now, but like Brother Owl, I feel that he can see in the dark. . . ."

"Today," Flint In The Face hissed, "I might have killed him when he turned upon the ground like a snake. Instead, I let him live. With the next sun, I will track him. When I find him, I promise you that I will eat his liver before his very own eyes."

Colter shivered in his treetop perch. With the coming of evening, his teeth began to chatter, his limbs shook. Hugging his knees to his chest, he pressed his back against the rough bark of the tree. Occasionally figures moved in the deepening dusk below him and men came to the river to fill water baskets and skin bags. Fighting against the night chill, John Colter made his plan of escape. Wait until the night was deep and the men in their blankets were dreaming. Slip down the tree, crawl to the river, swim downstream to the backwater of the beaver. If luck lasted, find a beaver den, spend the rest of the night there, then strike for the mountains.

There was the river the Crow called Mirepeawnzah and from the ridge that overlooked it, you could see the junction of the Stinking Water and Big Horn Rivers. Facing south was the empty bed of that ancient inland sea, hemmed in on the east by the Big Horns and on the west by the Rockies. On a clear day you could see Owl Creek and the mountains that were the boundary of the Big Horn Basin more than a hundred miles to the south. The mountain that gave view of this—what was it called? Colter searched his memory.

Ammahhahpaishsha.

Whispering the name, hearing it spill like the Fork rattling under the cottonwood tree, Colter dropped off to sleep.

And dreamed.

He was hunting again for Lewis and Clark and the black-tailed deer were spread out in front of him like a great brown lake. Moving in among them, walking sleepily through the blue-tinted shadows of the sage, he and Potts didn't know what to shoot first. There were so many animals and, not afraid of men, they were calm and unhurried in their browsing. Colter knew from experience that it took a deer and an elk, or perhaps a five-hundred-pound bear, to feed the voracious appetites of the Lewis and Clark crew. They ate as if there were no tomorrow, which surprised him because he always ate as sparely as a winter possum.

How could men consume so much animal flesh, he wondered. He was a hunter and he loved the call of the wild, the scent of the hunt. But he was not a great eater of animals, nor a great killer of them. He was a hunter.

"—y'know, John," Potts said, "we don't have to shoot these critters. All's we 'ave to do is hit 'em over the head with a stick."

"Truth be known, I'd rather browse on groundsel like

they do," Colter replied evenly, "than shoot a living one of them."

"Don't that beat all," Potts spat, "look yonder, them wolf pups playing in the dusky light with them fawns."

"Reminds you of the Good Book, kind of like," Colter said, keeping his eye on the herd.

"Well, sir, back to work." Potts raised his piece, took aim. "You know how the boys back at camp favors flesh of the fawn."

Colter, in the dream, raised his hand to prevent the shot, but too late. The blue smoke filled the air and hung in the windless air like a veil about their shoulders. Then it was John Potts who was dying, not the poor little fawn. "Colter," the strangled voice croaked as it was taken downstream. Potts was in the stream where he'd been shot by the Blackfeet, his mouth choking with blood and creekwater. Colter watched as Potts' open mouth widened, gave birth to a bison, a black-tailed buck, a spotted fawn, a beaver, a woodrat, a shrew, the latter poised on the edge of the dying man's lip.

"Speak to me, Potts," Colter said.

But John Potts remained in the stream, open-mouthed and dead-eyed, a shrew hopping about on his underlip.

Then the dream melted away from the autumn stream and John Colter dreamed himself crouching on a winter battlefield, with snow underfoot. Out of loyalty he had stayed with the Crows and their friends the Flatheads, but together the two tribes were down to about five hundred men. The Blackfeet had swarmed down from the surrounding hills, some fifteen hundred in number. Colter was the only white man in the fight.

The Crows and Flatheads were being driven towards a stand of pine. Bunched, back to back, they rotated like a medicine wheel, firing arrows and what guns they had, into the advancing Blackfoot horsemen. Colter, already badly hurt, hung on the ragged edge of the wheel, loading and reloading, ignoring his fractured leg.

Suddenly a rider on a black and white spotted pony thundered out of the throng. "White Eyebrows," the man called.

Colter looked up, watched the horseman guide the nimble mount around the fallen and the slain. The smoke of battle rose around him, but he paid no attention to it. The man had a black face shaped like an obsidian knife.

"What are you called?" Colter asked the man.

"Flint In The Face," the man answered, "and when you next see me, I will kill you and eat your liver before your face."

Then the whole battlefield roared and over the snow a black river of blood coursed and swept away the fallen men. Colter scrabbled like a wounded crab, grabbing hold of a tree which ripped away in the burst of blood. Groping in the darkening flood, he reached out, helplessly, and his outstretched fingers closed on a human hand. As the roar of the black bloodtide grew, the hand's grip drew Colter to higher ground.

He looked up and saw that the thing that had saved him was a black-boned skeleton. Upon its neck it wore a red, white and blue ribbon with a pendant of bright gold.

The Jefferson Medal, given by Lewis and Clark to win over the hostiles to the cause of the Great White Father.

"Give it back," John Colter warned and he jerked the

medal from the skeleton's neck. Yet as he did so the forest all around him collapsed, as if the ribbon and the skeleton fastened to it were the epicenter of the world. He pulled and pulled, crying out: "Give it back, you savage—" And as he tore at the ribbon, trees crashed, mountains flattened, and the river of black blood ran out of the wounds of the earth.

"Give it back. . . ."

Then he was awake, clawing for a cottonwood branch, plummeting to the ground like a fallen nestling. The whipping of branches, the meaty thud as he struck hard ground. He was on all fours, trying to remember where he was. It was still dark but the sky was beginning to pale. In front of him, a pair of beaded moccasins, the leggings of a man—no, not a man, John Colter realized, a boy.

From where he stood by the river, holding his elk-belly waterskin, the boy had witnessed the falling of a god from the sky. Yes, he was sure of it—a deity had dropped out of the starry night like the dew on the grass and was presently looking at him. The boy wondered: Was he two-legged or four-legged?

FOUR

GLASS

Awakening, Jamie's eyes beheld the mound of earth even before they regarded Hugh. The previous day returned to him in its entirety in that instant, and it was only with effort that he lowered his gaze to consider the final face of his friend.

Yet still was there movement. Yet still were those shallow breaths linked each to each in the feeble chain which held these days together. Whether it was anguish or joy that he knew in that movement, he could not tell. Whichever, the pang filled his breast so that he gasped. Then he sat upright.

"Hugh . . ." he said then, and it almost seemed those breaths hesitated at the naming. But that was all, and though he spoke again, there was no change.

He lay back again, and his mind drifted to dreaming. Again, he rode forward, and the shaggy bear-form, upright, waved its paws. Almost, it was Hugh now— Beckoning? Warning away? Both, somehow. . . .

The world tumbled and fell together then, and it was as if many hoofbeats passed. . . .

When he felt the warmth of the day about him, he lay,

eyes unopened, awareness seeping in, knowing what he would view in a little while, wanting to delay it, wishing to remain within the shadow of sleep. At last, however, he looked. First at the masses of excavated earth, then at Hugh.

A few moments passed. Then he saw that the faint breath continued. He realized that he had been holding his own, and he sighed it out.

He visited the spring, washed, drank, fetched water for tea. On his return, he saw that Le Bon had pressed an ear to the ground. The man raised a finger to his lips as he approached.

He waited for the water to heat. Several minutes passed.

Finally, "I heard something," Le Bon told him, rising and brushing at pantleg and shoulder.

"Hoofbeats," Le Bon went on. "And we know the major's cleared out. Now, I'm not saying it *couldn't* be bison—but it *could* be Ree."

Jamie nodded.

"Seems like a bad chance to be taking," Le Bon continued.

Jamie's gaze shifted to Hugh, whose shallow breathing had grown erratic again.

"Poor Hugh!" Le Bon said. "Right at the edge. God knows what the man had inside him to keep going this long. Well, it's almost over now. Look at him! Struggling to breathe. Lord! if he only knew what his friends were going through! I guess he'd give it up right now 'stead of a little later. Listen to the ground, Jamie! Put your ear to the ground!"

Jamie lowered himself and put his ear to the earth. He heard the beating of his heart and echoes of his breathing, the cries of birds, stride of the wind through the grasses. Within it all—faint, how faint must it be—there could be another throb, a pulse. Or not. He continued to listen. Perhaps a faint thrumming. . . .

"I don't know," he said. "Maybe. Yes, maybe there is something moving out there."

"Uh-huh," Le Bon said. "Doesn't mean they'll come this way. Of course, doesn't mean they won't either. Just thinking of them being out there is scary, though, ain't it?"

Jamie nodded, picked up his cup, went to check the water.

"Two of us wouldn't stand a chance," Le Bon said, and he looked back at Hugh. Then he dropped to the ground and listened again. "I hear 'em, Jamie! So help me, I hear 'em!" he said.

Jamie stared at Hugh. Had his breath ceased, finally? After a long pause, he saw a small chest movement.

"I think we ought to pack our stuff and saddle up," Le Bon said. "Have everything ready so we can move out fast."

Jamie licked his lips, searched the horizon with his gaze.

"All right," he said.

Le Bon's movements were fast, almost panicked, as they were about it. The frenetic pace communicated itself, and Jamie found himself hurrying, almost stumbling with the saddle, missing the buckle with the end of the cinch strap, first try. Le Bon kept glancing into the distance, all directions.

When they were finished, Le Bon returned to stand at Jamie's side.

"Almost, Jamie," he said. "Almost."

Jamie's eyes began to sting. Le Bon stooped and picked up Hugh's rifle, which lay beside him, and slung it over his shoulder.

"Might as well pack those things he won't be needing, too."

He raised the great hunting knife in its leather sheath by the belt from which it depended, hung it over his other shoulder. He shook and folded the blanket.

". . . And his flint," he said, searching, finding, and pocketing it.

Jamie sobbed once and looked away. He heard Le Bon moving off with the gear, toward the horses.

"Hugh, I'm sorry," he whispered.

How long he stared through clouded eyes he did not know, before he felt Le Bon's hand on his shoulder.

"I know it's hard," the man said, "but he'd understand. Living on the trail the way he has, he'd understand about being practical."

Jamie looked away, nodding.

"Look, I don't like suggesting it," Le Bon continued, "but our lives are in danger now, and losing our scalps to pay our final respects won't make a bit of difference to Hugh, in just a little while. He'd understand that, too, you know. Do the same thing himself, if'n he had to. You know what I'm saying?"

"Yes," Jamie replied.

"So I think we'd better ride out of here—the sooner the better. Those Ree could show up real sudden-like."

"I want to be alone with Hugh for a little while."

"Surely. I understand. I'll go wait over by the horses."

Jamie went and knelt by Hugh, talking softly. Le Bon stood beside his mount, staring off into the distance. After a time, Jamie rose and approached his own horse, mounted.

"Let's ride," Le Bon said, "west," and he shook his reins.

Jamie looked back, but all he could see was the pile of earth.

Floating, he stared down at the white shape in the blue, seeing it alter in form—bird, mountain, fish—and slowly take fire, break apart, go away. Another came into view, this one wholly incandescent, a tipped shield, breached, joined again. And then it was a burning boat, and it, too, drifted away. He watched the blue—waters?—take on a deeper hue. Somewhere far to the side there were brighter colors. Abruptly, he wished to move. When he tried, there came a blackness. Everything went away.

Lying, head upon his shoulder, he felt the light. He regarded the fire against the blue. The word "morning" came to him and went away again. He blinked and watched it happen.

The sky continued to lighten. It was easier to watch just one place than to turn his head. There was red, with pinks above, then orange. After a time these colors fled and the ball of sun coming above the land's edge grew painful to look upon. He shifted his gaze upward and his head rolled back. Cooler on his eyes this way, yes, with just the blue. He drew a deeper breath and sighed it out, becoming aware of pains in his chest.

Sudden then, he recalled the bear, squeezing the breath from him, giving him its own, rank and sweet. . . . He remembered the speed with which it had approached and seized him. And something about its face, as if it had flowed through other features as his mind swam and his spirit spun away. . . .

His breathing deepened, despite the pain. And Jamie? Jamie had been there, hadn't he? He seemed to recall his voice, as in a dream, talking to him over long stretches of time. Jamie. . . .

Blue unbroken above him, earth beneath. . . . He felt suspended. Sky and ground. This place was his, had become so by virtue of wordless, physical familiarity, grown over an age. So long as he did not move, did not disturb the bond, time would stand still, the place would protect him, and some hidden, lurking awfulness be ever held at bay.

Yet he had to move, now his spirit had returned from its wanderings. It bade him rise from the sleep of earth, go forward into day.

He drew his hands upward along the sides of his body, elbows extended outward, palms upon the ground. He drew a breath and held it. Then he began to push downward, raising himself, leaning his head forward. Slowly, his shoulders came up off of the ground. He heard the rushing of blood in his ears, felt it swell his face. He pushed harder.

He began to shake. It started in his arms, spread quickly to his shoulders, neck, head. His left arm gave way and he collapsed. There was a pounding inside his head even before it struck the ground, and waves of red and black passed through him. His awareness slipped away.

He remembered breathing heavily, and his brows grew damp. It seemed only a few moments had passed before he opened his eyes again. But now he no longer felt suspended. Time had lurched forward, like a wagonwheel jerked out of a rut. The waiting thing had moved to touch him.

He stared up into the blue, breathing deeply despite the aches this caused. His face throbbed now, as if a hot mask lay upon it. His eyelashes were caked with grit; he felt it each time they came together and parted. Dark, bead-like clusters in them framed his seeing. He raised his right hand and stared at it, lowered it again.

Then he clenched his teeth, leaned forward, pushed himself up with his elbows, slid them to the rear to rest upon. His sides and back added their aches to those in his chest, till it felt as if a hot tight band encircled his upper body. He drew a deep breath despite this, then let it go.

He looked about. His horse was gone, bolted, he was certain, when the bear had attacked. But where was Jamie? He was sure he had been near, that he had heard his voice in ghostly converse during the long dark time.

And the ground. . . . It was scuffed, as by the movement of many horses, and there were the imprints of boots. Had Major Henry been by? Then why was he alone now? Where had everyone gone?

And what was that huge pile of dirt for?

He dropped his hands to the ground, pushed himself into a seated position, braced against the dizziness he was sure would follow. Nor was he incorrect. His head swam. He drew another deep breath and held it, waited till his vision cleared and the wave of vertigo passed.

Next, to stand. He drew on his legs and pushed. The left one responded, but a terrible pain gripped his right thigh, squeezing to something near the bursting point. His arms gave way and he fell back again, striking himself witless upon the earth. And the pain remained, throbbing with a red pulse. He clenched his teeth, face twisting into a grimace.

After a long while it subsided. He moved his hand to the leg. Tender to the touch, there was an extra aliveness there, a fiery awareness of the gentlest exploration. Broken. It had to be broken.

Where had everyone gotten to, with him in this condition?

He raised himself slowly again, turning to his right as he did so. On his side, he moved his left leg over the top of his right and lowered it, knowing what was coming as he raised his hips and continued to turn. The twisting of the right leg brought a return of agony, but left him on his belly, panting, head raised, elbows beneath him.

He regarded the dawn and the long shadows it lay upon the land from tree, branch, and rock. Soon Major Henry would be riding west with his men. So he must return before that, come back for him. Mustn't he? Something was very wrong, and it was hard trying to think it into place.

Instead of thinking then, he began to crawl, dragging his useless leg behind him like a heavy branch. He turned his body and pulled himself in the direction of the heap of earth. Perhaps something about it would give him an idea as to what had been happening while he lay senseless.

He approached the mound and his gaze went to the pit. He worked his way nearer. What could it mean, such a large hole here in the wilderness? He studied its depth, its corners neatly squared. . . .

A grave. Of course. It had to be a grave. Empty, though. Waiting. A grave. . . .

Whose?

He began to shudder. And his brow was damp again. How long? How long had he lain there? How near had he come to filling that hole? Had his friends actually been ready to put him in it? Yet—Why wait with him to that point and depart when his fires burned again? He shook his head.

The movement made his throat feel as if it were stuffed with dry leaves. Immediately, he knew a thirst which pushed everything else from his mind. Straining at the ground again, he turned, letting the leg drag, and began crawling toward the spring.

Several times he halted, when the strength went out of his arms, his shoulders, his good leg. He lay with head upon outflung arm, breathing heavily, wondering at the cost in strength of his ordeal. And each time he rose again to drag himself nearer to the water his thirst had been compounded by the heavy breathing and the strain.

When finally he came to it he was unable to restrain himself. He had planned to cup his hand, dip it, and sip slowly from it, but instead he let his face fall into the water, sucked in a great draught and swallowed. Again, he drew in a mouthful. And this time he choked. Coughing, he drew back, sides aching, and his face began to burn. His wounds awoke, feeling as if he had suddenly been scalded about the brows. His throat, too, felt momentarily burnt, but this quickly subsided. Now he used his hand, cupping it, drinking more carefully. But he was unable to stop. Slowly, he swallowed handful after handful of water till his stomach felt a cold presence within him. At last, he forced himself to draw back, lowered his head, slept.

When he woke once more he drank his fill again and washed his face. Then, carefully, he drew himself about and regarded the litter of the camp. It could hardly have been the Ree who had been through, his body left unlanced. The major then, and tracks headed off into the west. Had they waited about for him to recover, finally giving up or frightened off? The ready grave and himself still breathing seemed to argue the latter. . . .

Or. . . .

How long? How long had he been unconscious? More than a day? Several? Could that explain it? Had they waited and waited, then had to be off? Still. . . .

He crawled to the left, making his way to the hoof-marks in the sod. He studied them with a tracker's eyes, then reached forward and crumbled a clod with his fingers.

Old. Dried out. He probed the depression. Several days, he judged, had gone by since the troop had passed this way. Might they have had to move on, but left someone to watch him? That small lean-to of branches near to the spot where he had lain. . . . He took a course toward it, pulling, pushing with his good foot. Yes, it would have sheltered a watcher should bad weather have blown this way.

Reaching it, he sought the interior with his gaze. The grasses within were flattened, the earth compressed, at both sides. Men had slept here, probably for several nights. A flat piece of bark, ringmarks upon it as from the bottom of a cup. . . . He could see Jamie sitting here, drinking his tea, watching over him.

One shelter. . . . Large enough for Jamie and one other. . . . *Only* one shelter. . . . So they had remained behind to care for him when the major's men moved on. Of course.

But why were they not here now?

He turned again, dragging himself clear of the lean-to, away from the area where he had lain, beyond the grave and its mound. He regarded the well-trodden area the horses had occupied. No. . . . But if two had remained behind where might they have tethered their mounts? Near those saplings, with grasses in ready reach of the horses. He might have hobbled his own there, had he the time. He commenced crawling in that direction, pausing several times to rest.

Tracks. . . . He had been right. These were more recent than the others. And there were droppings only a few hours old, he judged.

He rested his head on his arms again, trying to paint a picture of what had been.

The troop had left some time ago, Jamie and a companion more recently. To wait and then go so. . . . Why?

He raised himself up, scanned the horizon. Nothing.

Again, he began to crawl. When he reached the lean-to he was shaking. Thirsty again, too. There were things to do, but he lacked the strength to do them.

He crawled inside and sprawled.

When he awoke his leg, his face, and his sides were

throbbing. And he wondered again where he was. Somewhere a bird was singing.

He lay there for a long while, and his morning's journey returned to him—his visit to the spring, his exploration of the camp, the signs he had found. He listened carefully to the world. There were no sounds indicating that anyone had returned, or was returning.

He hauled himself up, waited for the dizziness to pass, crawled outside. He paused then, crawled, paused again, scanning the horizon. Nothing.

Turning then, he dragged himself back to the spring. This time, he was able to drink with full restraint, swallowing slowly till he'd had his fill. Afterwards, he splashed more water onto his face and daubed at it gently with his sleeve. The cold still came as a shock, and again the throbbing followed, though somewhat lessened. Then he turned and looked back at the camp.

Could it be that Jamie had simply given up on him? Could he have grown tired of waiting for his friend to die or recover? Had he thought of the major and his men riding farther and farther into the west—making his own journey more arduous, more perilous by the hour—and finally given up on old Hugh and ridden off? He did not like thinking this way, but the signs could well be read so.

He decided it was possible that no one would be coming back for him. Was that really the case? He realized that he could not afford to think otherwise, that his own wellbeing required he assume the worst.

Then he collapsed again, head upon his arms, and a great sob racked his body. It was true, it had to be true. His friend had betrayed him.

"Jamie . . ." he said, in a small, rasping voice.

At the word, a flood of memories came over him. His rescue of the orphaned boy on that day of battle, his taking him to him as a son, of teaching him to hunt, of the wind in the boy's yellow hair as they rode through the prairies, his laughter. . . .

No. If Jamie left him, it had to be for good reasons. There was more to this than he could see. They had grown too close for such a shoddy trick to pass between them.

What was most important now was that he plan, for he realized he could trust no one to aid him. He could still shoot game, make fire, shelter beneath his blanket. He must calculate the best disposition of his energies, then follow that course.

He drank again. Then, teeth clenched, he dragged himself back to the lean-to once more. It was time to assess his supplies.

He sought after his rifle in about the lean-to and the place he had lain, even looking around the mound and into the hole. It was nowhere to be found. And then he realized that his knife was missing. He searched his pockets. His flint was gone, too. No blanket anywhere about, either.

His fire, his food, his shelter. . . . Gone. Jamie had taken them all. He'd grown tired of waiting and made off with . . . everything. His life. Gone. The boy was a thief. How stupid to have cared so about one you never knew.

And again the image of Jamie was before him, this time wearing a certain sly expression he had never noted before. Blind. . . . Blind he had been to the boy's true nature, to the selfishness, the ingratitude that lay within. But now. . . . Now he knew—and how could it serve him? A feeling of doom had come into the air, wrapping him about as surely, as firmly, as that grasp which had crushed him, reduced him. He had seen wounded animals, trapped animals, animals waiting to die. He knew now what they must have understood. That when the time comes, you are alone.

He cursed. He was not an animal. He was Hugh Glass, hunter. Dying was easy. The doom was always there—sometimes far off, other times, like now, so near you could almost smell it.

He cursed again. Betrayed by a whelp who'd dug him his grave, stripped him of his chance to live, and left him. He pounded his fist upon the ground. A snarling sound came up from his chest, and he struck again. He would find a way.

After a time, he rested, bloody images dancing behind his eyelids. He dozed, and they continued on into dream. When he awoke the rage was still with him, settled now into a steady, smoldering thing.

He blinked his way further into consciousness and regarded the sky. The sun was now approaching its midday mark.

He crawled to his left till he reached the excavation. Turning then—slowly, painfully—onto his side, he unbuttoned his trousers and pissed into his grave.

FIVE

COLTER

In the half-light, Colter looked at the boy. He saw the knife in the quill case fastened to the boy's waist and his hands shot forward, grabbing the boy by the ankles and jerking him off his feet. Taken completely by surprise, the boy fell heavily to the ground, groaning.

But before Colter could make good his pounce, the boy rolled back off his left shoulder, and, knife out and flashing, jumped to his feet and took a quick swipe at Colter's chin. The steel edge of the knife nicked him on the chinbone. Colter felt warm blood run down his neck.

The boy was amazed. The god was evidently not a good fighter. The blood coursing down his chin . . . perhaps, just as some said, White Eyebrows was a man. . . .

Curious, the boy advanced. Swinging the knife with mock friendliness, he made some playful passes at Colter's belly. Colter dodged these feathery thrusts, and pretended to stumble.

He put on the impression of a drowsy bear, big, awkward and slow-thinking. The boy took the bait, coming in with reckless abandon. Colter caught the wrist with his left hand, and, unbalancing the boy, threw a hard right-fisted blow that connected, glancing off the cheekbone and hitting between the eyes. The boy twisted, ever so slightly, head flopping on his breastbone, and whistling softly through his teeth, he folded and fell. Then he lay on his side, a bunch of leaves in his left hand, the fallen knife shining in the grass.

Taking the knife, Colter placed it between his teeth and, without making any more noise, he stepped between the sawyers, drew a deep draught of air and slipped silently into the water.

Tendrils of fire crawled across his skin, the burn going deep into his chest. The extreme cold hurt his bones, but he needed to widen the distance between himself and the sleep camp of the Blackfeet. The boy would soon awaken and become town crier. And before he went into the water, Colter saw the dawn light between the pines. He swam out into the fast current and came up for air.

The river carried him and as he floated on its back, he saw two dawn-drinking elk raise their muzzles, eye him curiously as he swept past them. The current was strong, but he recalled how it tangled again in smaller tributaries of the Fork, breaking the land into swampy borderlands, home of the beaver. His plan, if he could achieve it, was to swim another mile, find suitable shelter in one of the large beaver lodges.

Two years ago he and Potts had trapped heavily here, and already he began seeing evidences of gnawed alder where the beavers had worked. He chuckled, remembering how they had seen a whole team of beavers gnawing the same log for weeks, all summer it was. Finally Potts had gone over to examine the downed tree. It was solid rock, petrified wood.

By now, he figured, the sleep camp was up, wakened by the boy. They'd be on his trail, the scouts. But now he'd come to the place where the dams and fords began, the acres of swollen, timber-toothed country, backwash bottoms of soaking earth. A man couldn't get in or out without leaving his track in the mud.

Unless he could swim like a beaver, and think like a man. A man hunted, a man wanted. . . .

He would walk on fallen trees wherever possible . . . double-back like a fox . . . float on his belly in water inches deep. He knew some tricks. He also knew that the Blackfeet knew them.

And would be looking for them.

Flint In The Face studied the place where the boy had fought with Colter. He could smell the big man—or thought he could. Pressing his nose to the grass, he smelled the thing he was looking for, some rankness not his own, a bit of blood from Colter's face.

He smiled.

And nodded knowingly. Pointing to the south, he told the scouts to go that way, to follow where the water went into the willows. Then he looked at the sun and said his morning prayer: "Oh Sun," he chanted, "make us brave, make us strong. Grant that we should live this day in your honor." He had in his hand some pollen of the tule that grew in the swamp, and he sprinkled it on the crown of his head and on the place where the droplet of Colter's blood stained the grass. Then he motioned his men to follow, and they started out into the red rays of the sun.

John Colter was less than a mile off. The water was bitterly cold and his muscles were beginning to cramp. He had to get out into the tule grass where he planned to leave a track as big as a grizzly's. It would throw them off—something they could readily see and easily follow.

But then—somehow—he would make the track go away, make it disappear into the thin air. He had seen the face of the boy, the open-mouth, amazed look at the sight of him. Whatever it was gave him an edge, a chance to bedevil.

The tules were taller than his head and sharp as swords. The mud underneath them was treacherous. In places, quicksand lay in wait of the unwary. It was a good country to get lost in and he stood in the reeds, ready to run. The early morning sun touched his closed eyelids and set them aglow. He said his prayer then: "Oh, God, give me this day."

Then he set off, crashing noisily through the tules. He bent them down as he pushed through them. The mud grabbed at his feet, but he went too fast for it to trap him.

In a short while he came out of the tules and found himself in a hammock of small grass and sedge. Here the beaver marsh had begun and the land spread out far and wide into a lumpy vastness, an intricate web of watery hammock.

Looking ahead, he saw something large and indistinct reflected in the murky water. As he drew near he recognized the shadowy form of an elk that had gotten stuck in the swamp. Sagging half-submerged, dead. Chunks of shoulder and haunch had been ripped clean by predators and carrion-hunters. He observed that in the nearby spruces a clatch of magpies quarreled, waiting for him to leave.

An idea came to him then. Perhaps it would not save his neck, but it might—if he were quick about it—gain him some time. With the stolen knife, he began sawing the front and back hooves of the rotting elk. Holding his nose, he worked at the sinew and bone. The hooves came away more easily than he had suspected owing to the putrefied flesh. Once removed, he lay them on the grass. Then he climbed on top of the elk's head, placing his full weight upon the horns of the dead animal. The sagging skull collapsed upon itself, exuding the stench of excrescence.

For a moment, Colter thought he might vomit, then recovered himself. The elk's great horned head and body began to sink into the boggy mire. Colter stood on it, and quickly it was gone into the ancient silt. He stood on the animal's horns until even the tips were consumed; then he jumped clear of the quicksand and landed on a clump of grass.

Placing his knife on the thong that held up his breech-cloth, he then took hold of the hoofs and slipped back into the shallow water. They might see where he had entered, but not, he hoped, where he would come out. There was an island of sun-parched, gray-blue pine. He headed for it.

The water was only about a foot deep, but he sucked his belly in and disturbed nothing. He made the island and hid in the scrub pine where he cut four strips from his buckskin breechcloth. Then he crudely fastened the elk's hind-hoofs to his own heels, so that his feet would rest on elk-bone while driving the hard hoofs into the mud. His hands held the severed forefeet.

He had seen the Flatheads dance the deer dance, holding the hoofs in this way and when the idea struck him, he knew that it would work, especially in the water—and especially if the trackers did not see anything of the sunken elk. No, he had made sure of that, it was completely sunk in quicksand.

Flint In The Face knew where Colter was going and he knew full well what the man would do next, for it was what he would do, if he were running for his life. The safety of the swamp beckoned.

"He will hide in one of the lodges," Flint In The Face told the warriors.

A man with a knot of magpie feathers in the topknot of his hair spoke up: "There are many lodges. It will take us days to go through them."

Flint In The Face smiled. He had thought of that him-self. In fact, there were more than a hundred of the big bea-ver homes in the Valley of Waters. True, they could not pos-sibly search through all of them. White Eyebrows was clever, but—

—"He will not bother with the large ones, for they will be too easy for us to enter."

He laughed wisely. It was obvious to the gathered men that Flint In The Face knew the ways of White Eyebrows better than anyone else.

"It is," he announced, "the small lodges, the difficult ones where he will try to hide himself. These we will burn—tonight, when he thinks we are making camp. The torched lodges will light up the dark. We will see him and we will capture him. Alive. He is mine, remember."

The warriors then turned to the work of tracking Colter through the swamp. It was not hard work, Flint In The Face noticed. Even for a wounded man, floundering in the reeds, the trail was too plain. It was another of White Eyebrows' tricks.

"Stop!" he commanded, just as they reached the elk place. "This is not the way he went . . . this is the way he wants us to think he went. He came this way, then doubled back, crawling like a snake through the reeds. Let us not trouble ourselves here, but go directly to the beaver lodges. We will find his tracks in the black mud of the banks."

Colter measured the broken lope of the wounded elk in his mind. Add to it, he considered, something peculiar, something out of balance. The hindfoot, dragging, only partly touching the ground.

Thus he elaborated mentally the disconnected dance of a mortally wounded animal. And holding this thought, he danced it into his own weary bones, so that, in hobbling, he became the thing, the elk itself, running out the last hours of its life. He staggered, always in the swampy water where his tracks would be somewhat lost in the settling mud, pressing his hands and feet deep, but reminding himself of the broken hindfoot, barely touching down, leaving a scrape where the hurt foot dragged. Finally, when he got out into the deeper part of the lake, he swam to the entrance of a beaver lodge and deposited the hoofs inside the tunnel leading in. They would assume, he hoped, that the animal had swum to the other shore. Meanwhile, they would find nothing that might indicate a man on two legs had passed anywhere near.

So far his luck was holding out. But now he heard voices ringing in the pines. They were very close, almost on him. He sighted his objective: the largest lodge in the lake. He swam underwater to the place where he suspected the tunnel might lead to the entrance. The big lodge would have a long and tricky tunnel and would be built like a fortress.

Hidden in the fern bracken, he found the hole in the bank. The lodge, twenty-five feet out in the lake, was enormous, maybe forty feet across, with a ten-foot ceiling. He shoved his head and shoulders into the twenty-five-inch tunnel and writhed his way in. Half-filled with water, as he had supposed, the tunnel wound circuitously under the mud. Pulling and kicking, he dragged himself along. It was not hard to get air, for all he had to do was raise his neck and breathe like a turtle, then press on. Wriggling this way and that, he forged along. Finally, he felt the fresh air that indicated the entrance of the lodge.

Yet though he could feel cool air on his legs and knew that he was almost there, his shoulders were wedged in the small entranceway. He took a long breath and reversed his position by somersaulting forward and turning, wrenching himself sideways, so that he might back into the lodge, feet first.

He made the turn, but got stuck again, this time against

the narrow margin of the tunnel. It occurred to him then that he was just too big-boned to make it through. Nonetheless, he had no choice. He could breathe—but barely, the tunnel was almost full of water now, and it was beginning to collapse around him, letting more water in.

Colter thought: Is this the end of the line? The hole that empties into hell. . . .

But as the tunnel fell in on him, the entrance of the lodge widened some and Colter found that while half of him was outside the lodge—the lower half—the front half was still hung up in the collapsing tunnel. Then there was no more air, and water from all around smashed against him. This widened the entrance even more and Colter hooked his feet on some branches in the lodge and drew himself in. Once in the entrance he again found sweet drafts of life-giving air. Then he was in the lodge, breathing deeply.

For a long time he did not move, felt the rise and fall of his chest, listened to his heart. There was no other sound. After a while, his blood slowed. Still, he drank the air down into his lungs and lay, exhausted. Outside, in the bright sun a surprised bittern boomed an unsociable call. Somewhere, far off, a marsh hawk cried. Colter did not try to move. Completely spent, he lay on the floor of the lodge, trying to assemble some human thoughts, trying to impose order on a mind that kept going blank.

He needed food—and soon. He felt faint, and sick. His heart beat more evenly now, but every so often it skipped a beat and ran off like an undisciplined child. Colter felt prickly all over.

"Don't give out, heart, not just yet," he said prayerfully.

There were many sounds. But, as yet, no human voices. He dropped into the dreamless sleep of a dead man. And as he slept, unmoving, the furtive sounds of the swamp came and went. Wood frogs clucked like chickens. Leopard frogs snored and rattled. Pickerel frogs made a sound like cloth tearing on a nail. And, always, in the midst of these smaller sounds, there was the bass boom of the bullfrog.

When Colter woke—although he did not know it because of the darkness—it was the end of the day. His only thought was that he was still safe. Somehow, though, he could feel them out there. He had no idea what time it was, or how long he had been lying there, but he felt very stiff in the joints and there was an achy, feverish feeling coming on him. His throat was sore and it was painful to swallow.

Rolling on his stomach, he put his face close to the entranceway, and drank some water. It didn't taste brackish and was rather cold and mossy-tasting. He drank long and deep, swallowing the fever out of him. Then he backed deeper into the lodge and sat up. It was cold, shivery.

Then he remembered something about beavers and their dens. Curious creatures, much like men. They had a place to live out of the weather as well as a separate place to store their food, a kind of kitchen or cache, usually quite near the main lodge. They slept on a sleeping loft, off the wet floor of the lodge. Reaching around in the dark, he felt something hard about fourteen inches from the floor. The loft—covered with fresh strips of newly peeled alder bark. Bless their rich little hides, he thought, and crawled onto the loft, burying himself in the good matting. In a few moments, he felt warm. And his mind began to work again.

What was it they called the beaver?

Amik.

He placed the word on his tongue. Amik, he said, thank you, for making me warm. Then, feeling a little foolish, he thanked God for keeping him alive.

But for how long?

That inescapable furry feeling came over him. Images in his mind blurred, fuzzed out. The big dead elk jumped out of the mud and shook itself. A beaver twice the size of the lodge emerged from the water with a water lily in its mouth. Colter shrank to the size of an ant and fell into a vortex of whirling water. Spinning, he again lost consciousness.

When he awoke he had but one thought.

Food.

He had to have something to eat.

He considered the food caches he and Potts had dug up. Beavers were vegetarians. Yet their simple fare consisted of both inedible sedges and edible berries. Colter began to stir, moving about on all fours, feeling for the exit hole, which he believed might lead to a food cache.

The lodge was huge. As he went around on all fours, he thought about the lives of the beavers, their constructs of canals, locks, dams. He marveled at the thought of their mud and log lodges, walls four feet thick, clay banks well-wooded with aspen, alder and willow. They stored plentiful food, had plentiful water, and created as much safety as any man could want. Their worst enemy, aside from coyotes, wildcats and the occasional wolverine, was man. And now, secreted in the walls of a beaver lodge, Colter reminded himself that he'd taken the lives of so many of these good-hearted little animals. One morning, all by himself, he'd trapped ninety-six beavers. Now, his life was worth no more than theirs, and he knew what it felt like to be one of the hunted.

Searching around with his hands, he touched a hole in the wall of the lodge. Perhaps another exit. He leveled himself into it, his broad shoulders shoving hard against the conical curves of wood and mud. Once in, he dragged himself into an adjoining room. The entrance of the room was quite large, owing, he thought, to the possibility of bringing food-stores into it—branches with lots of leaves.

I may have found myself a larder, he thought.

And so it was: a dining chamber. But the clicking of incisors woke him to a new reality. There was a beaver somewhere very nearby. He could almost feel the warmth of its body and he could certainly hear the clicking of its razory teeth. Colter knew that beavers were not given to fighting among themselves. They hardly fought against their foes—they were too clever for that. But occasionally he'd seen them get their backs up and then they were ferocious. Those teeth that chopped wood could cut through flesh like butter.

Hissing a warning, the beaver backed away from Colter. Colter covered his face. Without being able to see, he was completely vulnerable. The beaver rattled its teeth.

Then Colter understood that he was blocking the animal's only way out. Slowly, he drew himself to the side of the lodge. At once there was a clicking of webbed claws and the beaver escaped back into the big lodge. Colter, having backed even further away, bumped his head against a row of sticks. He fumbled around with his hands.

Then smiled. Pay dirt. The open kitchen was his. And full it was: a great pile of beaver food—sedges, berries, spatter-docks, nettles, mushrooms, cow parsnips, rushes, bur-weeds, blossoms, iris bulbs.

Sighing with satisfaction, he felt among the pile for something really tasty. The berries were fresh and he ate of them greedily, juice dripping down his chin and sting-ing the knife wound there. When he had eaten all of the berries, he sought out the parsnips and mushrooms. Un-like the sweet berries, these were dry and bitter-tasting. The eccentric, almost meaty flavor of the mushrooms made him think of how he liked to gather the big red and gold chanterelles. Death caps and poison pies he'd seen plenty of too, in the forest, but he and the beavers knew the difference. These mushrooms, though very dry, were good to eat. He continued randomly to stuff his mouth. Swallowing hard, his throat hurt, throbbed. But his stom-ach was beginning to feel a little less crampy. He selected something almost delectable—the fruit of the royal fern, and it was freshly picked. He ate it down. In among the grasses and roots, he found some watercress, also fresh. Crunching it up with his teeth, he discovered that he badly needed another drink. This time he really drank his fill, the icy water soothing his mind and soul and easing the pain in his throat.

After eating, Colter felt tired again. Full for the first time in two days, he decided not to drag himself back into the main lodge but try and make do here. Although there was no sleeping loft in the food cache, he did find a slightly ele-vated place lined with an aspen bedding, probably a place for beaver kits to sleep while their mothers worked at the winter's drying. He covered himself with soft ticking, and immediately fell asleep.

In the beginning," Long Arm was saying around the camp-fire as the flames leaped in front of his face, "the beaver people were all about this place. But they did not make it as you see it today because it was their wish, but instead they built these watery valleys as a defense against the whims of Coyote. He made his dams out of mountains. They made theirs out of mud and sticks. But as you know, they were the better builders and they won out. Beaver is a holy person and he must not be taken for a fool. To burn the lodges is a bad thing and in the end we will suffer for it. That is all I have to say."

The fire, leaping on the spruce logs, cracked loudly. Some members of the party nodded and said "Ai" so that Long Arm knew they were one with him. But the fire that danced the loudest was in the eye of Flint In The Face. To him there was no other way. They had passed the entire day, looking for a sign, and all they had turned up was the faded footprint of a wounded elk. Once again, White Eye-brows had left the forest without a trace.

"The man we seek," Flint In The Face said, "is but a man. I have seen his blood and it is red like ours."

"Let the boy, Raccoon's Brother, speak of what he saw," one of the men said.

All eyes turned upon the youth.

The boy licked his lips and stared emptily into the flames. The spirit of speech was not in him, but he would, if they wished, tell them what he had seen. A purple bruise between his eyebrows showed where White Eyebrows had knocked him out.

He spoke not like a boy but a man: "As you know I have seen the one they call White Eyebrows. He came from the sky and landed on all four of his feet. He looked me in the face. I could not look upon him for long, so I do not remember what he looked like."

Raccoon's Brother watched as the silent trail of smoke went up the great smokehole of the night and mingled with the fires of the star people.

"His blood," he continued, "may be like ours. But they say even the great bear in the sky drips blood on the earth this time of year and makes the leaves turn red."

"—White Eyebrows is no more than a man—" Flint In The Face scowled.

Some of the others grumbled their assent. One or two of them even laughed, but afterwards they peered over their shoulders into the shadows.

"The time has come," Flint In The Face announced.

The warriors got to their feet and each one took a fire-brand from the fire.

"See to the small lodges first," Flint In The Face told them. "And if you see White Eyebrows, make the sound of Owl so I will know."

Only the boy, Raccoon's Brother, and the old man, Long Arm, stayed by the fire. The others took the flames out into the night.

Outside the lodge where John Colter slept, the noises of the night had changed their pattern. A fox barked, clear and cold, far away. Then, close inshore, the throng of the frogs stopped. Like a great rippling blanket, the night noises changed shape. Colter awoke, listened. There was a lisping of water, other sounds he could not identify. He listened, craning his neck.

He rubbed his hand over his arm and felt the hard-caked mud. Then he felt his face, his chest. The mud covered him like a casing of darkness.

Good, I will not be easily seen.

At the crown of the cache, Colter knew there was the weak point, a place where the beavers left a hole to allow fresh air to enter and stale air to exit. It was identical to the smokehole of an Indian lodge.

Reaching for his knife, he got to his knees and poked the blade up at the curved inner dome of the cache. He began a steady probing, forcing the blade deeper and deeper into the roof.

Suddenly there was a crash.

Footsteps.

There was a man walking on the roof of the cache. Colter listened as the man creaked above his head. Some of the sticks he'd been prying at cracked and fell. Then, all at once, a foot dangled in front of Colter's face. He reached for it and with one pull, jerked the man's body into the chamber. He came down hard, crashing.

Colter was on him, with his knife. But the warrior moved quickly and the knife plunged into the aspen bedding.

Then the man had Colter about the neck and the two of them rolled, grunting and kicking, and seeking a lethal hold. Colter had lost his knife in the tussle; it was somewhere under them.

A knee out of nowhere jolted Colter in the skull. Lightning flickered around the edge of his eye sockets. He fell heavily. The grip on his neck tightened, choking him. Sputtering in the dark, he clawed with his fingers, snared something loose and soft, drew it powerfully downward.

He had a handful of hair with which to bargain for his life. . . .

Now, as the man closed on his throat, Colter pulled the hair back, pulled and pulled until he felt the hold on his own neck loosen. Then, unexpectedly, he snapped the man's head as far as the tension would allow.

The darkness groaned, the head swiveled, and regained itself. Again he pulled the horse's mane of hair, and again the head rocked back. Each time, Colter heard the vertebrae pop, but the man who had a deathgrip on his throat would not quit.

They were rolling around the lodge, banging against the tooth-sharpened beaver poles. Suddenly, Colter felt the burning coil on his neck slip. The choker hold broke off. Wasting no time, he put all of his might into his own hair-grip until the sickening crack told him it was done.

He felt behind the dead man. In his shoulder he found his missing knife and against one side of his neck there was a gaping wound where one of the beaver-staves had punched a hole.

There was no time for anything except escape. Colter ejected his body through the opening made by the unexpected warrior and crouched on top of the cache. The night was ablaze with lodge fires, beaver lodges burning eerily. Men dashed wildly from one to another, trying to set fire to them all.

Colter saw that his best bet was the long dam that led to the middle of the lake. It was but a few feet away from him. Once on it he could run for the cover of the marsh.

Leaping into the darkness, he landed without slipping on the long dam. Then he ran along its length toward the shore. There was a whiz of arrows. He dived into the tamaracks just as a fire arrow stabbed into the trunk behind him.

Again John Colter was running for his life.

He tore through the woods as through a spiderweb—a brown, mud-caked man, stumbling through a swamp filled with the howls of those who wanted his blood.

He broke through a copse of willows and staggered into the circle of fire. No one was there. A green spruce log bubbled with sap. Colter came up to it, rubbed the hot sap through his fingers, ran it into his hair.

Then he stuck the top of his head in the fire. His hair, mud lacquered to the roundness of his skull, was alive with little blue lightnings that sputtered about his head.

The old man and the boy, who had just come back to the fire, saw the thing standing there. The brown body, the perfectly round bluish head that glowed like a star.

S I X

GLASS

Hugh Glass drank his fill at the spring. From the gray-leafed bush nearby where the flushed bullberries grew he fed himself, stripping it of every fruit and downing them mechanically, despite their measure of bitterness. And he drank again, forcing swallow after swallow till he felt distended, till he gurgled when he moved.

Then he turned himself to the south, for to the north lay the bad lands of the Little Missouri, burnt black as the Devil's backbone. To the south ran a little stream, some vegetation beside it, and that way took one farther from the Ree. He dragged himself a body's length in that direction, then paused to rest.

It was over a hundred miles to Fort Kiowa on the Missouri. He knew it was madness to try crawling that distance. Yet, it was death to remain. He dragged himself another body's length and rested again. And again. As soon as a measure of strength returned he pulled himself a few inches forward. South. The stream would deviate, go dry after a time, the land grow harder. But there was no real choice. There was no reason to wait, and many not to.

Pull a little farther, pause and gasp. Pull again. There must be an ideal rhythm to it. He would find it. Pause. Pull.

Dragging the injured leg, he pulled himself along, sometimes pushing with his elbows, sometimes raising himself up on his hands. He tried pushing with the good foot. His ribs ached at the sternum when he rose up; his back hurt when he stayed low. His injured leg dragged like a dead thing, a piece of metal, a stick of wood. This, too, caused his back to ache. After a while the pain in the leg awoke. No longer dead, but of no use either, it began to throb as he moved, a thing of dull fire and occasional stabbing pang. But there was another fire in him, as well. Born of a different pain, it burned hotter, and it overrode the protests of his body, making him dig in with his elbows and push downward, backward, pause to draw breath, and do it again. He felt it in his gut, and it burned behind his eyes, casting unwanted pictures before him. . . .

. . . Riding into the melée, swinging his rifle like a club, snatching the boy away from his attacker. Later, he spanked him to teach him good sense. And the bear walking like a man on its hind legs come forward to embrace him there in the field where both held rifles and he taught him to brace it properly elbow out hold the breath exhale squeeze and his hair catching sunlight bright device on a flag seizing him with inexorable deathclasp urgency breathe exhale squeeze musk and honey and berries and rot and Jamie riding before him laughing twisted snakes in his hand down openings in the earth following hoofbeats into darkness and damp. . . .

He woke with a growl. Immediately, he raised himself

and began crawling again. The shadows had lengthened, the earth was hard, and knobby roots projected, gouging him as he moved. He was going downward, into the creek's gully. Grasses caught at him. A small thicket barred his way.

He drew himself on, finally pausing, both to rest and to figure the best way through the thicket. He wanted to reach waterside before nightfall, to drink, to have it there in the morning for further refreshment. It seemed a difficult enterprise, though he could smell the water, could hear it if he lay very still.

He essayed the course, and tiny, brittle fingers caught at his clothing, poked at his flesh. He extricated himself from one entanglement only to discover that another held him. And his dragging leg. . . . He seemed never to be aware when it was trapped until pain lanced along it.

Gasping and sweating, he worked his way through the thicket, resting frequently, plagued by insects, coughing at the dust or pollen he breathed. By the time he emerged from the reedy stand the day was perceptibly darker. Halting, to wipe his eyes, to catch his breath, he could feel that it had grown cooler, also.

A feeling of near-despair came over him, for he knew that, had he been on higher ground, he could look back to the camp he had quitted. Were someone there, he could conduct a shouted conversation with him. To have spent the entire afternoon to travel this short distance. . . .

Farther. Just a little farther now. He was feeling spent, but the water was near. It seemed to take forever, inching his way along over this irregular terrain. He could not allow himself to stop now, not when this small goal was so near. The pain in his leg grew worse and he forced himself to concentrate on the trail. He was panting steadily as he topped a small rise and looked down.

Water. In sight. A final effort then and he came up beside the stream, dropped his face down into it, felt it, sucked it in. He drew back coughing, then chuckling, drank again, sighed, drank again.

It had grown darker during this last leg of his journey. He shifted a little to one side and cushioned his head on his arm. He realized that he was hungry. But even more, he was sleepy.

He heard the birds singing above his grave. Dreaming, he lay in that hole, back in camp, mound of earth beside it. His friend had put him there. Now, though, he felt a cool breeze, and birds were calling. He stirred, remembering, and the rage beat in him like an extra heart, and he would rise. He moaned and clenched his teeth and swallowed. He would rise. Rise, and make his way again. For somewhere Jamie waited, laughing now. It would not always be so. For he would find him. He would come crawling, insect-slow. Crawling now. Not always, though. He would live and walk again, would find the one who had put him in this place. He opened his eyes. Birdsong, breezes, light: morning.

He gathered his strength, moved to the left, and took a long drink. Then he sought the area with his gaze now it lay in full light. And there were more berries, and plants he knew whose roots were edible.

He stirred himself again, to breakfast. Afterwards, he harvested all of the additional bread-roots he could locate, stuffing their gnarly twists into his pockets. There would likely be few such more to be found between the Moran and the Grand. Moving streamside again, he swallowed water to fullness, rested for several minutes.

Then he pulled himself upward from the stream and commenced to crawl. The coulee he had entered would deepen, he knew, widen, and continue as a great gulch before it brought him to the vast plain. He would lose the stream, and perhaps his life, somewhere ahead. He drew himself farther, paused, crawled on. He was off on the best start he could make.

The coulee twisted and angled through a slow rising, its stones scoring his body in a double-dozen places. Winds teased him, bringing dust into his mouth and eyes. A pair of crows investigated his presence, decided that he moved too much, passed on. He labored up the rises, pulled himself over sharp bits of detritus in the level areas. The day warmed about him, and he felt the first touch of sweat upon his face. He spat and continued, checking the creek's dwindling flow at each rising of the land. Finally, the waters diminished to the point where he knew he must drink his fill once more, against a long time without.

Sucking up the last from his hand-scooped basin, he thought again of the one who had left him, reduced him to this animal-like scrabbling for sustenance. If his stomach was not full at least his heart had a bitter food to sustain him in his traveling, to drive his effort to return to balance accounts.

He turned away from the muddy depression and continued his journey, rage taking his mind from the pains in his body. Inching along—uphill now—he rehearsed the words he would say, to have them perfect when the grand day of vengeance arrived. He said them over and over in his mind, changing them slightly each time, seeing the startled, frightened face of the one he addressed, on each occasion, anticipating responses, fresh remonstrances. It seemed to buoy him as he went—anticipation, master of will.

It was a strange sort of happiness that filled him for a time then, as he crawled through the widening coulee, dreaming of vengeance. Then he stared too long at the boy's face in one of the visions, and he cursed and put them all aside. Southward. . . . Dragging himself through the growing day, nibbling a root, dozing, waking hot and sticky, continuing on.

The coulee continued to widen and its sides rose about him, nothing to eat or drink at either hand. He clawed his way up an incline, slid down another, leg aching all the way. His hands had stopped stinging, developing a certain measure of numbness. His face still throbbed, however, thick scabs cracking and oozing as he went. His ribs continued to ache.

He worked his way forward as the sun climbed to its noonday height. A measure of use and fatigue, he discovered, banished some lesser pains. And he watched the sun fall from its height, still hauling himself forward, and his thirst grew. He thought of it only periodically at first, but as the sun continued its descent it came more and more to occupy his mind, until at length it was his constant companion. Coming upon a patch of spongy ground, he sought a spring, but none was to be found. He tried digging in it with his hands, but no trickle, no exhalation of droplets came into his wells. Finally, half-crazed, he pressed his lips to the earth and sucked. Spitting then, he rose with a curse, so like his life of late was the taste—mud, grit between the teeth. And his rage came upon him again. Upward then. This could well be the sign of some spring above. His thirst added speed to his crawling. Upward, over dirt and stone, and he came to another muddy area, too like the first for halting. Yet it drove him on, sign of something that could await, above.

More damp spots occurred along the way, driving him to a greater frenzy. The sun continued its westward slide, and the gulch's walls quickly grew shadows out from their talus. The clouds were already pink when he saw a shimmering ahead.

Yes, it was a pool. He drove himself, panting, toward it. Undisturbed, it reflected the colorful sky.

Coming up beside, he plunged his head into it. For a single moment only, it was blissful. Then he reared back and spat. So bitter! The water had leached its way through an alkaline deposit, and his mouth felt singed at its taste. He spat again, and again.

Moving back, he drew his shirt up over his head. It was relatively easy, despite his aching sides. It was the trousers that would give him trouble, going down over that leg. He unbuckled and unbuttoned, turned slowly onto his back, sharp pains shooting up his right leg as he did so. Working them down over his hips, he raised himself into a seated position and slipped the trousers down to his knees. Then he beheld his right thigh for the first time since the day of the bear. It was swollen enormously and purpled all about, dark red about the purple. It almost hurt to look at it. Gingerly, he reached out and tapped it. Nothing. Almost a numbness. He pressed, then bit his lip to keep from crying out as the pain came to life again. Waiting for it to subside, he studied it, wondering how it would mend, should he live long enough to see it heal. He could not tell whether the bones lay badly within all that swollen flesh. Still, dragging it about this way must not be doing nature any favors with her work. He shook his head, pushed the trousers down farther, held them in place, and slowly extracted his left leg.

He paused to recover, then pushed the right pantleg down as far as he could. There, at midcalf, the problem began, with the upper leg's immobility. It was easiest, he finally decided, to lie back, catch the trousers with his left foot, then work them the rest of the way off. Immediately, he saw problems in getting them back on again. But he also saw that it could be done, and he continued. Then the rest, slowly, a bit at a time. . . .

He turned over again, and slowly he crawled. It felt completely different, crawling with skin bare against the earth. Not bad, only different, as the sand and the stones brushed against him, bare as a snake's belly against their gritty caress.

Pulling himself steadily, greedily, he moved forward until he touched the water. Then he drew himself on into it. He shivered briefly and went ahead, feeling it rise along his flanks, his sides, up his wrists and forearms, almost like sliding into a dream. Farther still, until, save for his upraised head, he was entirely immersed. To have the tug of gravity grow slack, almost to float, after a day so close to the earth. . . . He turned easily onto his back, stared up at the sky. Could he absorb water through his skin, or was that an old wives' tale? It didn't matter, he decided. It felt good just to try.

The sky continued to darken above him, arched from black to massy black of the gulch's walls, and night came on, scattering stars. A breeze blew over him, all but his face insulated from its touch. A high wisp of cirrus grew incandescent from the constellations it held. The wind began to murmur amidst the stone, and after a while he felt warm, or warmly numb. The stars drifted, as if the night were tilting, doubled, grew hazy as his eyes began to close.

It seemed that Jamie sat at a campfire with him, all their troubles past, listening while he talked, telling the tale of his crawling, of rocks and sand, bread-root and berries, of his encounter with a bear, of his soaking by night in a poison pool. . . . The smoke kept shifting around Jamie's face. . . .

He woke to dawn, sprawled upon the pool's rim to which he had crawled sometime during the night. Half of the sun shone across him from the top of the wall to his left. He withdrew slowly from the dreaming, not wanting to crawl another inch, ever again, on the doomed journey he had undertaken. Better to stay here till the end, soaking, drowsing.

The sun moved higher and he entered the pool once more, bathing, soaking. At last, he came forth and began the long rite of donning his garments, dry now from a washing of their own last night. When he had done, he ran a hand over his beard, through his hair, turned onto his belly, drew away from the pool, headed upward again. No sounds came to him but his own, and their sometime echoes off the stony walls.

He crawled, not with yesterday's first, manic intensity, though the thirst was still there. His way wound steadily upward now, and occasionally he had need to seize hold of projections to drag himself higher. Today, he resolved to pace himself. No more pushing to the point of exhaustion, collapsing into a panting heap, going on when his breath and strength returned. Today he would move in a more measured fashion, resting periodically whether or not he felt a need to halt.

So he crawled and rested, crawled and rested, husbanding his strength. At noon, he lunched on a handful of roots, and he fell into a light sleep afterwards. Awakening, he commenced crawling again and the sun made its way across the sky above him. When his thirst grew fiery he found a smooth pebble and sucked on it as he went.

Slowly, the walls descended at either hand. More and more vines and shrubs now appeared upon them. About him, a few small trees reared, and grasses dotted the ground.

At length, ahead, dark patches appeared amid the vines, and the trees came in thicker stands. At first, he deemed the irregular spots but recesses of shade within their spreading leaves. But, pausing to rest, his gaze came upon them again and the world redefined itself within his vision.

Grapes! His throat constricted and a bit of moisture came into his mouth. Purple, juicy. . . . Turning, he hauled himself toward the cool vines. Thoughts of the visions of dying men—mirages, dreams, wishes—played within his mind. He crawled. The grapes did not waver, but grew more clear within his rapid blinking. He pulled himself along as he had to the pool, faster now, exerting himself to his limit, slumping only once. Grapes. Yes. A simple abundance. He would not depart, he vowed, till every one within his grasp had been chewed, swallowed, its juices flowing into the streams of his body, cooling.

Then they were before him. He extended his hand, realizing it to be shaking. But they did not fade as he took hold of a bunch, gently, and pulled it free of the vine. And then he was eating, crushing them in his mouth, letting the sweetness slide back, swallowing. His stomach protested but a moment, with a single sharp pang, as if surprised from sleep. Then this was gone, and he was swallowing again, and again, reaching for another bunch.

The second one went down quickly, also, and the third, and the fourth. He did not slow in his harvesting and eating till he had stripped away all of those ready to hand. Then he crawled to the next place of clusters and began again. Finishing these, he moved once more and, as he did so, something about the several nearby trees took his attention.

Small red fruits hung from them, some fallen to the ground beneath. Plums, he realized, there were plums here, also. He kept eating the grapes. Afterward. . . . With the plums, he could continue with a full belly. Those that he might reach or knock down, anyway.

He stripped the grapevines, a feeling of fullness coming to him as he did so. And a great lassitude. He sprawled then, resting from his exertions. Lowering his head to his outflung arm, he closed his eyes.

He awoke shaking, his paws—his hands—extended before him. A piece of dream which had almost drifted away returned, and he had had hold of Jamie and was squeezing the boy's throat. The young features were distorted, all the slyness fled, fear widening the eyes, an unnatural redness suffusing the cheeks, the forehead. He was readying a bearlike shrug to snap that neck. And there was a wild joy in him as, teeth clenched, he growled the words, "Thief! Betrayer!" Jamie's lips moved, but he could not hear the reply. He realized, as he relaxed his hands, that he still felt the joy, that it would be a good thing to give that shrug, to execute in that final moment the end of the feelings he'd held since his awakening beside that grave the boy had left him to.

Seeking neither to dismiss nor retain these thoughts, he raised himself and looked about, knowing of a sudden that he was stronger, that this was the best he had felt since that awakening. The shadows had lengthened, he saw, and he regarded the empty vines almost with affection for the succor they had given him. Turning his attention to the several plum trees then, he began crawling in their direction.

Partway there, he halted, staring at the ground. Old, dry, crumbling about the edges, was the impression of a massive foot. He reached out and traced it lightly. Bear. And old enough to have been left by his bear, foraging among these same vines, back before their encounter. Strange, this message from a time before the mauling. Finding it here. A recognition of how things were, or how they yet might be?

He shook his head. What strange musings. . . .

He drew himself past the mark, approaching the trees. All of the fruits still on the branches were above his reach, but there were some on the ground. These he gathered, eating as he went along, sucking, chewing, spitting pits. And there lay the stick he had hoped for, a fallen limb, off to his left.

When he had eaten all of the fallen fruit he crawled to the trunk of the tree and pushed upon it, several times. It began to sway, leaves rattling. Three more plums fell to the ground. These, he gathered and ate. Then, with the branch, he struck at those within reach, dislodging a few. These, too, he garnered. When no more could be obtained in this manner he moved on to the next tree, repeating the gathering, the shaking, the striking, the eating. Somewhere along the way, he realized that he was sated. Yet he resolved not to depart until he had taken all of the nourishment available. At the final tree he simply gathered all of those fallen into a mound, to which he added all of those he could shake or knock down. Then he rested from his exertions, dozing again.

When he awoke, with no memory of further dreaming, he lay still for a long while, breathing the smells of the grasses, the fruit, and the earth, so close to his face. When he saw fit to move, his limbs creaked, then he scratched a number of itches, and massaged his right thigh above the break where a tingling sensation persisted. Afterwards, he ate the rest of the plums and threw the branch into the tree. Two more were dislodged. He threw it again and it caught, hanging, above his reach. He shook the tree several times, but it remained. He had reached the limit of the place's bounty.

He ate the two final fruits then, trying to savor them. But their taste merged with his fullness and could not equal the flavor of the first.

Again he rested, loath to depart this place of refreshment, and again he drowsed, and the day worked its way to completion above his head, weaving shadows into a dark entirety. When he woke again he studied the night, then, turning, felt his way back to the broken slope he had crawled up. Upward then, toward that place where the rim joined with the plain, feeling his way, crawling.

He passed through the darkness, wondering at its cooler qualities against his exertions. Better, he decided, as he mounted the incline, to travel thus, by night, resting during the day, sweating less, preserving those fluids the sun drew forth to soak his garments, to evaporate away. As easy, it was, to mark his passage by the stars than the hot orb's comings and goings. For the plain would be hot by day. . . .

Drawing himself upward, resting at intervals, the black line of the gulch's rim near now beneath the stars, he found himself hurrying, postponing a rest period to achieve that boundary. When, at length, he was upon it, he lowered his head and panted, counting this as a victory, though a small one, in his struggle. He waited till his breath had grown regular, the tingling in his hands and arms subsided, the throbbing in his leg diminished, before he pulled himself forward again, two feet, four, six, ten, onto the level terrain beneath the big sky.

He raised his head then, gazing aloft. The Big Dipper hung to his right, halfway down the sky. He crawled forward then, to pass a field of broken stone. Then left, turning his back to the north. He felt, at a great distance, the plain all about him. In the faint starlight it stretched on into immensity. And that star-occluding mass far, far ahead—a butte, by which he'd take his way.

He dragged himself toward it, feeling grasses already, rather than bare earth, beneath him. These thickened as he advanced, making a sighing sound along the limp leg he hauled. Distantly, he heard a coyote howl across the night.

As he moved away from the mouth of the gulch he felt as if he were coming free, coming up out of the earth beneath which he had wandered, coming free of its tugging against which he had struggled as he had mounted the long slope. Roots and tendrils no longer wrapped him, trapped him, caught at him. Now the grasses slid by, softening his way, their hillocks nothing compared to the rocks he had fought with below. And this open night was somehow cleaner, free of the close dampness that did not quench any thirst. He moved more rapidly on the level, sometimes clutching fistfuls of the tough grasses and simply pulling. Now he felt he could hasten the day—whether it be the day of his undoing or the day of his vengeance. Either way, he hied toward it now, dark mass across the plain, and the wind could almost be singing as the stars wheeled in their great stately dance and the air came clean into his lungs. His movements grew more fluid, the need to rest lessening; though he continued to pause periodically, he lengthened the intervals between such pauses. He felt a hint of his old strength coming into his arms; even the pains in his ribcage had subsided by more than half, so that when a chuckle arose, unbidden, it did not hurt him.

After a time, his movements became hypnotic in their regularity. Flashes of alertness came to him at some unexpected obstacle, recalling him as from unremembered dream; one time of rest he dozed and dreamed that he was crawling. In a way it was the same. Continuing was all.

Later, the moon came up and spilled a glow across the plain. The grasses and low shrubs were touched with silver.

The contours of the butte were limned in greater detail. He adjusted his course slightly. He had shadows now for company; his own reached out a little before him, like his dark spirit drawing him onward. It amused him to feel that he could not die till he'd covered the space it had claimed, always just slightly ahead.

He followed his shadow, slipping into and out of dreams. Sometimes it seemed a daylight meadow through which he passed, flowers all about him. He could even smell their scents, borne on light spring breezes. It was almost like home, and him a child again, crawling among them, playing at deerstalking or war.

His shadow shifted and the moon rolled down the sky, changing the face of the butte. He crawled and sometimes rested. The grasses tickled his face. A coyote's call seemed to reach him from another world. Once, a startled rabbit burst from the grasses beside him, bringing his mind back into the focus of his body from the great distances to which it seemed to have spread. Then the moon was overhead, all shadows hidden; then it hung to his right like a lantern beside some invisible wagon. Now his mind was all moon, even as he rested. Now the moon grew nearer the butte, transforming that still entity yet again; it now became the stump of a great tree, himself perhaps the upper body seeking to reunite itself and stand. Crawling, he felt the desire for wholeness, for union with the shattered limb that hung useless. Other times, it was as if the leg pursued him, malicious entity catching hold and dragging back. He muttered to it then, telling it to let go and leave him to his business, cursing it. The moon continued to ride into the west. He felt his shadow pulling him to the left. But always the butte. He looked to it, called to it, feeling now as the leg must feel, dragging, seeking to be reunited with its larger self. He apologized to the leg. He called out again to the butte. A pair of birds fluttered into the air before him and he collapsed, panting. "Come back . . ." he said. He had come back to himself. He found himself thirsty. He licked the grasses for a little dew, then commenced crawling, slowly, again, pausing to lick at the grasses after each advancement. After a time, he felt as if he might be leaving a smeared trail, like that of some giant, single-footed slug. Gradually, the damp taste of the grasses cooled the dryness in his throat. The moon came down to touch the horizon, which sliced it, each time that he looked, until it was gone.

Later, eastward, came a paling. The stars went away, a field at a time. Hate, now. He felt it warming his bowels. Still he drove himself onward, despite his resolve to rest at dawn. Jamie would be that pile of rock, and he would reach it. He pulled himself forward, gnawing at his lower lip until he tasted blood.

SEVEN

COLTER

By the fire he snatched up a blanket of soft trader's wool. Wheeling about, he crashed into the bracken, leaving the two watchers standing, mouths open. He ran but a few feet into the tangle before he plummeted to the ground and sank his head into the mossy soil. His was a thick head of hair; the mud and pitch had saved his scalp. Chuckling, he imagined the effect—wet blue curls licking across a pirate's pate. The boy and the old man would not soon forget that sight. Now he dampened his head in the spongy swamp moss that came away in his hand like fleece. A tenderness around his forehead suggested he'd not guessed right—in the madness of the moment, he'd not felt the burn. Now, tenderly touching his forehead, he winced at the risen welt.

Add that to the tab, he growled. And took off through the thick growth, thinking: Still, to my credit, I am alive.

There was but one thing to do: Get out of the Forks.

And but one way to do it: Climb.

He knew the country like that of his own palm, all the familiar whorls going southeast. Out of the swamp, there was a treeless place, a grassy knoll where he'd camped with Potts, eating beaver tail, succulent, fat-broiled beaver tail. His mouth watered, thinking of it. Beyond this, going steadily uphill to the butte were the caves the Crows called Blue Bead, and which he and Potts had renamed The Quarry. In these caves they carved their curious stone pipe bowls, of the deep blue plumstone that lay around.

Such thoughts flitted through Colter's brain as he came to the starlit knoll, lungs on fire from the uphill run. Behind him he could hear the shouts of his pursuers, and through the stately columns of pine, he saw the torch-lit runners coming after him.

He'd been carrying the rolled blanket about his neck. Now he took it, slashed two armholes, pushed his arms through and mounted the blanket around him like a sheath. Already, though his body was sweaty, he could feel a fresh bite to the air. And for the first time since the chief had waved him on and he had begun the run for his life, Colter's heart ached for it to be over: to lie still and not move. The pain in his calves was unendurable, his hamstrings hurt like flayed flesh. The burns and contusions and bruises had taken their toll, and the cactus nettles he'd been unable to extract were pustulant reminders of his weakened state. All over his body ached. Pushed beyond capacity, his old leg injury flamed up, and he limped, dazedly.

Again, he wondered: What are my chances?

Yet if he turned himself over to them now, he knew what they would do. First, a feast in his honor, fete him, honor him; then stake him to a barked tree, open his belly and unwind his entrails, dance them around him—ring-around-the-rosy—in a bright spiderweb of blood; then, cook a chunk of his own buttock, serve it up to him on a hot plank. He'd heard the most gruesome tales, some of them invented, some of them true. One time he witnessed a man being dismembered, one limb at a time, until he was just a trunk, propped against a tree, still alive and gouting blood from his mouth. The man had not stopped screaming, even after they'd severed his head. The head, mindless of its death, had screamed. And screamed, hissing itself bloodily into oblivion.

No, if death was the way, it would not come through surrender. He plowed on, bashing his forearms into saplings that barred his path. The land rose steeply—who chose to follow would have to climb.

Soon the leaf trees thinned, their place taken by jackpine sunken into the iron beginnings of the great-headed butte. The solid green fell behind, the grey-blue rock lay ahead, bathed in shivering starlight.

Colter made for the rock, the gaunt stone tower the Crows called Heart Mountain. Somewhere to the south, across forest and thicket and plain, and through the place where the land heaved up into spumes of foul, burning water, was the fort . . . running, clawing upward, he could not remember the name . . .

. . . Fort Manuel Lisa, the last "civilized" outpost he'd started out from two years ago. Started out fresh and eager, hurly burly, to seek his fur-trader's fortune. Fatten his purse by stealing furs off the beaver's back, selling them to fat merchants in St. Louis, who'd turn around and market them in England, so that fine English folk might trip down Hodding Lane in the latest fashion: beaver felt, beaver collar.

He spat to think of it. Greed, unmitigated greed, had gotten him into this. And only guts would get him out.

Now stunted pine was all that held him to the trail, if trail it was, more like broken talus in vast orifices of rock, broken plates of talus which fell away like huge china chips at his touch. Barefoot, he arched his back, and seizing the jackpine roots, clenched a hold, worked his way up, tenuously, using his legs like posts. As he crawled, he bested the worst places and came, finally, to a seamless face of stone that soared straight up in front of him.

I will not think about falling, he mumbled.

Only climbing.

Below, in the enclosure of the pines, he saw the pitch-flares stab at the night.

On they come . . . will nothing stop them?

Flint In The Face called for his men to stop pawing the ground.

"We rest here," he said, "go no further."

"Given time," Raccoon's Brother said, panting, "White Eyebrows will ascend to the Beaver Moon. She will catch him in her arms, and she will laugh at us—"

A few of the men, tired of the chase and wishing they were snug in their tipis, laughed.

The others grimaced in the cold, said nothing.

"Yes, there is Beaver Moon," Flint In The Face agreed, "and maybe she favors Seekheeda. But there comes, now, one he did not plan to greet so soon—Old Man Snow. He comes. Do you not feel the soft tread of his moccasins in the trees?"

By then Long Arm had hobbled up to where they stood under the canopy of pine, by the long downward flow of talus.

He was gasping for air, his long white hair fallen down over his shoulders. In the light of the pitch-torch, he himself resembled Old Man Snow, and the warriors saw this.

"Rest, Uncle," Flint In The Face chanted softly, "Take your ease. Tomorrow we decide if you climb, or stay—"

"I shall go no farther," the old man wheezed. "Far is far enough. You are right about the things you say. It is time for me to rest, and it is time that Old Man Snow put all of us to rest—at home, where we belong. I can feel him drawing his great, silent bow in the air. Soon we will all feel the sting of his arrows."

They nodded: for the sudden, unexpected coming of it was a palpable presence. The damp, marrow-claiming cold caught the cheerless group, nipped their toes and fingers, weary from the futile hunt. The torches were dropped in a circle on the earth, dry wood heaped upon them. And they drew close to the flames of their squaw-wood fire under the bald head of Heart Mountain, and they felt the cold bow draw back from the north.

For John Colter the world had narrowed to a single rock, the purchase of it, the tremble of his hand as he took it in his grasp, and made for the next handhold. He was no climber, but he had been on this rack of rock once before, on the Sunlit Basin side, climbing, hand over hand, his life tethered to his breath.

In the pulse of stars and the milky light of the shrouded

moon, which he knew hinted of early snow, he could see. Far below, the voices rose and again, the insane smell of meat. He pushed on, glad of the blanket that girded him from the meanness of the night's chill.

There was a chance, just a small chance, that the snow would hold off until the dawn. In that case, though he knew he could not possibly reach the top of the mountain, he might find a chute, a spot to shelter himself for a time, wait out the storm when it came. As such, his gamble was two-edged: It would make difficulties for both the hunter and the hunted. Yet if he could increase his pace, get high enough, he might yet see the morning's ice confound them—or the noonday's runoff stop them in their tracks.

Whatever, his task lay before him.

Rock.

Minions and pinions of faulted stone. Once, reaching out too quickly, his hand broke off a rotten piece of stone. Another time, as he drew himself agonizingly upward, a small white owl was frightened from its perch above his head. Climbing, he heard the soft downy ruffle of startled wings. Once, an arcing, bouncing thing fell from above— reminder that rock is alive and moves in the dark as it dreams its sleep of stone.

After a few hours of slow climbing, he wedged his knees into a fissure, wound his arms about a miserable knob of stone, and sagged to a restful position. Here, after a while, his breathing slowed. Heart came bubbling up at his ears. The rest of him, poor, broken body flesh hung like bacon on a hook of steel.

But Colter always reminded himself: I am yet alive. And hung on, sucking air. Way up, somewhere, he felt the faintest fuzz of droplets. Rain? No, it had to be spillage, a little wristlet of water flowing out of the upper reaches of Heart Mountain. His lips were dry, cracked. Swallowing, his Adam's apple rose in his throat, blocked his faulty breathing. He was drenched in his own sweat, frozen to the bone. And sick, he knew he was sick. But there was nothing for him to do but climb.

And climb.

The fearful cycle continued long into the dire cold night. While the fevered flesh inched its worm's way up, the sky began to loose the flakes foretold by the Blackfeet. At first, just a few of them floating about teasingly in the air. Then, dozens, then thousands. And the night clouded over, making sight an effort, forcing Colter to hug the rock, cheek to stone.

Yet this was what Colter wanted, had prayed for. They could not follow him in a storm, and storm it was coming to be. Toward dawn, his toenails still clicked the rock, his fingernails taloned the little interstices between the awful flat-nothing that vertically ironed out into a world of white, with no separation between mountain and night. Down, way down, looked up to him—but for the note of gravity in the whirling, ever falling flakes. The white world had swallowed him.

The rock beckoned his delirium. Seductive, it called to him to make swift, unwary reaches. He came to the end of his climb. Suddenly there was nothing more to grasp. All that fused him to the rock, it seemed, was his crazy heart. His fingernails were all broken off and his hands refused to grab. The cold penetrated beyond his bones, into his soul.

He seemed to have reached the end of something, the

place of no return. There was not an angle, anywhere, with which to use his stubborn, unyielding hands as wedges. The snow blinded him and the rock maimed him. Dumbly, he hung on—to what he did not know. . . .

Perhaps merely the pressure of himself, against himself. . . . Had he finally grown into the galvan of stone . . . was his skin ice-burned into it? It felt so. Now he neither moved, nor tried to move. The droning white-moth world went round and round, and he, with it, pinwheeling into space.

He came to, clutching, scrabbling. He'd fallen asleep. Slipped down. Like slime, oozing, pizzling down the stone face. Off to the right: black lip, a crack. He dripped himself into it. Found it, his right hand burrowing fast, forming a fat fist that stuck in the crack, pinned him solid. Then his whole body seemed to yaw like liquid into the crack, which opened up as he flexed himself into it.

His bones melted—then arm elbow shoulder head— poured into the widening hole. Falling, he landed on a ledge. The crack in the rock had turned into the chute he was looking for. Now Heart Mountain accepted him, cradled him. He was too delirious to question his good fortune. He curled up in the stolen blanket and slept.

Dawn came and more snow spilled out of the sky. Midmorning, it stopped. Teeth chattering, Colter awoke from a slippery dream to confront his dilemma. He'd fallen through a big fissure onto a small ledge, in back of which was a dark passage, a funnel. Catching up some snow in his fingers, he sucked them, thirstily, moistening his swollen lips and tongue.

The snow water tasted sweet, but was hard to swallow.

His throat felt like crushed glass. Tears came to his eyes when he tried to drink, when he tried to force the muscles to do their job.

He edged over toward the side of the ledge, keeping the weight of his body well behind him. Below looked like above: white both ways, sheets of frozen, wind-swept snow, curling up and down, skirling around the stone cliffs.

He smiled with mute, pained satisfaction.

They would not follow him in such a maelstrom as this.

Thank you, Lord Rock, he said, trying to shake off the fever. But it would not shake. No more climbing, then. And he sighed, looking at his bared, bruised, welled-up knuckles.

Yet even in this boiled up and frozen state of mind, he could see that the only sense lay in back of him. To go out, or up, would mean death. The escarpment was aglitter with ice. But back of him there appeared to be a chute of some kind.

He explored it and it did, indeed, wind upward into the inner chambers of Heart Mountain. So, the Heart's heart. . . .

Was that the reason they had named it so?

Using all fours, Colter clawed along the darkness of the tunnel, which spiralled ever upward. There was flotsam under his bare feet, dead sticks, which meant, somewhere up ahead, there had to be access to the top of the butte. The stuff had been carried down in a storm. After a while, though, the angle sharpened steeply, then shot straight up, a chimney of wet, wet rock.

Bracing his shoulders against it and planting his feet

on the opposite wall, he could crank himself up, a little at a time. The dull sky refracted light off the ledge where he'd slept. The snow glare followed him up, as he cranked, with pressure of shoulder and heel. But the higher he went in the chimney, the darker it got. Twin bores of light, now; one down below, one way up above. Above was like the barrel of a long-rifle, pointed at the sun; he aimed himself for it, scrunched his back and shoulders into the nasty, inching maneuver, first one shoulder, then the other, then the first carefully planted foot, then the second.

As he went up, little by little, he felt the old familiar feeling of fear. Colter did not like heights. Oddly, the space below him seemed to magnify as he ascended. It was one thing to traverse elliptical rock that was before your face, but quite another to be positioned, head down, staring into the infinite maw of your worst fear. The bore, the sun glare, the spill of white space, through which he could just faintly make out the tops of snow-laden trees, these hundreds of feet below him. The fluttering in his belly trickled like unwanted sweat into his groin where it tightened the skin around his testicles. He wanted badly to look up, but his feet seemed always to be below him.

Pulling them up, one at a time, he had to look down, to bring those maddening numb limbs up to level. Slowly, then, one foot, then the bastard other. Forcing the back into the rock, lifting the frozen foot, rooting it, bringing up the other foot. The sound of silence, winching his way up, the spasm of flakes down the chimney, the tickle of sweat in his groin. The tightening gyre in his testicles.

It began as a trickle of water on his head, a desultory drop, then an irregular cascade as he came to the chimney top. Finally, the roar of snowmelt. He'd backed himself up and out of the chimney—elbow height—and white, blinding daylight assaulted his eyes. The cascade coming off the upper reaches of jumbled stone splashed all about him. The sun was out, the snowstorm was over. And John Colter was on the top of Heart Mountain, with but one small, graspable, traverse left.

In the small basin where the snowmelt had collected he drank his fill. The ice water made the back of his skull ache. He felt squeezes of exertion go through his belly muscles, as they came undone from the climb. His facial muscles ticked nervously and his calves quivered painfully. The sun beat down on him and the world, what he could see of it from the promontory where he lay, was a white blaze of black ice.

Look at your poor servant, Heart, Colter said through distended lips. Body beaten, mind gone, what's left of me's not fit for carrion. Yet—here am I, on top of the world!

He spoke to the mountain, affectionately, as one would speak to a lover in whose arms one had lain for many long hours.

Drinking more water, he sank his face into the basin, opened his eyes underwater, blinked. Then he tried to stand, sank to his belly again, lay out flat, completely done in.

I see, he mumbled. All right, then, Heart. Have your way—that I must continue as your servant, and worm my way out of your grace.

And he began to crawl over the slick rock, less a man than a thing that scribbled itself on the surface of things. His limbs, on fire, spoke of many complaints, dirges of them. But his brain felt lax, enfeebled by the strain, and took no notice of anything he was doing. In the end, he urged himself, chin-dragging himself over the final verge.

On top of Heart Mountain the wind howled, cutting him to the quick. He tugged at the blanket, now shorn to rags. The dry snow came in fits, dancing around his head, teasing him. It looked, in his snow-blind state, like waves of golden water. He squinted at it and saw through the veiled light a dark figure, something hunched, furtive.

Too tired to go on, he clutched the snow that no longer burned. Tried to throw a snowball at the darkening shape. It came near him.

Fish breath. Fangs buried in black gums. It sniffed him from head to toe, bit him once, tentatively, to sample his condition. He did nothing, he felt nothing. Nerve sensors shut down.

John Colter was nearly unconscious. But the last thing he saw through the slits of his snow-shut eyes was the face of a wolverine, the pinched and wrinkled nose, the overbite, the starved animal eyes, ready and mean.

In the dream of the beast-brain, he saw the animal heft the man upon its shoulders. Its fur like plumage, touching his cheek as he flopped. And it took him then, like the monster the tribes called Windigo, and walked on the wind with him, leaving no track, or one that was marked only by a single droplet of blood. He saw himself, no longer himself. He was only what the creature carried, a burden of bones, a deadness, meat for the winter cache.

Where are you taking it? he asked the wolverine.

To the place where it stored the furs, the wolverine answered through the teeth of the wind.

Ah . . .

He knew the place: a cache, two years ago.

So the wolverine would take it there and store it with the other stuff to be eaten, slowly, one winter chew at a time.

So be it, for he knew it was dead.

But he saw it turn into the boy it once was, the boy from Stuart's Draft who could write his name and upon whose shoulder a bluejay sat and pecked . . . accompanying the boy were his two cousins, the Ray brothers, on their way, all of them, to meet Meriwether Lewis in Maysville, Kentucky. . . . "You have the countenance of Mr. Daniel Boone," Lewis exclaimed, amused, liking him immediately and he was hired just like that on the spot and entitled to thirty-five months and twenty-six days of service at 179.33 1/3 cents which went to pay for twenty traps and tools and two years supply of ammo, knives, powderhorns and hatchets . . . now where had those things gotten to? . . . He saw them buried now along with four pounds of powder, six pounds of lead, an axe, an auger, planes, files, a blacksmith's bellows, hammers, tongs, flour, parched meal, two kegs of pork, a cooper's awl, some bearskin, beaverskin and horns of the bighorn sheep. . . . The cache was a safe place to store things built like a kettle or a pot, wide and squat at the bottom and narrow at the top with a sunken gravel floor overlain with shagbark and then hay and finally fur. . . . A man could hole up in a cache and live out the rest of his days. . . . Then the things a man must climb to find himself alive came to the fore and the mud embankments were too slippery to climb and he slid back down into the churning coffee-colored water of the Missouri; using his tail as a rudder he mud-bellied up until he hit white sandstone rain-eaten into a thousand grotesque parapets and well-worn statuary and columns and pedestals and pyramids of conical structure with niches and alcoves all of which a man must climb one at a time and overcome . . . in his hands the elk hide rope and under one armpit the Minnataree football he'd found in the rapids caught up in the foamy cobble . . . and he'd made it to the top at last over gravel mud sand box alder branch and cotton root and through the thousand and one carcasses of the buffalo driven over the edge of the mud bank to die in a heap where the Minataree had driven them and now poor what's-his-name had to drag himself through this maze of harp bones sun bones wind bones to the top of the world. . . .

The wolverine was an elegant host who wore a long fur frock and served up chokecherry tea. He couldn't read but he kept many books. There was a buffalo tallow lamp that cast a gold haze about the cache and piles of mouse-nibbled books that belonged to Meriwether Lewis. The wolverine couldn't read but he liked the atmosphere of good books lying open and if his claws tore at the pages sometimes when he walked over them, it was not to be held against him.

In the night the tallow lamp wavered in the wind that seeped through the smoke hole of the cache. The copper pot of pounded charcoal mixed with beeswax flamed occasionally where something like a rabbit cooked. Outside he heard the hailstones fusillade the earthen roof of the cache and sound like the drumming of hooves. He had once seen a man killed by a hailstone that struck him just above the eye socket. But the wolverine seemed not to mind the din and offered him broth of weasel and more chokecherry tea. There was a buffalo horn with a note in it, yellow with age. A parchment message from Lewis to Clark about the size of mosquitoes in these parts. They wrote each other notes and left them in sheep horns along the way whenever they were separated. These mosquitoes, Lewis told Clark, were larger than coneys and would devour a man if they did not rather like to drain him.

He began, over time, to share what he knew of these two noble gentlemen with the wolverine, who liked to curl his lip and laugh at the stories, sometimes spilling his elderberry wine across his striped shirtfront. The wolverine especially liked to hear the one about Lewis passing through the willow bar and being accidentally shot in the ass and calling to Cruzat, his companion, to come out of the bushes so the two of them might find better cover both of them hobbling along Lewis holding his hands over his injured hind as he stumbled and fell most indecorously.

The wolverine howled with mirth, showing a spectrum of back teeth in his cavernous mouth. Then he would when he stopped guffawing shamble over the open books tearing their pages with his outrageous long claws and place a wild onion poultice over the swollen glands of his companion. He sponge-bathed him with tea water using a moss scrubber so gently Colter thought it must be a woman doing the work with only an occasional slip of claw cutting his flesh.

When he awoke knowing his name, the storm was past.

He sat up and was surprised to find a willow-backed

upright covered with beaver pelts behind him for support. Yes, he remembered the place well, the cache he'd put in with Potts. He was wearing a leather overshirt of deerskin and a pair of soft buckskin trousers. His skin stank of bear grease; someone had rubbed him down with a mixture of crushed, boiled wintergreen and bear's fat. His mouth smelled of fish.

Somehow he remembered the chokecherry, a black decoction for making up a night-sweat, to break a fever. He saw the bark cup at his elbow. Someone—but how?—had seen fit—but how?—

He sat in comparative warmth. The stuff in the cache, all that wasn't iron, was chewed on and mostly eaten by rodents. His Crow-made pair of rattlesnake suspenders were gnawed to strings, hanging from a tripod of cast iron. The light filtered in, smokily. Everywhere, all about the dim walls of the cache, were evil-looking roots; the place was strung with them.

His eyes roved the old cache for things he might use again. Sadly, there was not much left. In the darkest corner he saw the remains of the bull-boat, the round cup-like hideboat made by himself and Potts from the pliable stems of willow and the wetted and dried skin of an elk. What was left, not eaten by rodents, was winglike: two pieces that might fit over a man's arms, that is, if a man were a bat.

John Colter, he mused. He savored the name, his own.

Alive. Who would've believed it. Not Potts. Lewis, maybe. Manuel Lisa, perhaps. Which brought him to the thing that stopped such loose thinking: Who, pray tell, had brought him here? Who had dragged him over the snow and stored and cared for him here? He recalled with distaste the image of an animal—a wolflike thing—that he'd dreamed up as his nurse. Ridiculous.

He looked about him. The roof of the cache was just over his head. If not an animal, a small man. If not a small man, a boy. Yes, that was it. It came to him then in a burst of light, a boy like the boy he'd once been: a boy with a wolverine's headcap and a robe of similar fur about his shoulders.

A boy . . . so that was it. And it came to him in shreds and bits, little salted biscuits of memory, quick to the taste.

Behind the wolverine's musky face had been a boy . . . and then it struck him—the same boy he'd tackled by the river, the boy he'd bested had somehow brought him back to life! How his sorry carcass had been found on that sad windblown height at the top of Heart Mountain might never come to him, yet he knew that this boy had saved his life as surely as he knew his life was saved.

E I G H T

GLASS

Hugh awoke to a brightness that still hung in the air. When he had sprawled and slept, he was uncertain. The night's travel was a jumble of waking dreams, movement, and mixed emotions. Now the sun hung low in the west, touching banks of low clouds with red and pink. Hugh rubbed his eyes and touched his scabs, turned his head and sought the butte. Half of it was ruddy now, as if a cataract of blood splashed down its westward face.

He made a tentative movement forward and his throat constricted. Dry. More than dry. Parched. He tried to summon saliva to dampen it, to ease the near-abrasive chafing that came with his efforts. But nothing flowed. He tore loose a handful of grasses and stuffed it into his mouth, chewing, chewing. Nothing. It was as dry as he was. He spat it out, aligned himself with the butte, and moved again.

The leg dragged like time at his back. The sun eased itself out of the sky. He found himself resting so frequently that he set a quota of forward movements to be met before he might halt and take his ease.

His head began to throb. Later, the call of a coyote echoed painfully within his temples, his brow. A great lassitude came upon him then, and his limbs felt heavier, his movements slowing. The next time that he rested, he slept again. It did not feel as if he had dozed a great deal, but the world was completely dark when he opened his eyes, and the throbbing in his head had subsided to a dull ache. His mouth and throat felt as if they had been burned.

He began crawling again without resolve. Volition had no part in the process. It was only later that he thought it might have become a matter of habit, that his mind was no longer needed and might be set free to wander in realms of its own choosing while the meat where it made its home twitched, tightened, relaxed, moving itself as meat had done down the ages, across the earth.

. . . He walked beside a cool stream in the shade of fruit trees. Kneeling, he dipped his hand and raised it to his lips. He felt the water splash upon his cheeks. Red apples lay in the grass. His hand sought one. He raised it and bit. . . .

The grass. . . . He crawled through the grass toward the butte, his vision fled, thirst unslaked. It was not only his throat, for his stomach, his whole body cried for water. He licked at the grasses, but they had not yet acquired a damp condensation. He felt that he might have cut his tongue in the attempt, but it was too numb for him to know for certain.

The smell and memory of the apple orchard stayed with him for a long while, and the memory of water upon his face—fairy gold now. Yet— He returned to it again and again, almost tasting the thought.

He groped in his pocket a little later, where some of the bread-root yet remained. The chewing of it was a dry affair, the swallowing a forced thing, painful upon the lining of his throat. Still, some moisture must remain, must come into him, he felt.

. . . And the butte—sometimes far ahead, sometimes near now—took on a bluish cast, as if water now flowed down its slopes, fountain-like, to flood the landscape. How long till its cool waves reached him? Knowing its falseness, he rode the tides of this feeling, also, for the touch of distraction, the dream of relief that it bore.

The hate, like the movement, was no longer a conscious act. It flowed, a thing of will itself, along with him as he advanced. It informed all that he did, saw, thought, dreamed, having become an environment. Perhaps it *was* the movement, the thing that pushed his limbs forward, again and again, toward the ever-changing yet somehow constant monument of stone. The stars were gone, behind the banks of clouds, yet somehow it knew to drive his limbs in the proper direction, through darkness. It invented his way before him, black trail within blackness.

It overrode the thirst. It overrode the knowledge that he would probably die soon. It directed the energies of his life and it seemed that it would do so until they were exhausted.

And so he crawled, and it warmed him and fed him, though it ate him and burned him as he went. Into and out of dreams of the hunt, where sometimes he crawled along game trails, tracing obscure markings of his quarry's passage upon the ground, weapon in his hand. That which he must find and kill had left its track. He need but read and follow. Somewhere ahead, he would come upon it, no matter the course it had taken. So long as his strength held, he would pursue. And its life would come into his hands, and he would take it. For he was the hunter. His breath came to him rank and sweet. Bearlike, he advanced.

. . . In the orchard the apples had fallen to the ground. The stream gurgled nearby. He slogged his way to it. Lowering his head to drink, he beheld his reflection—crusted ridge of a brow, hair everywhere, dark glaring eyes. Bear or man? The same, the same. He raised the head to drink his image. . . .

. . . And was crawling, still crawling toward the dark lump, wind sighing above him now. The thirst was upon him again, and a series of cramps caused him to double and seize at his stomach. When they ceased, he massaged his bad leg for a time, groped after splinters in his hands, sucked at his cheeks, hoping that moisture would flow.

He became aware that the winds had stopped, the stillness in the air seeming almost unnatural. The winds had been with him for so long that they had gone almost unnoticed, till now. He began to wonder how long it would take him to die if he just lay there and waited for it. One day? Two? A matter of hours? As he thought about it his mind slipped away again. He dozed, his body jerking periodically.

Minutes later, he awoke, barely aware of the interruption, coughing and sucking air. It was as if he were at the bottom of a sea, the pressure suddenly shifted upon his lungs, his aching sides. He wondered whether this was an answer to his question. Was it to be now? Were these his last breaths?

But they kept coming, kept going. It was no longer a pain that he felt, but it seemed as if there had been some change in the air itself that had caused him to labor in taking it. His puzzlement quickly passed as the demands of his thirst rose again. A dull fire traced his throat, followed it downward to his stomach where a queasy tenderness still resided. The effects spread outward from there to his limbs, weakening them. Perhaps it were easier simply to lie and wait.

Yet, there was a choice of sort, even as he regarded the end. If it were a matter of waiting and dying or of going on, his nature gave him the impulse. He must crawl, he must continue with his remaining strength, must go on, until it caught him.

He straightened, thrust with his good leg, pulled himself ahead again. It seemed more of an effort this time than before, but he clenched his teeth and went on. Several times more, and the rhythm had returned.

Before he had crawled very far a low rumbling began. At first he thought it might be the sound of his blood rushing in his ears. But it grew, mounting in intensity to an audible growl from beyond his person. And then there came a flash of light, and something in the sky cracked like a whip. Now there came a hissing sound and the wind returned. He halted.

A moment later it fell upon him—a great wall of water, driven by a smashing wind which pressed him to the ground. The light flashed again, and the thunder boomed about him. He was immediately soaked by the downpour, and he struggled against the wind and his game leg to turn himself onto his back, tongue slowly tracing the area about his lips after droplets that ran upon his face.

Succeeding, he sprawled, mouth opening wide to the

heavens. The rain which pelted him was not gentle. It came down as multitudes of small blows upon him. Yet it ran within his mouth and he did not care, did not care that it pummeled him, so long as his throat was moistened. He gagged at the first swallow but continued. He drew his drenched shirt from his waist, raised it and began wringing it out above his mouth, swallowing repeatedly now, oblivious to the cold cascade upon his belly. He lowered it and spread it, raised it almost immediately and wrung it again.

His stomach knotted, relaxed, quivered, relaxed again. The burning in his throat was cooled, the dryness disappeared. He continued to swallow. He raised the shirt, wrung it, again and again. The water ran through his hair, his beard, softened his skin, seemed to soak through it.

The lightning flared once more and the thunder boomed. The rainfall increased in intensity. Shivering, Hugh drank deeply. It was life, he knew, assailing him while it benefited him, and he drew it into him, continuing past the point of satiation. Then, for the first time, he wondered when the rainfall would cease.

The waters continued to pelt him, the winds to buffet. The ground grew muddy about him, beneath him. The water had reached every inch of his skin. He closed his eyes and waited. The lightning flashes still came to him through his eyelids. The water still ran into his nose, causing him to turn his head and blow it out. He covered his face with his hand.

Lying there, he had images of the ground being so soft that he sank into the earth, down to that underworld he had so long inhabited—how long ago? It seemed a long while now since his awakening in the deserted camp. And it had brought him into another life, one where he moved slowly and regarded the world from the vantage of jackrabbit, prairie dog. The signs were clearer down here, but so was the vulnerability.

As the waters continued to pour over him, he began to imagine himself as being immersed in a stream, mountain wash pouring over him, flashing by on its way to the sea.

He recalled the ocean, running into it, letting it splash against him, knock him from his feet, falling, sputtering backward, drifting momentarily, struggling to rise, discovering the feat more difficult than he had thought—moment of panic then—and the waves, the big waves—like getting run over by a hill—he remembered. Soaked. Laughing—he had been laughing—and the waves. He remembered.

Somewhere, he was lost in the waves and the remembering. He awoke coughing. His hand had slipped away, letting the water come into his nose again.

Coughing, he sat up. It was still pouring, and water ran down his back, his sides. The next flash and thunder roll came more distantly, off in the direction of the butte, and the wind had calmed somewhat. The rainfall seemed a trifle more gentle.

After a time, he sucked more moisture from his shirt. No longer thirsty, still he wanted all that he could hold and he drank until he felt bloated. Then he lay back again and let the rain pelt him.

Gentler now, the sounds of the storm's center continued to retreat. Muted. He lay panting, as if from exertion, belly like a cask that moved but slightly with his breaths.

Then, abruptly, it ceased. He lay puzzled for a moment at this change of state. Then he realized that it was gone, and he cried out. Gone. His entire body tingled, and for a time it was as if ghost-drops still fell upon him.

A little later, soaked garments plastered to him, light breezes blowing over him, he began to shiver. A vision of himself sneezing and coughing, nose running, came to him. It was time to begin moving again, if only to keep warm.

He flopped over onto his belly, his entire frame reacting to its liquid inertia. When he moved to crawl, his fingers sank into the ground. Nevertheless, he pulled himself forward to the accompaniment of a squishing sound.

Again, the cycle of crawl and rest, while the storm continued its retreat. Overhead, the clouds broke apart, starry rivers gleaming among them. A while, and the chill went out of Hugh with the warming of his exertions. And later—how much later, he could not be certain—the clouds moved away and he saw that the sky had grown pale in the east.

The butte was gone, though his body seemed to know its direction, hidden behind a wavering wall of white. Steam rose from the wet plain, clinging and swaying. He crawled amid its veils, keeping the growing light to his left.

More brightness poured into the world as he moved, and he saw water puddled about him. Today, he decided, today he would not rest during the light, but would drive himself forward. The coolness would offset the sun's glare, and he could drink as he went before it all soaked away or evaporated.

Crawling onward, he saw the sky clear above him. The mist slowly subsided. No clouds marred the blue. The ground still oozed as he moved. The butte came into view once more, just where he'd felt it to be, and he held his soggy course toward its now gleaming eminence. The morning remained cool, and he felt that he did right to pursue his way through it rather than rest and await the return of the dark.

He tried to remember how many days had passed since he had departed the camp, but time was blurred. All that he could recall was the crawling itself, through areas of especially difficult terrain—uphill in the gulch, thickets, brambles—and special places, such as the pool and the spot where the grape vines and plum trees grew. The rest was smeared together into a near-eyelevel landscape of dirt, rock, grass. Time was a uniformity of low exertion, prospect of slowly passing terrain. But the recollection of the grapes and the plums stayed with him, no longer for the thirst-quenching sweetness, but rather for the juicy bulk that held it. He remembered each swallow, with the feeling of its stomach-filling solidity. He craved something other than water, something he could chew for a filled feeling of digestion. Groping in his pockets, he sought a few remaining root-ends. Quickly, he placed them in his mouth, chewed, and swallowed. Their initial crunching between his teeth was memorable, but in moments they were gone.

Shortly, a terrible hunger assailed him. The roots had served only to remind his body of how long, within that time-hazed span, it had been since he had really eaten. He studied the grasses at either hand as he crawled, searching for signs of anything edible. At each puddle that he passed he paused to suck up water, to keep his belly filled. There was no thirst left in him, but he might trick his appetite a little with the pressure.

As the morning wore on, he found that his regular

pauses for rest were growing longer, were becoming harder to conclude. He closed his eyes on several of these occasions and dozed, awakening when his head struck the ground. He came to fear resting his head upon his arms; finally, he fought even against closing his eyes when he stopped.

For a time, he forced himself to crawl a little more slowly, resting slightly after each pull, to husband his strength, forestall fatigue. Then he realized that he was closing his eyes at each of these rests. Once his head dropped into the mud. A pang in the wounded forehead awakened him immediately. He tried crawling faster, driving himself, but then when he halted an even greater lethargy took hold. He drank from a nearby puddle. He rubbed his eyes. He decided upon some distraction then, each time that he halted. Rub the leg, take a good look around, stare off at the butte, massage the shoulders, blink the eyes, glance at the sun, blink again, drink, take deep breaths, find a pebble to suck, hum a tune, spit out the pebble, run a hand through the hair, touch the wound, feel the pain, look for something to eat. . . .

The hunger. . . . That seemed to work. Since he could not satisfy it, perhaps he could use it. Think of food, think of eating whenever the tiredness reaches the head. . . .

Crawling, he thought of steaks and eggs and bread, coffee, tea, and wine, a piece of chocolate. Solid, heavy, a filling mass for a man's center. And after a big meal, sleep was such a fine thing. . . .

He started again, with bacon, fish, onions, cornbread, apples, a piece of cherry pie. . . .

He felt a pang in his stomach and he stopped to drink

again. Blink now, massage, hum. Crawl again. Stop thinking of food for a while. Too many juices flowing.

After a while, the sleepiness returned and he found himself yawning. He fought with it again, rehearsing his earlier tricks. Later, as he crawled, there came a burst of movement from his right as a startled jackrabbit leaped before him.

It halted, not too far away, nose twitching, head turning. Hugh licked his lips. He slid his left hand back along his leg, caught hold of his boot, tugging, and began to work it loose. Not to frighten the rabbit with sudden movements, he pulled the boot free. Thinking of the animal's death, thinking of killing, he thought of Jamie—out of reach now, but not perhaps forever. He transferred the boot to his right hand, drew back his arm. Jamie. . . .

He cursed as he threw it. The rabbit bounded away. Jamie.

He crawled ahead and recovered the boot, sought about after the rabbit, could no longer see it. With another curse, he lowered the boot, worked his foot into it. Some good had come of it, though, he decided, for he no longer felt like sleeping.

Immediately, he commenced crawling again. If there was one rabbit about there might well be more. He would exercise more control the next time he attempted to take one.

But he did not see another all that day. He drank at every puddle and bison-wallow he passed, but he found no food, wherever he looked. Somehow he made it through the day and most of the night without sleeping. Or did he sleep? He was uncertain. Crawling and the dream of crawling were so similar. He remembered crawling into the night and passing out before the dawn.

And now it was evening. He stared at the butte. He would be passing to its left, as he calculated his course. How far had he come? Difficult to say, when he was not even certain how long he had been crawling. But there was something else. . . . Now, in the distance, beyond what had been his goal, he could discern the rough line of a ridge along the southern horizon. This was the crest of the divide. There, once he'd crossed it, would lie valleys and meadows, fruit trees, streams. There lay his life, could he but attain it. At least to have come this far, to have it in sight, seemed a small triumph. Yes, the butte was nearer, to have yielded its prominence. A small rush of strength passed through him. To have a real goal in sight, no matter how far removed, changed his perspective on the geography of his mind, his feelings. All that he had endured had given him this moment, and he might trade more of the same for an even greater time.

He moved ahead with a new vigor which sustained him long into the night. Waking dreams still came to him, and visions of food tormented him, but there was water in the depressions along the way, and his limbs moved with the deliberation of purpose. Perhaps tomorrow there would be food. . . .

The stars were bright throughout the night, moving in their eternal wheel. Coyotes called across great distances. The breeze was cool but not chill. He would go for so long as he could, trying to re-establish his sleep-by-day, crawl-by-night cycle. He would push on. Staying awake seemed almost more important than distance covered.

Crawling and resting, he passed most of another night. But the rest periods grew longer. Before the dawn, he slept, dreaming of the land beyond the ridge.

He woke to the warmth of day. Raising his head, he studied the ridge. The butte was off to his right now. The sun stood well-risen, aimed at midheaven. He massaged his leg, wondering whether any water remained at surface level in the area. He cracked his knuckles and yawned. He rubbed his eyes and touched his scabbed forehead. He licked his lips. He stretched. He scratched his neck. The hunger had not started yet, though he knew it must, soon. For the moment he almost felt entire, of a piece, as if he could stand and walk away. As soon as he began to move, though, he knew the illusion would vanish. Yet . . . move he must.

He put his hands forward, straightened his body, pulled, pushed with his good leg. At least the ground had dried to the point where he wasn't dragging his way through mud. He reached again.

Through midday he crawled. Then, from off to his right, he heard a small chirping sound. Immediately, he identified it as a gopher's call, and he felt his stomach tighten. He halted, made certain of the precise direction, then crawled slowly, quietly toward it. Parting the grasses carefully, he came at length to a clear area, where he beheld the creature beside its burrow.

His hand went once again to his boot, working it off from his foot. This time he did not cast it, but set it aside, to slip the heavy woolen stocking down off the foot. Raising this before him then, he set to work unraveling it.

Breaking an end loop, he worked a strand free, saw

the others loosening. For several minutes more he spread and tugged at the fabric. He encountered worn areas, holes, which required that he tie pieces together. At last, however, he held a lengthy strand which he stretched and smoothed, coiled and uncoiled.

Then he formed the loop, and he drew the boot back onto his foot and crawled forward. The gopher ducked back into its hole as he advanced.

Carefully then, he situated the loop about the hole and smoothed it. Holding the strand, he retreated, eased himself into a relatively comfortable position, and waited. As it might well be some time before the creature emerged again, he prepared himself for a long wait. Thoughts of meat began passing through his mind almost immediately, however.

He changed positions several times, rehearsing the meal. Occasionally, he lowered his head, pressed an ear to the earth, listened after sounds of movements below ground. He heard nothing on any of these occasions but was not disheartened thereby; his quarry must have several entryways and exits, and many galleries below. There was no reason to expect it to pass this way with great frequency. Still, it had done it once; it would do it again, sooner or later.

He kept the string fairly taut. He had positioned himself so that his shadow lay nowhere near the hole. He kept his breathing quiet. The shadow moved farther into the east. He glanced at the ridge occasionally. It was noticeably nearer now. He thought again of eating, contracting his stomach muscles against a growling that ensued.

An hour might have passed, perhaps two—Hugh

could no longer tell—when it seemed that a shadow stirred within the hole. His hand tightened and he realized that he was holding his breath. There came another small movement. He waited, breathing quickly again. Minutes passed. Nothing. The minutes dragged on.

And the afternoon wore on. The creature had changed its mind, he decided, found something else to occupy its small attention. He adjusted his position, massaged his leg, considered the length of his shadow. He could wait. He had learned the art of waiting long ago.

He thought again of food and eating, and of how Jamie had reduced him to this—waiting outside a rodent's burrow, hoping to snare a miserable meal of raw flesh, and savoring the notion. Ah, Jamie. . . . Where are you now? Dining on buffalo steak and fried potatoes with Major Henry and the men? And thick slices of bread and perhaps an apple? Do you ever think of old Hugh, wonder what became of him? Or am I gone completely from your memory?

He listened again to the ground but heard no sounds from below. The sun continued its plunge into the west, and now he was thirsty as well as hungry. He cursed soundlessly and continued his vigil.

There! A small movement within the hole. He readied himself. Another! It had advanced slightly, was peering out now. He thought of Jamie and of his hurled boot. He willed the creature to emerge, felt himself inside its small body, urging it forward.

It advanced a little farther, made a chirping sound. Hugh felt saliva come into his mouth. It continued to move then, head coming up out of the hole.

Just a little farther. . . . There. It rose.

He jerked the string. It caught perfectly about the gopher's neck. Then the string snapped.

With a howl, Hugh threw himself forward, reaching, trying to grasp it before it retreated. But it had vanished back into the hole, amid a flurry of wild chirpings, before his hands arrived. He could hear the scrambling, squeaking noises continuing below ground as he lay there, his eyes suddenly moist.

He cursed long and loud, as he thought of his belly and his long wait and of Jamie. A hunter with nothing to show for the day's stalking of a rodent. . . . It could almost have been laughable, had his life not depended on it.

He turned away, his face to the ridge, and commenced his crawling once again. His belly growled and his mouth was dry. Cursing, he made his way into the twilight.

NINE

COLTER

Colter winced at the light that intruded into the dark cache, his eye roving the disarray, the ruined goods of some forgotten mountaineer. From the rootbound walls to the caved-in lodgepole roof, the cache was a seep hole of ground water. He found himself in the middle of it, getting dripped on.

How had he gotten here?

His hand wandered feebly across his face, tracing the stubble of beard. Covering his chest and legs was a four-point Hudson Bay blanket, in sad repair, slash holes cut for the arms. Running his fingers over the damp wool, though, he knew he ought to be grateful, for the blanket and the cache had saved his life.

Hollow voice from within: Who are you?

For which, temporarily, no reply.

He was something, though.

He felt of his skull. It told him only that his hair was uncommonly long, yet favorably clean, as if recently washed. A scar on his forehead felt cold as ice. An old burn, perhaps; he couldn't remember it. His bones ached, but told him little else. A beard furzed his chin and jaw.

Itching but otherwise unobjectionable. His scarred legs were mostly healed. His feet seemed to have been used for battering rams; toenails broken, toes blistered.

For a long while he lay, thinking of the poor thing he'd become—or was he always that way? He didn't know. All he knew was that he was a thing which hung in the balance of another thing which was unknowable. God or fate held him in the palm of the world. His ancestors in the isles had once called their god, who was none other than fate, by the name of Wyrd—so his father had told him once. Scratching his beard, he wondered if old Wyrd watched over him now. Or whether Wyrd, headless and bodiless, was nothing but a series of fated footsteps into which pitiful, helpless men fell and scrambled, trying for another foothold.

Yet there was nothing to do now but try to get up before this hell-heap of dirt crashed down upon his head. He groaned as he sat up, propped on his elbows. Through a hole that was the entrance of the cache, he saw the sun. Nearby he heard water tumbling over rocks. . . .

Hadn't he once been on a mountain? And wasn't he—? His thoughts broke off. He began to crawl the earthen floor, looking at the ruined stash of goods. Casks of powder, wetted, congealed, long since given over to the earth's grave. What was left of some rusted axeheads and augers was undiscernible—a clotted afterbirth of oxidation. Planes, files, all of them rust-encased; kegs of once edible meal, now all but mouse-eaten, foetid; bearskins, shorn of fur, sinew still good, maybe a pair of moccasins left somewhere. He looked again at his bare and swollen feet. Then turned to the stuff of the cache—what had not been claimed by rodents—now embraced by giant white roots, great fat snakelike things that had insinuated themselves into the cache and made conduits for the groundwater from above.

Suddenly, Memory's bold knocking fist—

—I remember storing this stuff, heaps of winter bounty, passing it down the hatch-hole to Potts, him grumbling like a pot of boiled molasses down in the dark.

And with the name Potts came a whole panoply of self. The old armored rigging of who he was in the world, and what he was supposed to be doing.

Chuckling, he knew who he was. He tested himself. Most recent nickname: Seekheedha. Most recent occupation: trapper. Former occupation: hunter. Reason for being: staying alive. Reason for staying alive: being.

Satisfied, he clambered out of the hole and into the sun, and was instantly blinded. Hands over eyes, he peeked through the cracks of his fingers, a little at a time, as pain would allow.

Damned if I don't feel like an old man. . . .

Then: How old am I? Don't know, for sure. How many winters, the Crows used to say. . . .

He counted, lost track. Thirty-four, thirty-six, maybe.

He dragged out the fleshed bearskin with its odd spots of fur on hard grey-blue board of skin. Alas, it wouldn't come up through the hole. Cursing, Colter let it fall back into the dark.

So it's just me, blanket on back, knife on belt. . . .

Sitting in the white autumn sun, he let his eyes grow accustomed to the light. Just beyond the cache the river roared, full of snow-water, twisting through the spruce trees, disappearing round the bend. There came to his ears, then, a bright, loud, crack of timber. He looked up and saw a showering of embers. Halfway up the mountain above the raging river was a dead spruce, burning.

The meaning somehow clear to him. Living among the Crows, he knew sign. Someone, damned if he knew how, had set the tree ablaze. This meant good weather ahead, prayer to the creator for more of same, blessing and thanks, tree set afire, blazing unto heaven.

The wind from the northeast tickled his cheek. Colter shivered, turned his eye from the tree of hope, looked to the river that crashed among the boulders and slipped round the bend. He knew that it went south. Knew that it plunged through chasms, ripped through whited meadows, ghosted prairies, lands full of grazing game. South lay the broad path of the sun, all the way to the canyon they'd named after him, the place called Colter's Hell.

So be it, then. Take the sign, follow the creek. The way of the blazing tree.

And them that wants me, let them follow me down to Colter's Hell. Let 'em foller. He shook with laughter.

The popping spruce exploded into stars of coals that arced out over the river, leaving cool tails of smoke in their wake. Colter followed the fire-coals with his eye. And where they led was another surprise—most unimaginable—for there, by the river shore, hidden in a patch of red willow was a wonderful thing. . . .

The crude boat made of willow and elder, covered with sun-dried elkskin had once belonged to him. Memory knocked again, and he remembered the day he'd built it with Potts, storing it that same day in the cave up above the cache. They'd used beeswax, buffalo tallow and pounded charcoal to caulk the holes of the stretched out elkskin. The stitches had pulled apart in the two years since they'd framed it, but it was still sound. Two years—was it that long ago? He limped over to the boat, his feet bluish in the sun, tender as an old woman's.

You'll get another pounding ere I'm done with ye, Colter crooned, spitting on the ground.

The spruce paddle he'd carved lay inside, with his initials on it. A stark J.C., over which was the familiar cross, his mark. Private joke—the initials and the cross. Next to the paddle a pair of moccasins, double-soled with buffalo parfleche. For the first time since the Blackfeet had surrounded him, Colter smiled and the fatigue and long-stored pain seemed to ebb away.

Blanket and knife, he sang. Boat and beaded mocs, he sang. And danced a fool's jig, around and around, in the sand.

Where might a man go? . . . Man might go where Man might go, he chortled nonsensically.

Ha!—all the way to St. Louis . . . and if I'm free of this passel of savages, O Lord, I promise thee, once and for all, to lay aside my meddlesome ways, make a safe home in the long grass, quit my running around, give myself over to your care. . . .

He looked heavenwards, saw, in the fluttering of an eye, a dark hawk cross over the sun. The claws closed over a mouse, he saw them. The long, black made-for-digging claws and the lordly, well-toothed mouth wrinkled over the short-furred snout, the darkened nostrils pointing up—

—Hawk?

He saw the sun-blurred image melt away. The cruci-fied hawk's blood gone in the corona of cumulus.

Colter shook his head to rid himself of the image.

Scree, scree.

Hunters sometimes hung hawks on trees, spiked-out wings, alive, crying for humanity.

Humanity?

He wondered whether it was an animal's world or a people's world. What an un-animal animal, this human ani-mal, who could not get along with man or beast. He'd seen it all in the windy world, the wooded ways of the trek, pray-ing to the mist and the waterfalls of the eagled islands where white bears made their mark on trees two hundred feet tall.

The men on the expedition prayed, he remembered, to gods unknown, or to gods known only in the blood. Christ Himself was half-forgotten, wedded into the wood-land in such a way as to bring curses upon the heads of men instead of luck. And they cursed Him back for it, and begged, in the same breath, for His blessing because it was all new here, a new and terrible, if somewhat promised, land.

Which was why Colter left his own bear's mark wher-ever he went, that curious signature—J.C. with a cross—on wood and stone and on the walls of caves and on the trunks of tiny saplings that would, one day, grow large with grace, and carry his totem mark on their living flesh.

Hunter. He was a hunter, a killer. But only to live, to

eat. But that, at times, seemed a transgression to him. He'd seen a thousand buffalo die, blasted on the plain, merely for their tongue and hump. Meriwether Lewis shot one through the lungs while it grazed with its calf. Then he shot the calf and the sibling of the calf. And he would've shot the calf's calf, if such there'd been. . . .

Why did a hunter always keep such keepsakes of death?

He'd heard the bones of these beasts make harps of the wind that played in the prairie sun and he'd watched the oatbeards grow out of the hollow eye sockets of their bleached skulls. And the men of Lewis and Clark carried thunder in their hand and lightning in their belt, and thunder and lightning their ally, their lord—so saith the tribes.

Not until the following day, far downriver, did Colter truly consider his good fortune. He recalled, now, his collapse on the top of Heart Mountain. The rest was hoary memory—someone tending his fever, someone saving him from the frozen night.

There was a dribbling dream that clung to his consciousness. Himself babied by a mother wolf, the way the shamans of the Crow took care of their wounded, licking them all over. He had a sense that some such had actually happened to him, but he couldn't salvage any of the details, save the feeling of the motherly nursing, the warmth, the smell of woodsmoke and tallow and the breath of fish, and the feel of fur.

The river kept his mind clear. Luck and his leaking bullboat kept him afloat until nightfall when he caught up with a drowning antelope. It wasn't the first time he'd seen this. Manuel Lisa's barge had poled among the dead carcasses, more meat than any of the men, even with their mountainous hungers, could reckon with. Drownings by the hundred, so that the river, where it slowed among the wild tansy, was overripe with death-stench. But where the wild, reckless current caught the young beasts—buffalo, elk, antelope and deer—and the meat was still fresh and ready for bleeding, there was a portion of veal and a potion of rum for every man on the trek.

Colter missed the rum, the warm, upward-moving burn of it in his belly, but now he had his first real meal of antelope haunch, which he roasted over the coals. Some sage was growing about in the clearing where he made camp by the river and he threw it on the roasting coals to make sweet smoke for his meat. Second day on the river, the mountains dropped behind him like a theatrical backdrop, the river turned the color of coffee-milk. He ate gooseberries, wild currants in the cottonwood scrub. All round him as he feasted there gathered the amiable herds of white-tailed deer, unafraid and docile, nudging him out of their way to get at the berries. Overhead, blue-crested jays scolded and abused the man and his unlikely friends.

By noon he'd traversed the worst of the rapids. Now the granite cliffs fell away behind him, and like the mountains before them, disappeared. The river opened up full, rank and muddy, its banks striated with red and white clay where the various tribes ferreted out their warpaint.

This country was like home to him. Always, in the past, the mountains called to him. But once he was in them, they treated him harshly. Mountains made scars, the plains healed them. For here the black-tailed deer followed his boat like dogs with nothing to do. Together they ate white apple, what Drouillard used to call *pomme de prairie,* the turnip-shaped root of the bean family, that fed a man or a team of men, for days and even weeks, when nothing else was available. The deer of these broad, park-like prairies were well fed, not like the starved mountain deer he'd seen with Potts. Famished for salt, the blacktails licked his face, as he sat there lazing in the sun.

There was, of course, the imminent feeling of the hunted man: the hunter who was hunted. Given his escape on Heart Mountain, he was now fairer game than before. Yet he believed they'd not go over the mountain, they'd come around to the east, on fine willow-woven snowshoes, taking their ease. First, repair to tipi, eat meat, tell tales, feed the heart, sweeten the chase with sleep. Then, surely as he'd moccasins on his feet, they'd come for him, the best runners there were, the open plains runners, the ones who would not stop at night, the legendary hundred-mile runners.

Truth was that the real hunt for John Colter had just begun. That he'd escaped them, twice, was their own good fortune, not, likely, his. So the game would continue with Colter's life on the line.

He knew that pausing here by the river, feeding his own weary heart with sun and the faces of friendly deer, was a time of dangerous dawdling—yet he couldn't help himself. Something in him fed on the knowledge that they were on the way, that he was wasting precious time, that it would soon be too late. And, hell's fire, he liked that feeling.

After eating the prairie apples, he went back to the

river and examined the bullboat, saw that it was now taking in a bit too much water. This reminded him that Lewis's prize bullboat had been an abysmal failure. The forged iron frame that had taken weeks to make, the heavy boat leaking at all the seams. Then, that same day the bullboat sank, the unlucky omen came—thirteen axe helves broke. The new ones, fashioned of wild cherry, were not as good. The men looked over their shoulders all day.

Shrugging off the recollection, Colter took to the river again, measuring the height of the sun on his southward course. Along the banks of the river, the margins of meadow grew wider and the prickly pear flashed waxen blossoms of yellow and mauve. Sunflowers, also blooming, hung over the bank, and Colter noticed an abundance of lamb's-quarter, wild cucumber, sandrush, narrow dock. The earth was still summering in these lower elevations and the growing things that greeted his eye were plentiful, and made it hard for him to believe that his life was in danger.

I'll not starve, not here, anyways.

Presently the timber turned from pine to cottonwood, and then to wind-bitten elder. The wide bottoms continued to roll into rich, moist meadowlands, giving hint of the great plains that lay further south. Paddling, he saw otter and muskrat. Over each vale the sad toll of the river-dead: deer, antelope, and buffalo caught in the fast current, unable to get up the slick banks. Once, in midpaddle, he saw a grizzly bear looking out of the red, stripped ribs of a drowned elk. The bear's whitish face soused in blood. The beast raised a paw, less threatening than curious. Colter raised a paddle, as if greeting a fellow oarsman, then was gone around the bend.

Three years earlier, when Lewis had shot one of these monumental animals, it followed him into the water, clapping its paws and pretending to play. Lewis fired nine musket balls into it. And the bear threw up its paws, circusing around in the spray, unhurt, as far as anyone could tell. Colter and others poured more volleys into the dancing bear and it roared when it was hit and swam after Lewis, who tried to hide in the water. But the beast kept coming. Finally, all that was visible of Lewis was his nose and white-knuckled hands gripping his firing-piece. The water covered the rest of him. And still the bear advanced, paws clapping, and the men closed in, guns booming.

In the end, the great beast took enough musket balls to level thirty men and, at last, it sank below the surface of the water, but not before it uttered a queer crying noise that reminded the men of a child, dying.

Colter thought of the dying bear as he made camp on a tiny island of stunted birch. Lightning, he decided, had burned out the middle of the island. Or maybe Indians had done it; at any rate, the heart of the island was all burned-out, and recently, too.

One old gnarled oak had withstood the conflagration. He walked up to it and found a circle of blackened stones which had been carefully tended at its base.

He backed up, then, knowing that the tree was sacred. There were tie strings on its longest branches, sinewy offerings of small beaded shields, dangling in the wind. At the base of the burned trunk, in the eye of the fire-blackened circle of stones, there was a flat porphyric rock, which the fire had not touched. To Colter, who had seen something like this on the trek, the circle resembled a Mandan fortune wheel. The people prayed to the sacred stones in the center of the wheel. They fed them all kinds of food, blew smoke upon them, slept in the woods beside them. After making obeisance, the man or men who asked of it the future lay about, smoking kinnikinic, holy smoke, waiting for a sign.

Kneeling in the ash of the ancient oak, Colter bent his head toward the center stone, which was ten feet in circumference and nearly lilac in color. It seemed to shimmer in the late day's afterlight.

No, I must provide it with something. . . .

He went back to the boat and fetched his small roll of antelope jerky, his last supper.

Well, I won't eat. . . .

The stark outline of the tree was etched in the fading light. Yet the stone—which appeared to have the northern lights snared in it—gave its own light. He did not need to touch it, for he knew how it felt. Soft, like a woman's breast. He had watched a man and woman make love by such a stone, a Mandan woman who could not seem to carry a child. And in the fall, her belly swelled and toward spring her baby came, healthy and whole.

He stared at the stone, flickering in the dusk. The wind from the river blew soft ash around his head. He closed his eyes, laid down the bundle of jerky, which was all that he had to give. Once he'd seen a man cut off his right forefinger and place it where he'd just dropped the jerky, facing east, and in the morning the finger was pointing south, so the man had gone that way, certain that his fate lay in that direction. And it had, he had become a chief.

I've parted with enough personal hide to go around,

Colter mumbled. I've left it over all the hills and rills of the Forks.

He bent his head. The stone glowed. Somewhere within, there seemed to come a Mandan murmur, which mixed with the river and was lost in the emptiness of the night.

After a few minutes of silence wherein he thought nothing, his heart empty, Colter got up, went back to the boat, sat down on a rock, wondering what next to do. Across the river a drowned buffalo was being eaten by a confederacy of thieves: magpies, wolves, ravens. Hearing the ripping and feeding going on, his stomach growled. The little white tuber potatoes were long gone—his belly wanted more, wanted flesh. Yet so did the sacred stone. And it would have the flesh he would not.

He sat on the rock and watched the eerie wings over the bloody carcass until in the first wash of eventide, the grizzly from upriver appeared and chased the carrion-eaters away. He could hear across the river's babble, the gross munching, the grizzly-lapping of blood.

He bedded down with the blanket he wore drawn around him. Still, he was bitten with the cold. The night wind moaned as the grizzly bore down on the ropy meat of the dead buffalo. Colter convulsed with shivers and shakes. Then he got up and walked to the ash place and dug with his fingers in the soft sand. The deeper he went, the warmer it got. For several hours, then, he dug, making a hole for himself to lie down in, close to the light of the stone, near the old oak, fluttering with tie-strings and emblems of beads.

And, buried in the sundered earth, he felt warm. Asleep, blanket clutched around his chin. Deep into dream, into the smoke lodge of the Mandan where the old men sat in a circle, the young men behind them with their wives hidden under buffalo robes.

Colter and Lewis standing next to each other, having been invited to attend. What was the custom, what was going on? They knew it had something to do with the buffalo, but exactly what they couldn't begin to figure. The young wives naked under their robes. The elders approached by the young men, who whined and wheedled, in Mandan, begging the old ones to get under the robes and make love to their wives.

The long days on the trail had taken their toll. Out of the corner of his eye, Colter saw some of his own party getting into the fray. . . . "—Devil's jaundice," he heard Lewis mutter. "Pox upon those that defile these heathen who know no better—" Lewis left the lodge in his greatcoat, muttering oaths under his breath.

Colter could not leave, however. Something, more than fascination, riveted him to the spot. He turned his rapacious eye away from the fools of Lewis and Clark's paymaster, and watched the elders, sagging-fleshed, white-haired men, as they fell dreamily under the robes, one by one, until, like the narcosis of opium Lewis administered as medicine, they went into a dropsy of dreaming, falling, swooning, love-making. . . .

Colter fought with it no more. As she opened her robe, he went in, rolled with her. The lodge was loud with the grunts of the old men, the sighs of the given-wives and the weird whining of whimpering young men who were offering their women, by rite, to all takers who would come into the soft heaviness of the fleecy robes.

He rolled with her. Young, firm, she wrestled with him. Tears of gratitude ran upon his cheeks. Reaching out to her, he found that his claws . . . his hands . . . bore down, forcing his breast onto hers. He tore at her with his sharp mouth.

He awoke, shuddering in the steely dawn. The bear across the river was yet at work, face deep in the buffalo carcass. Over his head in the black oak, a hawk was perched, crying thinly on the wind. He was on his stomach, his face stuck out into the wind, his body wrapped in his blanket, oddly turned in the sand, hands clutching, hips driven, feet pushing at some feral, half-conscious act.

There was a rime of sand on his lips and he was sweating. He got up, clutching the blanket round his shoulders. Down by the boat was a chokecherry bush he'd seen the day before. He took out his knife and wounded the bark, slicing several strips to chew on, for he knew the potency of chokecherry would stem a fever.

Then he got up, disgusted with the mouthings of the bear—it was too gray and steamy to actually see it—and went back to the ash place. The hawk was gone.

In the center of the stone, he saw something.

All during the day as he trotted along, Colter thought about the thing he had seen. It played upon his mind, coming and going. Like the fever that he felt rise within him, then subside, the vision of the stone came and went, enticing him into a kind of waking dream. Abandoning the bullboat because it was taking in too much water, he found a good bank to cross over—safe from bears and wolves—and headed out, sweat cooling his burning brow.

The plains that ascended from the river were golden brown. The wind coming off them from the west warned of rain. He ran, wobbled, ran, wobbled, stopped, sucked air, dropped to his knees, listened to his heart pound.

Hate to get caught in a hailstorm here. Saw it pound a man into the ground—what was his name?—got shot by heaven's own fusillade of hail. Hail the size of musket balls. . . .

Which reminded him of Lewis, shot in the ass, but unable to think of a proper epithet, the kind of good man he was: "Damn you, you've shot me," was the best vehemence he could muster.

"I've not shot you, sir," Colter came back.

But Lewis was stubborn, obstinacy equally measured with decency, his cardinal virtues.

Come, admit the truth, man. You've blasted me in the backside; shot a second hole where there ought only be one!"

"You were wearing brown. You looked like a bear when you bent over—"

"God's hooks, man. Will you not shoot the mosquitoes? They're more capacious than fowl and . . . ahh, my shot butt, my poor broken-down hind end. . . ."

Then they both bent down and got into the wild onions, for there was a great patch of them here. Relishing the foolish memory, they grazed, Colter and Lewis, chomping like a couple of deer.

"My advice, Colter, is to put an onion bulb in each ear hole," Lewis said, in his doctorly way. "Tie two on either side of those swollen glands of yours, just under that dinosaur's jawbone you're wagging all the time."

He did as chided, feeling foolish, stopping up his ears, but Lewis was the camp practitioner and knew much of these things.

Presently, there was some relief. They were not running anymore, they were just walking. Passing through long, pleasant smelling fields of Mandan maize, squash and tobacco. As they walked, they talked.

"These red people, these Indians," Lewis was saying, "they're a fine lot as long as confined to the growing of gardens, which is the proper occupation for guileless heathen. By the by, whatever became of that man who took up with the Indians?"

"Do you mean Rose?"

"The very one! How fared Mister Rose, Colter, on those jaunts you took with him?"

"I recollect a fight twixt Rose and the old mountebank, Manuel Lisa. Ferocious fight it was, saved by Potts, who churned his way into it, parted the two just as they'd come to blows."

"—Potts took God's own wounds for his trouble—" Lewis interrupted. "Had the most confounded way of settling himself into the broil of any disturbance, didn't he?"

"Potts, to be sure, was pulped by Lisa, who then boarded his pirogue and set sail, and was later blasted by Rose who fired the Fort's swivel cannon on him. I watched Lisa duck down, while a feller name of Sooner hopped in the air. The charge from that cannon passed directly between his legs, whereupon Sooner struck the deck and swore to all assembled he was deader'n a coon!"

"If a shot was to pass between your pantlegs, I wager you'd do the same. Which reminds me, Colter, of that bear I shot. Do you recollect that six-hundred-pound menace whose fat boiled down to hog's lard? He was nine feet from his nose to his heel, three feet eleven inch around the neck, and with talons five inch in length—"

"What's the fat of the bear got to do with the charge of shot aimed at a man's balls, I want to know?" Colter jibed.

"Just this," Lewis answered demurely, "if his heart was as large as an ox, how large, then, do you suppose the bear's testicles were?"

"No bigger'n yours," Colter joked.

Lewis paid him no mind. "Those testicles were bigger than billiards, two separate pouches for the pair, instead of the usual federal issue."

Colter changed the subject. "Foot itch!" he stammered. The beard-seeds from the prairie grass had penetrated his moccasins and his feet were itching. He sat down, beckoned Lewis to do the same. The two of them slipped off their moccasins, rubbed their sore feet in the sun while gazing at the clouds.

"What I'd not give fer a good draught of springwater," Colter pined.

"What I'd not give to know what that smoke is, up yonder," Lewis pondered, pointing at the horizon from which a gray plume was now rising into the afternoon sky.

Colter smiled.

"What that is," he announced, massaging his foot, "is a life-saver."

Then, turning about-face, due north, he said, "And what that is, is a war party."

Lewis stared in surprise at the heat rippling off the dry grass. Dark shadows rose in wraiths off the heat shimmer, indistinct figures of men on the run.

"Will nothing stop them?" Lewis asked.

"Nothing that wouldn't also stop us," Colter said calmly.

Lewis did another full turn, rounding the opposite direction. The smoke smudge to the south was now gone.

"Whatever that was, no longer is," he concluded. "Best we be on our way."

They ran in silence then. Two men, side by side, elbow to elbow. The pace they set was an even one, metronomical, and their twin elbows, nearly joined, clocked the speed of their run. As their arms made half-circle arcs, their feet rose from the ground and made small puffs on the dry grass, and their breathing settled into a certain sway. Trusting to the monotony of their feet rising and falling, trusting to the rhythm of their hearts, trusting to the coursing of their blood, they ran on into the afternoon.

Behind, the black-blur of a death sentence. Ahead, Colter's Hell. How far they were between the two was hard to know. Only the soft, steady pounding of feet, the gentle brushing of elbows, the matched pace, had any definite meaning. Colter looked at his companion, and his friend and superior, Meriwether Lewis, was not there. Colter laughed, a short, dry, cackle.

"You never were much of a runner," he said aloud to the empty air.

And kept on. . . .

He ran until his feet were heavier than chain.

He ran until the sun went behind a cloud, and the

hawk that was following him dropped out of the sky. Then Colter felt a sudden cramp of pain in his shoulder blades. Crying out—screee! The hawk—

—hatcheting the wind with darkened wings.

Now, it was easier.

Move fast, glide. Take cloud, hook into.

Ride cloud, fly into. Sweep, hawk, scree!

Hawkscree!

Night dark the plain.

Shadow runners shadow into.

Night sky spits stars.

Then the wings on his shoulders settled for the night.

He sat, his hooks tight around the limb. Around him the sounds of earth and sky, vast burblings and streamings. He was not afraid, for he could fly. He drowsed, his head tucked under his wing. Again, eyes closed, he saw himself as he had appeared in the magic stone, wings outstretched. The night continued to devour itself. Water boiled, mud bubbled. Earth, old Earth sighed. And he saw Her in his hawkscape dream: how small and round and globular blue, with rivers of blue veins running through Her. From afar, from the impossible staraway far, She was lovely, wreathed in Her soft doe's dress of cloud, fragile blue egg, swirled, as he saw Her now from out the glass bubble of his eye. Hawks knew, dying men and visioning men with bubbles on their heads, and hawks with wings on fire, knew Her, loved Her, made love to Her.

T E N

GLASS

A notch had become visible in the ridge and Hugh made his way toward it. The skies continued to darken, matching his thoughts, and his strength came now from the rage which seemed always with him, coiling and uncoiling his limbs. He did not rest for a long while.

When he finally halted, he rehearsed his encounter with the gopher, till at last he drifted to sleep, dreaming of it. And Jamie was there, mixed up in it, smiling, at one point holding the broken string which might have been Hugh's life, hair tossled, eyes dancing. Then it all drifted away, and he dreamed of crawling again, toward the notch to salvation on the ridge's farther side.

He awoke by degrees, discovering that he was crawling. Had he stopped at all? Or had he simply gone on, dreaming the while? There was always fatigue; it was hard to judge from that. And long reveries often came to him as he crawled. He halted and massaged his leg. Sometimes it seemed as if he had always been crawling, the rest of his life a series of dreams.

He pushed forward, listening to the grasses as he slid among them. Sometimes he felt as if he were deep underwater, his movements as deliberate as those of a swimmer. Other times, there seemed no resistance, and he scrambled ahead with manic haste toward his goal, the ridge.

Finally, he had to rest, and he drowsed again, and the bear was there, and Jamie. He woke in a rage, crawled again in a continuation of fury. The night wore on, and he drove himself through it, dreaming briefly, always continuing after with a steady intensity.

He awoke, shaking. Had he been crawling or simply lying sprawled? He was uncertain. But daylight had come into the world, filtered through a bank of clouds. Immediately, he peered southward. The ridge and its notch were nearer now. He had come far. He sighed and rubbed his leg above the break.

That day he came upon a muddy gully—briefly a pond, he supposed, following the cloudburst. Still, the mud looked sufficiently moist. . . .

He crawled down its driest slope—that, by virtue of its rockiness. He plunged a hand into the mud. Wet, very wet. Immediately, he began scooping out a basin. Within moments, the water started filtering into it. As he waited for it to deepen he told himself he would also wait for it to settle, to grow clear. He wiped his hands upon the ground, then upon his trousers. He watched the level of the brown water as it deepened.

As soon as it had reached a point where he could scoop a handful and drink, he did so. And again. It was impossible, he realized, to wait any longer.

Twenty minutes, perhaps, and he had had his fill of water. The well seemed slower in refilling now, also. He turned and crawled back up out of the gully. That much, at least. Starving, yes. But no longer thirsty. He spat several times to clear the muddy taste and made his way toward the notch. He was certain now that he could make it that far. Then— Things would be better. He fell to creating the scene beyond the ridge—lush valley teeming with game, sparkling clear streams. . . .

He seemed to be moving more rapidly. Was he somehow grown stronger from the exercise of his efforts? Or was it the energy of anticipation that drove him now? Either way, he determined to use it to the utmost.

All that morning he crawled, hate forgotten, pain numbed, even his hunger held at a distance, as he slid over the plain and the ridge came clearer and larger toward him. A snake fled his trail. A few dark birds dotted the sky on a southward journey, passed over the ridge, were gone.

Nearer, much nearer, he decided, beneath the noonday sun, as he rested, rubbing his hip. Possible. It may be possible to get there today. Once the butte had seemed much farther, but he had passed it. Now it was somewhere to the rear, toward the west. He did not even turn his head to check its position.

He pushed himself through the afternoon, the ridge growing steadily higher before him, its gap widening. When the ground began to rise, he drove himself against it, still keeping his rests to a minimum, refusing to lengthen them. Steadily, he worked his way toward the divide over increasingly stony terrain.

Telling himself stories of the other side, he mounted the sloping way, recalling the rising of that first gulch and the bounty he'd achieved near its end. Ignoring the aches in his hip, his leg, he drew himself over stones and gravel, sometimes slowing to negotiate a particularly irregular passage.

And at last he neared the apex of his climb, towers of stone at either hand. Slowing, he realized he neared a place of viewing that prospect which lay beyond, knowing, too, that his dreams concerning it were only that—tales he had told himself to ease his passage to this place. Yet—

Slowly, very slowly now, he mounted the final yards. As the spaces opened before him rank after rank of yellow hills came into sight. He halted, studying them. The story he'd told himself had been so pleasant. He lowered his head onto his arms and sobbed.

He'd known, of course he'd known, he told himself. But seeing the sustaining lie come apart this way was a heavy rock suddenly laid upon his back, breaking his will, squeezing away his strength, leaving only these feelings—loss, futility, abandonment. The wind whistled among the rocks of the gap, and he clenched his teeth, not wanting to look upon that forward prospect again.

For a long while he lay there, after the sobbing ceased. Worthless now, all of his efforts. He knew he could never cross what lay ahead. Why move at all from here? This place was as good as any other for what was to come. Let it be, he decided, let it end here.

But after a time he raised his head, to turn and look back upon the waste he had crossed, to consider how small a thing it had come to. The butte, toward which he had striven so long and hard—where was it? When finally he located it he frowned and raised his hand. Tiny, it had become, to be blotted from sight by the tip of his little finger.

So far. . . . It was hard to believe he had mastered all of that distance. He stared. So far. . . .

Then he smiled, knowing he could go farther, into the yellow hills, through them, beyond. As far as was necessary. He turned away from the butte. He looked about. However far. . . .

He began to crawl. Through the notch. Over the divide. Down. Toward the yellow hills.

Easier, the downward trail. He descended the slope of the ridge. Over the divide now, moving quickly, sometimes almost sliding, his exertions were not so strenuous as before, each forward stroke overpaid in the way of progress.

The new mood stayed with him for a long time, down to the level land, on through the evening and into night. His leg and hip still hurt, his lower back and shoulders ached, and at times he felt it in his chest as well. Yet, for now, he was apart from the complaints of the flesh, atop a wave of euphoria from all he had managed, beyond the ridge.

He had found no new landmarks to pursue before he came into the night, and so he took his way from the stars. They seemed very bright tonight, above his progress, and he continued for a great while before a heaviness came upon him. Resting then, he slipped quickly into sleep, with no dreams that he could recall.

The day was gray upon his awakening, and a chill had come into his bones. Fog lay all about him, stirred by a cold wind. The hunger was there, as always now, but the chill pushed it from his mind, and he began moving as soon as he was able, to stir his blood and raise some warmth.

For direction now there were no landmarks, no stars,

no taking of his course from the position of the sun. He took his way from the alignment of his body, from the position in which he had fallen. His movements were rapid because of the cold.

Fog. Stirring. In a way, it was neither night nor day that he now negotiated, but rather that landscape of dream through which he had crawled so many times these days past. As his limbs moved and the cold was driven out he grew less and less aware of his physical being, coming more and more into the slow, wraithlike stirrings until they seemed a part of him and he of them. He became a part of their dance, they of his rolling senses, and he passed through meadows of his childhood in far Pennsylvania, a sound of sobbing coming to him. Was it himself or another?

Of course. It was Jamie. Why was the lad weeping? He could not remember. Suddenly, though, he felt tears coursing down his own cheeks. Somehow, they both shed the same tears. He did not know why. It did not matter. He crawled, weeping, through the fogs, and when this passed he was depressed. He thought of Jamie lying somewhere dead. He thought of a Ree war party approaching, about to cross his path. He feared a sudden crevice, unseen till too late, into which he might blunder.

He crawled through the fear, groping his way, panting when he rested. Too long a halt, however, and the chill came into him again. He made his way through what could be morning, and still the misty curtains persisted about him. He crawled on. The thirst was there, and the hunger. Stronger still were the icy strokes of the wind.

He went into and out of the sadness, and the wind was sometimes like Jamie weeping. Yesterday's feeling of victory was a faraway thing now, as from yet another dream, like Pennsylvania and the shadow of the bear. The fear would still come upon him suddenly, though, objectless now, and he would either lie shivering or crawl madly at its advent.

The ground rose and fell. The fog persisted. Once, from high overhead, it seemed he heard the honking of geese. When the land fell the winds grew quiet. As he mounted slopes they returned to torment him. So it was that when the fog darkened into night he chose a lower area in which to fall to his rest.

He fell asleep to the moaning of the wind. He dreamed of his last meal.

He woke numb with cold. The dawn was white. Below him, the hollow rolled with fog. There was a great silence everywhere. He did not move. A part of the dreamworld had come with him. His gaze drifting overhead, he saw branches heavy with plums, waiting to be knocked down. Yet he knew them for the fruit of dream, and he strove by an act of will to bring them with him into the world where his body lay, cold. He held them within his seeing until a rising hunger forced him to move.

All of his pains were with him as he stirred himself. But these were forgotten when the plums refused to fade. The gray-green smears above him on the slope were indeed the leaves of a plum tree. He raised himself and discovered many to be within his reach.

Tears filled his eyes as he took hold of one and drew it free. To have slept beneath them all night, unknowing. . . . He began to eat.

Daylight pierced the whiteness as Hugh fed, and the

fog began to thin. As the prospect cleared, he realized that he had slept at the head of a valley. A touch of warmth came to him after a time, and the air continued to grow clear.

Farther down the valley then, he could make out the faint line of what had to be a creek. Knowing what he did of the general area, he realized it likely that it eventually led to the Moreau; thence, the Moreau would find its way to the Missouri. He need but follow.

Light and warmth continued to fall about him as he ate. When he had obtained all that he was able, he turned and made his way downward into the valley. His hip ached from the previous day's exertions and the cold; his joints were stiff. He groaned as he set out; yet, hope lay ahead, reducing the pain by its presence.

Crawling, refreshed, he saw a little green far ahead. There was a rill, then, as he had thought, fed by a spring in that beginning place. Yes, as he moved, he saw that the green extended on, along that length.

Water. And once he'd reached it he would follow its course. No more thirst. Hunger perhaps, but at least there would be water, and a few fruits and roots and berries seemed likely along the way. He hurried. The last of the fog was burned away as he descended the land.

It was a long crawl, and the sun moved higher and the day grew warmer as he was about it. But at last he reached that patch of green where the water bubbled in a little pool, overflowed, and trickled southward. As he drank he thought again of the journey which had brought him to this place, of the journey which lay ahead, of the end of his journeying. Suddenly, he felt that he was going to succeed.

Having passed through all that he had he would master any trial that remained. Then, then there would be Jamie to deal with. . . .

He drank again and it was sweet.

He lingered at the spring, drinking, then sipping, resting, rubbing his leg, dozing. At last. For the first time since he had begun his odyssey he felt safe. It was good to savor the feeling.

He spent over an hour so, before he moved again. And then it was with a pleasure that he crawled, beside the tiny rivulet. He would accompany it, would watch it grow, watch it gain in strength. It would share this power with him, he knew.

And so he crawled, drinking each time he paused to rest. Roots and a few berries appeared along the way. He dined and drank that day, and the next, and the next, as he made his way eastward, watching the stream grow to his left. As his strength grew he thought again and again of what had brought him to this, and his anger rose and became once more his companion. Now, now it was much more likely he would live, would be able to take up that special hunt. As surely as he had tracked game would he find the trail Jamie had left, would he go hunting. . . .

Crawling through a morning's light he encountered fresh bear-scat. Later, he came upon a cluster of shrubs, berry bushes. Before them he found a recent bear track. The higher limbs of the bushes had been largely stripped, but several handfuls remained below. "The bear has left me breakfast," he reflected. Was this some recompense for his injuries, to be fed by the bear-spirit? If so, it seemed a bit niggardly. "He could have left me more." And it took his mind back to the day of the bear. In taking something from him, had it given him something as well? The plodding, implacable determination of the bear had seemed to fill him ever since. But was this a thing like the berries? Had the bear taken more than it had given? For the thing that drove him now—had it really been a fair trade? He smelled again the stinking-sweet breath. Death, and a terrible energy, and the sweetness of life. He had the energy now, but which of the others had been breathed into him? Which had he breathed into himself?

He studied the bear track again, then shook his head. Thinking like an Indian, he decided. Totems, and their power, day-power, night-power. . . . Was it the night-spirit of the bear that filled him? Even so, then. He would take its gift willingly now, for it sustained him, and somehow, he knew, it would take him all the way, to Jamie.

He sucked water from the streamlet, wiped his mouth with the back of his hand. He dipped his hands and ran moist fingers back through his hair, raked his beard with them. He touched his broken nose. Still tender, but not nearly so much as on the day of his awakening. It felt like a snout now. His forehead was still scabbed over, but it, too, yielded less pain to pressure than it had.

And so he crawled steadily, resting regularly. Clouds blew past the sun, alternately darkening it and letting it shine free. More geese passed into the south, their notes drifting down and back to him. He became more and more aware of his hunger. Now that his thirst was at last slaked the hunger came in waves, roiling his belly, sweeping up the front of his body, passing through to the back, creeping into his limbs. The berries and roots he discovered along the way seemed blessings each time he came upon them. But they never filled him entirely. There was always an ache for more. He felt his shrunken arms and counted his ribs. He wanted a regularly filled belly. He wanted meat. He dreamed of steaks and game hens. He smelled them frying and roasting as he slept. He wanted a rabbit, a bird, venison, buffalo steaks. Each time he dug up a bit of bread-root or swallowed a handful of berries it was in some way worse than nothing. Filling him a little without satisfying, it seemed to increase his hunger, made him think of the food that he really wanted—squirrel, trout, beef, bacon, salmon. He felt himself wasting as the days passed. There was an immediate energy to be had from his fare, but he was aware that he had wasted down every time he looked at his arms. His great biceps and heavy forearms were shrunken, his sinews standing out like cords. His reflection in the stream was a hardly recognizable, haggard thing, face thin and heavily lined, framed with heavy hair, eyes sunken into dark pits beside the bear-smashed snout, dark band of laceration above the brows. His hunger and his anger were one now, their source the same—Jamie and the bear. But crawling, grizzled, foraging, the bear had also given him something to sustain him, where Jamie had only taken. His crossing of the plain had worn much from his frame, his spirit. That which remained was that which had been strongest—rendered down, purified—elemental now. He had become a hunger, meat his object.

Jamie a feeling there must be warm and gory and filling come along. . . .

And he crawled, and sometimes he grew very warm though the breezes were cool and he moved in a shade. He knew then that he was feverish, but it did not matter. He would drink and crawl on, sweating, hearing voices out of his past saying things he had forgotten in places he had not been in a long time. He sailed again in the Caribbean, played in his Pennsylvania valley. He wrestled and hunted and feasted with the Sioux. . . .

At times, too, it seemed as if the fogs had returned, and, when they cleared, that he crawled through city streets ignored by passersby, strange bright buildings reaching to enormous heights about him, odd vehicles passing through him, no horses. . . . And sometimes it was summer and sometimes winter, rain, snow, and the colors of the season's passing. Crawling through years as well as places beside a stream, it seemed. . . .

. . . And the hunger was with him even then, as peculiar shapes passed through the air, strangely dressed people walked by. Beside the stream then, crawling, head burning, he could hear his voice raving, and he did not understand himself, and it did not matter. Forward, with the rush of the water, he went.

The stream continued to widen, fed by occasional creeks. The green area was greater now, the trees higher. Birds warbled and trilled as the day began, hunted insects, passed.

The fever eased and he soaked his face for a long while. He gathered a meager salad, ate it, continued on his way. A little later he collapsed and slept.

Awakening to the coolness of drying perspiration upon his body, his garments, he drank again and crawled. The valley narrowed as the day advanced, grew more rocky, seemed to deepen. A coolness of constant shade was with him now, and the earth seemed to be sinking and himself with it. He crawled along a pebbled bank rather than a grassy streamside trail.

Turning, in the shaded, afternoon light, he followed a sudden curving of the ravine. All at once, the world fell away but a small distance ahead, granting him a view of the flat, tree-lined, shrub-clustered farther bank of the Moreau into which his stream now debouched from his height, his gaze was taken across its dark and flowing width.

He hauled himself farther forward for a wider view of the area. The deep-worn bed of the stream fell away eastward, the yellow rock which held its channel rising to a high summit to his right. As he went he became aware of a low murmuring sound which he knew was not the flowing of water.

It was the most difficult climb he had made since he'd begun crawling. The way was at times very steep, and his leg and hip found new ways to hurt. The trail he had taken was circuitous, and three times he had to backtrack and choose another route as the afternoon wore on.

He achieved the summit before the light of day had gone. Lying there, low-hung sun at his back, he listened again to the sound that was not the river, and he sought its source.

Far down along the winding valley through which the river flowed he saw a large cloud of dust; outlined against it, the distant treetops shivered.

As he watched, it seemed that the volume of the sound increased, though he knew this might only be a matter of the focussing of his attention upon it. Staring, fascinated, at the cloud, he began to make out a line of movement low within it. Periodically, the dusky curtain swayed. It parted for an instant, fell closed again, opened once more. . . .

Through the gloom, then, Hugh beheld a migrating mass of buffalo. They would be headed for their winter pastures on the Platte, he knew. And he watched them—living troop of meat, passing, passing—till the sun fell away and the night filled the sky, and the sounds of their passage followed him into sleep.

Dreaming, he sat beside a campfire on which steaks and tongues sizzled, sucking the sweet marrow from a bone. Awakening, he heard a lowing sound, and the roll of hoofbeats had grown louder. A piece of moon shone upon the water, lightened the valley, displayed the shadowy, roiling mass much nearer now, passing, passing.

He slept again, trailing a bison in his dream through deepening snow until finally he could go no farther. He awoke to the continuing thunder of their passage, great masses of them right below him now, moving by into the west, none for him to eat. He watched the sun come up upon the spectacle; a single, long, living thing flowing by, it seemed, covered with dark knobs of heavy flesh.

It was unbearable to see it pass and be gone, to leave him unsatisfied. If there were some way to stay but a single member, to leave it dead till he could reach it below. . . . He cast about him.

There was a boulder. He knew he couldn't lift it, but it seemed sufficiently rounded that he might be able to roll it to the edge. Heavy, of course. Still, once he got it going. . . .

He crawled over to it, placed his hands upon it, pushed with his good leg. It shook, but remained in place.

He realized that he must get it to rocking. He braced his foot, relaxed his shoulders, flexed his arms. Then he pushed and released, pushed again, relaxed again, pushed. . . . It moved a little farther each time, in either direction. Push. . . .

It had come loose from the depression in which it stood. Release. Push again.

It moved forward over the lip of its pit. He maintained a steady pressure, and it tumbled forward.

Crawling to keep up, he kept his hands upon it, continued the pressure. Pushing. Forward. Toward the edge of the bluff.

And suddenly it was gone. Over. Down. He crawled the final distance forward, quickly, to observe its fall. It plummeted, struck a ledge, bounced. Rolling then toward the passing herd, it missed the flank of a cow, continued by, came to rest. The herd adjusted its course, flowed about it.

He howled, picked up a stone and hurled it. Another! Another. . . . They fell harmlessly among the herd, as inconsequential as a bit of rain. After a while, he stopped and simply sat staring.

Finally, he turned away, heading back down toward the creek. There, he drank, and he ate bread-root. Afterwards, he began following the stream, toward the low, level land. The way was irregular, his going slow, and all of his aches were upon him, his brow hot again. He felt the fever rising as he crawled.

As the morning wore on, the vibration of the land seemed to diminish. Passing. . . . The bulk of the herd must have gone by. About noon, he was certain of this. The drumming of their hoofs was fainter now. After negotiating a patch of boulders, he lay his head upon his arm and rested. No reason to hurry, to push himself, and he was hot and shaking. He closed his eyes and listened to the fading thunder.

When he woke, the shadows were much longer. He drank from the stream and washed his face in it before he continued along the downward course. Something was different.

It was several minutes before he realized what had changed. There was a silence now. The ground no longer vibrated to the hoof-falls of the passing herd.

He continued, slowly. Then there were two more rough places, and then the slope grew more easy to negotiate. When he reached level ground he rested again before crawling forward. The air was still foggy with settling dust, the river shallows muddy, churned by thousands of hoofs. All of the trees were stripped of their lower foliage, the saplings battered down, trampled to splinters. He advanced farther, for a better view down the shadowy valley.

The way was uniformly ruined for as far as he could see. In his mind, he marked his passage along it, then followed with his body. Crawling the trampled earth in the late afternoon light, he decided to travel as far as he could while daylight held. He followed the bending of the Moreau, eastward, by degrees. The rich smell of the watercourse still pleased him as he went.

Crawling into twilight, he heard a noise from beyond the next bend. A yipping and a screeching composed it, and his spirit rose with the sudden realization of what it might mean. He hurried ahead.

Rounding the bend, he saw a bison carcass dark with crows, crows flying above it. Round about them, a ring of dog-like creatures pressed in to feed—too large for coyotes. He cast about quickly for some weapon.

Over near the waterside, sticks. One of them had to be suitable for a club. He crawled that way. Considerable driftwood had been cast ashore at the bend. He searched among it for a piece a couple of feet in length with some heft to it. Shortly, he found one which had the proper feeling when he swung it, one which did not shatter on impact with the earth.

Crawling then toward the carcass, he cried out. He picked up a stone and hurled it in that direction. He shouted again, threw another stone. Some of the crows took wing, circling; a few fluttered away, to return again in moments. Three of the wolves halted their movements to stare at him for several seconds, then plunged back to the feeding. His fingers closed upon another stone. He raised it and threw it. It fell wide, and this time none of the feeders stirred.

Hugh felt the anger move within him . . . that he, a hunter, be forced to contest for carrion—and then ignored by scavengers. In a hot wave the anger flowed through him, its passage raising his hackles and seeming to swell his limbs.

He roared, then roared again and crawled forward in a steady lumbering, shambling, bearlike advance. He swung the club before him as he drew near, and the birds departed, crying protests. The wolves remained, silent, staring. It did not seem to matter what they did. If they fell upon him he would fight back for as long as he was able. If he were killed and eaten himself, so be it. He roared again.

The wolves retreated, slinking back from the carcass. Continuing his roars, Hugh hurled stones after them. He heard one of them whine as they withdrew into the riverside brush.

He rushed ahead to the bloody carcass, where he lay his stick aside and thrust his hand into the torn opening on its flank. The flesh was slippery in his grasp; it stretched and slid away. Whenever his fingers found purchase and he began to pull, it escaped. He cursed Jamie again for the theft of his knife. Then, with a final growl, he fell to the flesh with his teeth—biting, tearing, gnawing. He tossed his head as he swallowed, watching the shadows. Then down again, sucking and drinking, biting and ripping, all his dreams of meat swirling in mad dance to the tempo of his heartbeat, rush of his blood. He seized a chunk with his back teeth and twisted his head to the side, tearing it free. He bolted it without chewing and returned for another.

The twilight deepened as he fed, and he saw darker shadows emerge from the brush to advance slowly, tentatively, in his direction. He found himself growling on this discovery, and he saw that this caused them to halt, briefly. Immediately, he lowered his head and tore away another chunk of the warm flesh. When he raised it again, this time chewing slowly, they began advancing once more, as if stalking, moving their paws with silent deliberation, heads low. In the deepening darkness their eyes seemed to burn, and he felt of a sudden that the night belonged to them, that his club was no longer adequate against their new courage. Growling softly then, he retreated to climb a nearby bluff. Before he reached it they had fallen upon the carcass and were eating.

Red-bearded, his hands smeared with gore, he watched them for a time from the height, shouldering one another and snarling about their feast. Occasionally, he snorted and snarled himself, recalling the taste and texture of the flesh from which he had been driven. He licked his lips and smacked them, belly still writhing and growling about the unfamiliar masses it contained. The heat came into his face, and his limbs felt suddenly weak as he watched. Alternately, he shivered and sweated, and his mind was filled with a haze, the figures below at times seeming very distant, then very near, then wavery and dreamlike. He sprawled on the rocky surface, resting his head on his arms. Now the wind blew cool, but it did not chill him. Below, the wolves snarled and barked. In his dream he was down there with them, pushing his way through to the flesh, slavering and tearing.

ELEVEN

COLTER

Wheeling, hawkwinged, hawkwinding circuits dark-
skied, darkscrying blue incandescence of waters through
drifting clouds' veils, dark lines of mountains, clusters of
forested green, strings, dots of rivering blue, hawkswinging
high, hawkseye holding lights flapping over ice fields,
crawl of darkthunder herds under clouds' dust over furbe-
lowed plain, circular rainbows, firetipped peak beyond
ocean turning, darkened flyway of birdcalling formed to
wedge and arrow the seasons, descending then, plumed
plummet, out of equinoctial exuberance, downderrying,
down, through vaporous wisps, heatshield blazing, hawk-
call, huntcry, over Her eversighing mudstreaked Self,
breasting broken ranges, dipping valleyed declivities under
starshot blackspread sky, falling, falling now, amid pinna-
cles, buttes, talus, and scree, into caverndark opening,
down, eyes of fire, walls paintpotted mineralbright, low,
low, the weight of Earth heavy, so heavy it groans in the
turning, landing, perching, jerkstepping, jackbirded, lowering, lowering beneath world's weight, lengthening, widening, thickening, furred unto slow power, progressing, four-
legged, down, ever down, derry, into. . . .

T W E L V E

GLASS

• • • **P**laces of foundation, where dark streams through darkness flow, blind fish borne through caverns measureless, walls fungus-bright, delineating face and form of all the ancestors of all the tribes of the world, delicate fronds splayed amid coalsheet, beaver, deer, father to himself the bear, the cats, the fish people, bird he had dreamed lifetime but moments before, snake, bat, raccoon, wolf, coyote, and all the insect-folk, amber-cased, dreaming the dream of Her body amid jewels and lakes of oil, and hot rumble of melted rock flowing forever, deep, deep, and light of underworld about him now, and even man and woman, hairy hunters, wanderers in the earth forever, and the big flowers, the strange, unknown flowers, him padding by, blood upon his muzzle, in his mouth his throat, and throws back his head and roars that the underworld know that yet he moves, that nothing has stayed his course since the very beginning.

THIRTEEN

COLTER

The buzzing woke him, a soft, swarmy sound of bees around a hive. Eyes open, he saw it: the long boulder-colored coil, assembling itself, building into a fine figure-eight, then a handsome, six-tiered loop of rope.

Directly under the tree, looking up at him, the great rattler buzzed monotonously, a dry-leaved sound: shzz, shzz. The tail riding high above the triangular head, dusky and dangerous. The blur of the tail in the morning air.

He shook his head, looked down at the snake, which could not strike him. On the branch where he perched, he could see the foul-smelling land that lay ahead of him. His land, or so it would seem, for they had named it after him.

Colter's Hell . . . and right it is that I am so greeted this lovely pus-perfumed morn by one of Satan's crew. . . .

The great snake buzzed on.

And the clouds of yellow steam rose into the sky. The earth heaved, popped, sighed, subsided. Musing, he looked to the north.

If they dare enter, it'll not be where the founts break wind. The snake settled into a deeper, more menacing buzz.

Looking down upon it, he remembered Meriwether's diary entry, the time he slept beside a ten-foot rattlesnake.

"Rattles lined up like rows of corn kernels . . . mouth pink, fangs curved and white. For all its lightning striking, the creature would seem inaccurate with its blows, thing of limited vision. But what liquid line of beauty when it moved through the dry brush of an afternoon. . . ."

Yes, its signature was that death-head. Lewis was flat-out wrong about what it could do with it, too. Colter dropped a piece of bark, watched the sinuous coils reform into a fresh brown-gold diamond pattern, which revealed the custard-cream belly scales.

Bright-eyed head, he addressed it, Satan's walking stick.

The snake buzzed loudly, appreciatively.

Now, what? Am I to sit up here all day?

The snake shifted, diamonds flowing, the serpentine length of it sliding off the rock slab, slipping away from the tree.

That's better fer ye—and me! Colter mocked as the big snake slid like brown silk through the low chaparral, disappearing.

"Seekheeda," a voice said, quietly.

He thought the snake had spoken, then spied the rigid form at the base of the tree. Lean boy with a wolf-skin thrown over his shoulders. The rest of him daubed with red and black clay, dark rings around the eyes.

"What are you called?" Colter asked, in Crow, not stirring from the tree.

"Raccoon's Brother," the boy answered, in the same tongue.

They stared at each other, then. Not directly, peripherally. The eyes traveling semicircle, Indian fashion.

"Seekheeda," the boy said, again, lowering his head.

"What is it you want?"

Something in the boy's posture was asking, suppliant's hand and shoulder. The face, though, dark-blank.

The boy said nothing.

"You come . . . for me?" Colter inquired, his eye scanning the horizon. The northwest plain empty, the blue-grey grass of morning sun-shot, red hued . . . empty. . . .

Still, the boy did not talk.

Colter dropped from the tree.

The boy jumped back, reflexively.

They faced each other, neither one saying anything. Then the boy touched Colter on the arm. He didn't move, waiting. The boy's hand crept up the arm, brushed his cheek, stayed at the eyebrow, touched first the left, then the right. Then, like a small bird the hand dropped. A secret smile glinted on the boy's lips, vanished as fast as it had appeared.

The boy looked away, observing the rising steam of Colter's Hell. Across the clouds of vapor, there lay a watery land of scorching lakes, spouting fire, cool pools of aqua ice gleaming in the sun glare. Lavender lagoons, bubbling. Lime-green ledges, hung with yellow sedge, dripping. Crusted ochre outpourings, like lopsided omelettes, giving off wretched-smelling, sulfur fumes that cursed the air with their invisible vapors. Founts of limey green, great eyeholes of giant toads, oozing with putrefied mist.

The boy looked over these things with a face that betrayed no surprise. Colter wondered if he could read the scene, as he once did—when he first discovered it—in a moral dimension. Probably not. He'd heard, though, of the Mandan underworld, the red little devils therein, not far off from Revelation.

In the rising wraiths Colter recognized God's wrath. The souls of sinners were these high-flying clouds, forced up and pushed down, so that the whole thing was one great egalitarian combustion, a synchrony of rising and falling human aspiration. Fire, brimstone, the apocalypse where Satan was pitched into his lake of fire to preside thereafter over crusty fumes, soul-jets of mud and blood, pus and piss.

"Never thought I'd see the like again," Colter grimaced, shaking his head at his name-place, the birthing hole he'd vowed never to return to.

The boy looked on placidly.

"Well, to the baths, then," Colter mumbled. "Nothing to do but burn off the filth, scour the eyes, rinse the arse. . . . Come, lad, I know the place."

Obediently, the boy followed.

They walked through the wreaths of witchcraft, Colter hobbling around the boiling springs, the mud holes, the geysers, while the boy came up cautiously behind him. In the distance, the gouts of steam rose high into the sky. The rocks griddle-hot under foot. The earth constantly quaking. Tremors followed by deep-crusted rumbling, spasms of indeterminate grumbling. Colter traveled deer-like through the glades of skeletal trees which stood out deathly pale, burned bone-white in the frequent geyser sprays. The water over which he walked a thin crust, emerald blue.

They passed over terraces that rose steplike onto dun-colored hillsides of grayish shale. Pools of purple water gurgled at their feet, the rims spilling into deposits that glittered: draperies of piss water, dropping into successive descents, falling further into chasms—punch bowls of boiling excresence.

He chose to rest at the base of one of these: a golden chalice brimming with clear turquoise liquid. There he disrobed, sat himself down in the warm water. The boy sat on the bank of this place, surrounded by a hillock of snowy sand, tufted, here and there, with sprigs of pale, burned grass. Opposite the chalice, on the other side of the sandy hillock, was a thing that resembled sloppy green cake batter. It looked alive but it had been dead for centuries.

He bathed, rubbing the sand on his sun-dried skin. The boy looked to the north, as if something called him there.

Gradually, Colter began to crave the coolness of a nearby stream. He rose and walked to the rivulet, stones slime-laden and quick to the touch. Lying out flat in the cold stream, the slime cooling his back, Colter half-closed his eyes. Soon his body was chilled, he got up, walked back into the chalice, soaked himself anew. And so the day passed in this fashion, the man idly dozing, the boy looking out for something that did not seem to come, but remained ever on the horizon of his mind. He looked into the umber hills, beyond the opal terraces of Colter's Hell, searching, his eyes searching for what he knew must come.

By day's end, Colter was hungry. He'd found a station, a place built up high and from which there was ample vantage point of the surrounding landscape. Here he made camp, squatting, dozing, waiting. Far off, the honk of geese, trumpets on the lake, the other side of the burning fen. The boy, when he heard them, got up immediately. For the first time, Colter saw the bow and arrow tucked under his wolf-fur robe.

As the boy went away into the dead trees, Colter reflected on their chances. At the base of the camp was the throat of a small geyser, which emitted sulfur steam on the hour. Around this mouth-hole—he thought it resembled the open lips of a troglodyte—lay a fine, thin sheet of dry calcite crust, under which burning waters awaited the unwary. To mount the stand where Colter had made camp, it was necessary to cross a series of stairs covered with colored algae.

—A swan might fly over it, Colter considered.

—Or a little marmot hop up it. . . .

But no man, not without due notice, was going to usurp it, unannounced.

So thinking, he lay down, slept. When he awoke from a dreamless sleep, somewhat rested, the boy was with him again. Having roasted a goose, he offered some to Colter, who took a leg and tore at it greedily. They ate their repast in silence, the boy wiping the goose fat into his hair.

The banked deadwood fire flickered on the dry mount. The night was amply starred, the air sharp, cold. But where they had sought refuge, the steam rose thick, the hot rocks gave off heat. The commanding view of the gloomy gardens that were all around them led Colter to believe that, for the moment, they were somewhat safe.

He studied the face of the boy. Maybe he was deaf, Colter thought. They sucked at the marrow bones, listening to the expiring sighs of escaping gas. Colter, who pitched his bones into the troglodyte's mouth, thought he heard a belch of appreciation.

He lay back in the steaming darkness, studied the wheeling stars. He was, once again, most fully himself, a man born of recklessness. He felt the nature of himself coming to a boil in this mad place of his. Once again, he enjoyed the abundant health that set him apart from all others. And, feeling contentment from within, he closed his eyes, visualizing the great western plains as he'd first come upon them:

. . . The miles of tallgrass and prickly pear, the highlands covered with low sedge, the mountain currant berries growing on the sides of cliffs . . . the great plains were just as wide as Man's own mind, he had thought then, feasting his eyes on the deer that followed no roads or trails . . . here, there were only infrequent moccasin paths, heading into the sun. . . .

. . . And then it all seemed to tumble on him, his inviolate dream of goodness: the big bountiful bosom of the earth, the long rivers, the immense precipices, the shagged, spurred, pitch-pined mountains. . . .

He saw again the small rounded stones that the feet hated and the big rams or ibex, which, when shot, cooked up tough, the wild turkeys that tasted of boot-leather, the day measured by muscle-dragging effort, pulling the gorgon of a boat up current, the mosquitoes drinking down the men's lifeblood, the sun sapping their souls, the nights full of wild, marauding dreams. . . .

. . . Fair morning, cold night, heavy dew damping down the spirit—breakfast of buffalo, guts blazed on the fire, Mandan-style. Forests of arrow-wood, red wood, willow wood, and cotton, and one man with a tumor, another with a fever. . . .

. . . Lewis, supposing to shoot a wolf, fires instead upon a cat of the tiger kind, brownish-yellow, standing near a burrow preparing to spring, he shoots it fair, but when I sidle up to see, the wounded thing is gone, the first and only one of its kind; we put together a crude sketch that looks a little like it, but the effect is nothing compared to the sight of such an uncommon beast. . . .

. . . Cold night, heavy, night-hauling, river-roping, walking slick cobble, dragging cold spirits down, down, down. . . .

. . . To Hell? Potts asks from his invalid's bed.

I say, Naw.

He says, How come, couldn't prove't by me—

I say, Hell's a distinction you earn . . . it ain't free—

He says, Well, one thing: This here shore ain't Heaven. . . .

Lewis then, always interrupting: Whether I struck it or not, the tiger-cat, I could not determine, but I am almost confident that I did; my gun is true and I had a steady rest by means of my espontoon, which I have found very serviceable to me on the open plains. It now seems to me that all the beasts of the neighborhood are in league to destroy me, or that some mad fortune is disposed to amuse herself at my expense. . . .

. . . Oh, the craggy precipices and the river bluffs and the damp spirits of the wet, wearied traveler who longs for nothing more than his homey-hearth, but the wind's a wreaker of maladies and the rain wounds the skin and the beasts of the neighborhood are in league, are in league, I tell you. . . .

He turned in his sleep, cradling his head in his arms.

The boy rose from the fire, put another log on, covered sweating Colter with his wolf robe, listened to the night give off its ghosts, the waters whistling, shrilling. Somewhere, Colter heard men, voices pinned on the rising steam. Flickering fires. They were close, close to the lip of the geyser. In the morning they would come and kill him. He dreamed of this. . . .

The sermon was delivered over plumes of steam backlit by four burgundy moons. Lewis faced the men, arms folded. He rocked on his heels and the spermy fountains spattered the trees behind his head. The men daubed their faces with kerchiefs. Lewis, who was spotted from the explosion, did nothing but rock manically on his heels, lips pursed, prepared, like a tiger-cat, to pounce.

" '—Replenish the earth and subdue it,' " the Good Book says. " 'And have dominion over the fish of the sea, the fowl of the air, and over every living thing that moveth upon the earth—' "

Colter got to his feet, feeling ragged, but right.

"We have," he said, "worshiped the beast, the mark of which is on our forehead. We've drunk of its blood. The hour of judgment's come. Look at this place, look around, Hell's wrath, the wine of the beast. The Good Book saith, 'And the smoke of their torment ascendeth up for ever and ever and they have no rest day or night, who worship the beast and his image, and whosoever receiveth the mark of his name.' "

The crowd of men roared and fled, a multitude of drumming wings, ravens beating at the brimstone.

Rose bore the mark of the beast, verily, upon his branded forehead.

They'd all, each and every one of them, rolled with the Mandan women, despite Lewis's disapproval.

He'd prayed over flesh killed, flesh to be killed, flesh for the killing; he'd killed and killed, so had the others. There was no end to the blood they'd bathed in.

The four burgundy moons aped the sun for brightness.

There was a great quake. The men winged away in the wind, turned to ravens' feathers, became a monstrous black sackcloth of hair, the moons became blood. Out of the chalice came thunderings and lightnings, a sea of crystal glass, flaring, in the midst of which the beasts returned from the land of death with eyes that smouldered, horned beasts snorting in the lakes of brimstone.

He awoke, shaking. The boy sat crosslegged and barechested before him. The campfire, sending up wisps of smoke, was otherwise all but out. The boy regarded him with a certain kindly neutrality; a half-smile seemed to play upon his lips.

"You would not smile that way, if you knew what I'd just seen," Colter groaned, furiously rubbing his eyes.

The boy: "You have had a vision. . . ."

"Yes, that I have. . . . Do you know, my friend, that there will be nothing left? That it will all be gone? That your life, and mine, are not worth the spark they're fed on. . . ."

The boy listened attentively, the sometime-smile making his lips appear to curl gently in mirth, yet the face was stony-looking, immobile, the soft, young lines dimly cast in the smoky light.

"I have had a vision," the boy said.

Colter looked up, shook his head.

"When?"

"This night."

Colter examined the young round head with his eye. He felt his own shoulders; the boy's wolf robe lay round them.

"It was you, wasn't it? Otherwise, I'd've died—"

The boy looked coldly past him into the vapors that trailed the dark air. The little cat's smile gone. The face, in repose, was old, humorless, fallen, a turtle's wrinkled stalk of neck supporting a head that was ready to fall off and roll down the steps into the fiery waters. Colter eased himself forward to catch it.

The boy was frozen there. Overhead, the breaking stars. Below, the belching, farting earth. Between, two stone people: himself and the boy. Colter felt they had always been there, he and the boy, since the first fart of time.

"What did your vision tell you?" he asked the boy.

The boy moved his lips. The steam sneaked around him, obscuring his face.

"The white bears came," he said in a whispery voice, "they took me far up into the mountains. Where they left me, the war eagles picked me up, and carried me farther. I reached the tops of the mountains, where they join with the sky. There, I was asked by a voice to let out some of my blood. I did this.

"And where the drops of blood fell, a hole opened up in the mountains. I went into the hole and walked far, very far. I came to a place, deep in the earth, where the dead lived. There, a buffalo chief with great curved horns came up to me and said this: 'We are all dead. Once, we were alive, without number. Now, we are dead.'

"I told him that I did not believe so many of his people

could be gone from the earth. He assured me that it was so. The buffalo chief's eyes burned little fires in the darkness.

" 'Look,' he said, 'I will show you. . . .'

"And he called his people out of the earth, and the ground shook and rumbled with the passing of their hoofs. I could not count them there were so many. Hoofs, heads and horns passed my way, thundering to the surface of the earth.

"At last they came out of a hole—"

The boy gestured at the steamy mouth of the troglodyte.

"There," he whispered urgently, "that is the hole they came out of. . . ."

Colter observed the round mouth of gloom from which issued a delicate feather of sulfur.

"Is that all?" he questioned.

"These were not real animals," the boy said. "These were strange creatures of the dead world. They inhabited the living world, but they moved upon it strangely. They grazed like our buffalo do, but they did not raise their heads in recognition when I walked past them. Many lay down, but not as buffalo do. They were many and spotted, and strange. They did not make the sounds that buffalo make. When they spoke they seemed to make a low, sad foolish noise. The horns on their heads were small and short. Their eyes were large and round, their heads not large, but their tails long, and tufted at the end. This thing I have seen comes from a time not our own. I believe it is a bad omen of what is to come."

The boy finished talking. He looked away. Colter saw a tear in his eye. He made no effort to rub it away.

Snakes of steam came curling out of the barren, leaf-less, cold-limbed trees. The quaking ground expired breaths of death. The night replete with iced-over stars fogged like a dream. Colter rubbed his eyes, snorted.

"—So the damned bufflers're gone," he droned. "Won't Potts be vexed, he's with them now. . . . Did you see a funny pincushion-looking fellow down there in your Hell-travels?"

The boy looked away into the stubbly trees with the ghosts of snakes writhing through their limbs.

"They will come for us in the morning. They will kill us," he said calmly. "Now I must prepare my death face."

For the first time Colter recognized the familiar graying of the sky. Night was passing, morning drew nigh.

"Have no fear for your life, my young savior," Colter called out as the boy went down the slimy steps.

Then: "Mind the crust, it's but an inch from a watery and a fiery grave—"

But the boy didn't stop to hear his words, and suddenly the troglodyte belched forth an amazing froth of scalding foam. Colter leaped forward, hooked the boy about the waist, hauled him out of the way of the second jet of steam. This one went high into the air, but Colter dive-rolled, and the two of them fell into an adjacent cave mouth. The burning droplets spattered harmlessly on the cave's brow. They listened as the troglodyte roared fitfully, showering, now, the whole area with goblets of greasy issue.

"The whole place's rigged, don't you see—Mister Devil's got his timer working, just so. Now if I just knew what it was—"

The boy looked uncomprehendingly at him; it was as if he—as well as the boy—were already dead.

"All right, then. Go tend your death-face, I'll be here, awaiting your kin."

As the sky paled, Colter cackled. Soon the sun bled fresh blood on the unholy desert-swamp. The eruptions and permutations sputtered on and off, expunging the rocks, anointing the moonlands with noxious oils. The ungodly orchestration pleased the ears of the feverish man, Colter, who danced atop his slime-caked throne.

He cackled.

And far away, by another campfire, his cry echoed. A boy awoke, as from a dream, raised his head, listened.

They came on cat-footed feet with the dawn.

Colter, in a mad mood of distraction, was ready for them. He'd draped strands of algae across his shoulders and back, and overhung his head with the stuff. In his hands he had a braided rope of algae. The booby traps were set. He waited.

And they came.

Flint In The Face, first. Peering out of the stricken trees, he saw the distant image of a man dancing, whirling his rope. The bow shot was not what he wanted. He dropped the bow, unslung his quiver. Nodding to his men, some fifteen of them gathered at the swamp's edge, he proceeded.

Colter roared with glee, disappeared down the cave-mouth.

Within a few minutes, walking on fallen, stone-frozen

logs, Flint In The Face was at the base of Colter's camp. The steam rose around them in wreaths. Flint In The Face pointed his knife at the hole Colter had vanished into, and one of his men stooped and went into it.

Now, Colter whispered through his teeth, Come through the bowels of Hell, and I'll teach you the Devil's game of chess—

The tunnel led down, the walls too hot to touch.

Colter heard the warrior lose his balance, slipping on the slime.

That'll soften you up, he grumbled, as he readied the rope.

The warrior came around a fluted corner, the light behind him. A shadow, he walked right past Colter, who stood fast, a green, rock-like thing, a column of slime.

Then the slime shot out, took the man by the throat with his rope. They wrestled. The rocks in the sunken chamber rumbled. The end of the half-hour neared, the Devil's stopwatch. They rolled, Colter's uniform of green came off in the warrior's hands, as he choked him with the rope, which fell apart in the struggle. Now they swung wildly at each other. The cave walls resounded with the coming of thunder.

Outside, in the bright sun, the other tribesmen took shelter. The troglodyte sent its first preliminary blast of smoke, then the spattering of mercury droplets, then the convulsive heaving of the main fount, as thousands of gallons of scalding sulfur water raged out of the troglodyte's mouth.

Three men panicked, ran wildly out onto the whitish frost-crust, immediately crashed into the brimstone lake, and amidst screams, sank forever beneath its surface. The others scattered, sliding on the evil scum of the stairs, falling, running to the ridge of nearby trees. There, they crouched, and watched.

Inside the cave walls, unaware of anything but their own battle, Colter and his foe struck at each other with wild, loopy blows that made rubbery thuds in the half-light. Once Colter struck the exposed side of his throat, but too far back, his fist glancing off the breastbone as the man arced and turned, came lunging and shoulder-slamming into him, knocking Colter down. Then the man's arms clamped and locked, Colter felt himself backed up into the cave wall, crushed in the man's iron grip. He grunted as the Indian groaned, a great swallowing blackness threatening to close over his eyes.

Colter wavered, then, between worlds. His opponent was larger and stronger, and he felt his spine grate against the oven wall of the cave. There was but one thing to do, and he did it as best he could. With loose fingers, he pried at the man's jaw, reaching deep for the artery there; he felt his thumbs go in, then he drove them like nails into the soft flesh.

Instantly, a cry came from his opponent's mouth. The pressure on Colter's ribs slacked off, the other wheezed uncertainly, his grip broken. They both rolled free. Colter dived for the man's head, caught him by the ears and, seizing him like a head of cabbage, banged him thrice upon a rock outcropping. The man dropped into the gathering suds of the cave floor, unconscious.

Colter, though his hands were burning, was on all fours, unable to get up. His breath came in gravelly rasps.

His lungs, clamoring for air, ached. Tripping, he got to his feet, legs limp as water plants, and stumbled toward the steamy cave mouth.

The other Blackfeet had moved well away from the troglodyte. They watched from the empty woods of white-boned trees as Colter emerged, hanging on to the lip of rock, as if about to drop. Then one of them raised his bow, took careful aim, and loosed an arrow. The arrow traveled true. Colter saw it late, ducked, took it in the flesh of his right pectoral muscle, dropped into the cave.

Flint In The Face, angered, struck the bowman with his open hand.

"You should not have done that," he said angrily.

When he looked up again toward the cave, White Eyebrows was gone.

Colter fumbled, staring amazed at the arrow lodged in his chest, took three weak steps back into the darkness, collapsed. Moments later, when he became conscious, he saw the man he had knocked out getting to his feet. Clumsily, the Indian found hand-holds along the cave wall, dragging himself erect. He was moving very slowly.

Colter rolled painfully onto his stomach; then, one finger at a time, he pulled himself forward, bringing his right knee into a position of leverage.

The warrior was standing upright now, rubbing his eyes. Dripping with soapy water, he streamed and shined, a sculpture rather than a man.

Colter brought the bent knee up under his stomach and rolled with it, so that both knees came under him at the same time. The man's back was still turned toward him. Unsteadily, his head sagging as if it weighed a thousand pounds, he brought himself silently to his feet—but not without a tell-tale groan.

The cave whirled, spun. Colter clawed the air. Gravity knocked him to his knees. Now the man turned and faced him, brandishing a tomahawk.

His knuckles dragging on the cave floor, Colter felt something slurpy under his hand. The soggy remains of his algae rope. Cupping a knot of it, he wrapped his fist around it tight, buried his heels into the rough rock floor, and began to pivot.

The warrior, thinking Colter had only his bare fists to fight with, came on quick and leaned in close—too close— for Colter brought up his fist full of hot, dripping algae and cocked the man full in the face.

The blow threw him back. He moved a half-step to the side, swung wide with the tomahawk just as Colter blocked with his forearm, followed through, caught him with a right hook, sending his head high. The head jerked forward, bobbed, Colter landed a jab at the exposed Adam's apple.

Clucking, the man fell, plummeted heavily. His head bounced when it hit, eyes rolled back, snapping shut.

Colter held himself by his knees, and breathed hard. In that position, the feathers of the arrow touched his nose. He stood up, grabbed the fine flint-point, and rammed the feathered thing through the thin flesh of his pectoral muscle. Some of his skin came away with a cloth-tearing sound.

The arrow ripped free, Colter threw it clattering to the floor. Time again to make a run. As if on cue, the cave rumbled and belched steam. The troglodyte was about ready to throw another gout of sulfur water.

I wonder where this thing leads, Colter mumbled as he

headed into the tunnel. It dipped downward, made a plunge into a pool of cooler water, curved around another corner, and began to grow lighter up ahead. He headed through the straight bore, which brightened as he ran.

Could it be?—

Suddenly the cave was suffused with sunlight.

Colter reached the termination of the cave, the spilling-off place. He was standing before a wide cliff mouth; below his feet the rock fell away into open space. There was the last of the Stinking Water River down there. He followed it with his eye, as it spilled into larger, broader pools, until, feeding out into the swift white current, it became the Big Two Fork that led to the foot of the Shoshone Mountains.

The Shoshones were the last boundary between him and Fort Manuel Lisa; cross them and there was only the great open rifted valley to conquer. For a moment, he looked out into the sun and pines of a world unwarped by devilish configurations of hot rock; he was, all at once, back in the country God had not forgotten. The sky was blue and pure, cirrus flagging across the sun. Blood coursed his chest from his latest wound; he paid it no mind.

He leaped.

FOURTEEN

GLASS

. . . **D**reamt he lay broken beside his grave, his friends riding away into the west. He had heard them speak of going, been powerless to respond. Now he heard only hoofbeats as they went away from him. Felt them within the earth, heard a momentary exchange of their distant voices.

Vaguely, aware of light, he listened to the sounds. The words died away. A tired moon hung above him. He stared at it through a haze. Dawn had leaked a slight light upon strands of mist. There was no wind to stir it. The hoofbeats seemed to grow louder again. He remembered the taste of blood, the breath of the bear. And crawling. . . .

He was awake atop his bluff and the sounds of hoofbeats were real. He turned and peered downward. Passing through the fog, three Indian horsemen rode on the trail of the buffalo. Almost, Hugh called out to them, for they could well be Sioux, with whom he was on good terms. Yet, they could also be Rees, and he had not come all this way to deliver himself into the hands of his enemies. He lay still and watched them ride by to vanish westward into the mist.

They could well be the outriders for an entire tribe on the trail of the buffalo. He would wait a time and see what followed. With a larger group, slower in passing, he should be able to tell whether they were friend or foe. And then—If they were Sioux, he would be fed, cared for, his wounds tended. He would tell them tales at their fires, paying them in the coin of stories from his wanderings. Then he would walk again, be about his hunt.

He waited as the fog turned to gold, listening, watching. The sun drifted slowly out of the east, over the course of perhaps an hour. Abruptly, a flock of dark birds rose downstream, cawing and flapping, to move westward, settling in a stand of cottonwoods. Then he heard the barking of dogs and the neighing of horses. A little later a band of mounted warriors came into sight out of the brush, to pass the base of his bluff upon that westward trail.

He watched, suddenly aware of his heartbeat. Mounted on a piebald stallion, the lead warrior was an older man, face hard and craggy, hair streaked with white; and Hugh recognized him. It was Elk Tongue, the war chief of the Ree, and more and more of his people came into view behind him, rounding the bluff, continuing into the west.

As Hugh watched he saw old men and women, children, the ill as well as the hale, in the procession. This looked to be more than a hunt, for it might be forty lodges that followed behind Elk Tongue, and they bore all their possessions, not just those of the hunt. The Sioux must finally have succeeded in dislodging them from their eastern encampment. They were in retreat now, ponies dragging travaux bearing furs, pots, drums, baskets of food, a few metal implements, small children riding atop the heaped household goods; the forms of those too ill to walk or ride were strapped onto other carriers. Nursing squaws passed by, babies at their backs. All of them looked haggard. Hugh could almost smell their burning cornfields. They would follow the herd, to feed, then continue to the home of their Pawnee relatives on the Platte.

Hugh snorted. "Ree" was short for "Arikara." They had attacked peaceful traders several times, which led to the Leavenworth campaign, in which the Sioux had allied themselves with the whites, for they, too, had known unreasoned violence at the hands of these people. The Rees' cousins the Pawnees were more tolerant, less prone to battle and ambush without good reason. Having been a Pawnee, Hugh spoke their language fluently, the Rees' dialect as well, though he was certain that the Rees would not recognize his blood-tie with their kin.

Not that the Pawnee were exactly easy-going. . . .

As the tribe passed he let his thoughts drift back over the years. Where did it all begin? Beyond the Pennsylvania valley of his birth, what had brought him to this point? Chance, he supposed. Chance, and human meanness—the meanness of a white man, a Frenchman, as cussed as any he had met on the plains, white or Indian. No race, nation, or tribe had a monopoly on cussedness; it just seemed a part of being human. He remembered the sea.

After that war in 1812 he'd gone to sea, working on traders in the Caribbean. Never had any real desire to see the mountains or roam the plains. He'd known tropical ports, drunk his share of rum, survived fierce storms and damaged vessels. He had enjoyed the sea and its smells and moods, liked the bright birds and flowers and girls of his ports of call, liked the taste of their rich foods, their wines. He would likely be there still save for the doings of one afternoon on the Gulf.

When the sleek vessel carrying a lot of sail had first been sighted, no one had been particularly alarmed until she struck her true colors and fired a warning shot.

The captain tried to run, but this was a mistake. The pirate vessel overtook them readily. He tried fighting back then, but this, too, was a mistake. He was outmaneuvered, outgunned, outmanned. Actually, there was nothing he could have done that would have been right, Hugh reflected. Simple surrender at that first warning shot would also have been a mistake. Hugh was to learn all of this later, first-hand, though it was mainly confirmation of rumors he had been hearing for years. The captain could not have saved them from Jean Lafitte, who was not of a humor to leave any witnesses to his business that day.

Hugh saw the captain and the other officers cut down. The seamen were treated the same way. This decided him against any attempt to surrender, and he determined to sell his life as dearly as possible. Standing back to back then with seaman Tom Dickens, cutlass in one hand, belaying pin in the other, he killed everyone who came at him, gutting them, clubbing them, hacking at limbs and faces. The deck grew slippery with gore about him, and he bled himself from a collection of wounds. After a time, the attacks slowed; it seemed that the pirate crewmen were holding back, loath to rush in and close with him. Finally, he became aware of a tall individual who stood watching the slaughter.

Eventually, the man spoke: "Let up!" he ordered. "I'll talk to them," and Hugh heard the French accent and realized this to be the captain of whom he had heard stories.

"You two," the captain said, as soon as the attacks ceased. "Do you wish to live?"

"A foolish question," Hugh replied. "Would we be fighting so were it otherwise?"

The Frenchman smiled.

"I can have my men wear you down, or I can send for firearms and take you at a distance," he said. "Or you can join my crew and keep your lives. I find myself undermanned again, partly because of yourselves. I can use a pair of good fighters."

"Druther live," Tom said.

"All right," said Hugh. "I'll do it."

"Then put up your weapons—you can keep them—and help transfer the cargo to my ship. If you've any personal effects you care about, better get them, too. We'll be scuttling this scow when we're done here."

"Aye, sir," said Hugh, lowering his blade and slipping the club behind his belt.

Jean Lafitte's current headquarters were on Galveston Island. There Hugh and Tom were given quarters. While he made no friends, Hugh became acquainted with all of the pirate crew. There was some resentment of the newcomers at first, and while memory of their display on the decks of the doomed vessel prevented all but two from carrying this beyond words, those two were thick-armed, heavy-shouldered fellows with the battered faces of brawlers. The burly Hugh outwrestled his man and bashed him a few times till he lapsed into unconsciousness. Tom boxed with his opponent and, though his own nose was broken in the encounter, he laid the man out. After that, the two shipmates met with no further violence at the hands of the crew and found themselves on speaking terms with all of them. While no real camaraderie developed, the men were not particularly amiable to begin with, save when drunk, and then it only took the form of songs, gallows humor, bawdy yarns, and practical jokes. Hugh did not trust himself to get drunk with them, for they were inclined to the setting afire of beards and of the removing of a fellow's trousers and painting his bum with tar.

Hugh and Tom sailed with Lafitte. There were bloody encounters with merchantmen, for it became apparent that Lafitte's policy involved leaving no eyewitnesses ever to testify against him. Hugh fought in the boarding of vessels and he fought to defend himself, but he took what small pride he might in the fact that he never executed prisoners. This changed one spring day when they took a British trader.

Three able-bodied prisoners were taken that day. Lafitte faced them—a tall, graceful figure, elegantly clad, one hand upon his hip—and stared into each man's eyes until they fell. Then, as before, he spoke:

"Gentlemen," he said, "I find myself somewhat understaffed at the moment. The exigencies of this work do take their toll in manpower. So I've a proposition for you. Join my crew. You'll have a snug berth, all you want in the way of food and drink, and a share of the booty. There will be occasional shore leave in safe ports to enjoy it. It is a dangerous life, but a high one. Think hard, think quickly, and answer me now."

Two of them agreed immediately. The third, however, asked, "And if my answer is no?"

Lafitte stroked his beard.

"Consider it a matter of life or death, sir," he replied, "as you make your decision."

"All my life I've done what I had to and tried to be honest while I was about it," the seaman answered, "though God knows I've had my lapses. Cast me adrift or leave me on some isle if you would. I'd rather that than join your crew."

Lafitte raised his eyes and caught Hugh's gaze.

"Deal with him," he said.

Hugh looked away.

Lafitte stared a moment longer. Then, "Now," he added.

Hugh looked back, meeting his captain's dark gaze again.

"No, sir," he replied.

"You refuse my order?"

"I won't kill a defenseless man," he said.

Lafitte drew a pistol from his sash and fired it. The man toppled, the side of his head gone red.

"Pitch him over the side," Lafitte said to another crewman, who moved immediately to comply.

"Hugh, I'm unhappy with you," Lafitte stated, stowing his pistol and turning away.

Hugh departed and helped to transfer the cargo.

Later, when they had returned to their base, Tom said to him, "Word's going around you made the captain unhappy."

"I wouldn't doubt it," Hugh replied. "I didn't kill a man he told me to."

"I heard things like that have happened in the past, before our time."

"Oh?"

"Old Jean, he's a real stickler for discipline. They say that nobody as refused a direct order from him has lived too long afterwards."

"How'd he do 'em?"

"Sometimes he holds a sort of court and makes an example of 'em. Other times he just lets it be known to a few he trusts that he wants that man dead. Someone always obliges and puts a knife in him then—when he's sleepin', or some other time he's not on his guard."

"You heard he usually gets rid of them pretty soon after something like this happens?"

"That's what they say."

"Thanks, Tom. Maybe you shouldn't be talking to me much now."

"What're you going to do?"

"I've been thinking for some time about leaving. Now's as good a time to try quitting this business as any."

"You can't steal a boat, Hugh. They watch 'em too careful."

Hugh shook his head.

"Think I'll wait till after dark and swim for shore."

"That's a pretty far piece."

"I'm a pretty good swimmer."

"The water's sometimes sharky."

"Well, that's a maybe, and staying's a for sure."

"What'll you do when you get to shore?"

"Start walking for New Orleans."

"I'm coming with you. I don't much like it here myself.

Sooner or later he's going to ask me to do something like that, and the same thing'll happen."

"Make a little bundle of your valuables then. I'll let you know when I'm going."

Hugh waited till the others had started their evening drinking before he nodded to Tom and said, "Gonna take a walk."

They met on the isle's northern shore, lit by a partial moon and floods of stars. Small waves danced in their light as Hugh and Tom stared out over the waters.

"Looks like a long haul," Tom said, "but I'm still game. "How long you figure before they guess what we did?"

"Morning, if we're lucky. Sooner, if tonight's the night someone comes by to get me. Even then, they can't do much till tomorrow, and we'll either be drowned, et, or too far gone by then."

Tom nodded.

"I'm ready any time you are."

"Let's be about it then."

So they stripped, bundled their clothes about their possessions, tied their packs to their backs, and entered the water. It felt cooler than the night's air, but their strokes were strong and after a time the exertion seemed to push the chill away. They swam steadily landward, and Hugh thought back over the previous month's piracies. He'd wanted to leave before this, but the danger had held him back. Now he wished he'd left sooner. Stealing, killing, drinking too much every day, and being a prisoner much of the time made him think again of the world's meanness. There was too much of it, everywhere he turned. He wanted to be alone in a big place, away from his fellows, free. He wondered whether the man he'd refused to kill had had a family. He wasn't sure he ever wanted one himself. Another way to be a prisoner, maybe.

Crawling through the water, he lost track of time. There was the monotony of the waves, Tom's steady splashing nearby, and the sameness of the night all around. The two shores were dreams, the crawling was all. One must go on.

At some point, he remembered coming to shore. Now the waters of Galveston Bay seemed the dream, the land they waded toward the reality. He remembered laughing and hearing Tom's laughter. Then they threw themselves flat, breathing heavily, the tingling of ceased motion dancing over their skins. After a while, they slept.

• • • Lying there, still as a stone, he watched the latter end of the procession in its passing, through a haze of fog and trail dust—the lame and the aged walking with sticks, leaning on companions, more squaws with children and packs of supplies. They did take care of their own, he reflected, and he could almost feel a touch of sympathy at their flight from the Sioux, though it was their own cussedness had brought them to this pass. He and Tom had been captured by the Rees on their trek through Texas, but had managed to escape. They were wary after that because of the treatment they had received. But all the wariness in the world didn't amount to much for two men afoot on a plain when they were spotted again by a mounted party.

They tried hiding in the scrub but the warriors knew they were there and flushed them quickly. Hugh tried the few words of Ree he had learned during their brief captivity, and his new captors showed understanding of them, as well as of his raised open hands and his sign gestures. They made it obvious, however, that Hugh and Tom were prisoners by taking their knives and conducting them to be confined in their camp.

They were tied and guarded that night, and while they were given water to drink they were not fed, though they were allowed to dine from their own meager supply of fruit and roots they had obtained on departing from the Rees. The following day they were not molested, though they remained confined, and they spent the second night under guard, also. A considerable babble of discussion emerged from a nearby tent late into both evenings.

The next day they were brought food and treated with some kindness. They were given fresh garments and led about the camp. As the day wore on, Hugh attempted to communicate with their captors, hoping to win their release, but the only responses he received seemed to indicate that they would be permitted to join in a feast that evening.

The day wore on, and at sunset they were conducted to a gathering of the entire tribe in whose company they were seated. Fires burned at every hand, and the smells of roasting buffalo, venison, and fowls came to them. They sampled every dish, as their hosts insisted that they try everything, that they gorge themselves on their favorite fare.

They were infected by the tribe's seeming good humor and began to relax and try to make jokes themselves. Finally, sated and a little drowsy, they began looking forward to the feast's end, to retiring to a night's rest. Abruptly then, they were seized from behind by several braves and bound hand and foot with strips of rawhide.

"Hey!" Hugh shouted, then added the word he'd learned for "friend."

Nobody answered him. Instead, Tom was taken to a tall, upright stake and tied to it. Squaws cut away his garments, stripping him, and heaped kindling about his feet.

"Let the boy go!" Hugh called. "Friend! Friend!"

They paid him no heed, and the women went to work on Tom with knives, cutting away strips of his skin.

"Stop! Stop it, for God's sake!" Hugh screamed, his cries half-drowned by Tom's own shrieks.

The women continued about their business, taking their time, removing patch after patch of skin, occasionally poking and prodding with the points of their weapons. Hugh became acutely aware of the second stake which had been raised, not too far behind the first. He closed his eyes against the sight, gritted his teeth, and tried to blank out Tom's cries. It did no good. Not seeing was in some ways worse than seeing, leaving even more to his imagination.

The ordeal went on for a long while, till Tom finally pleaded with them to kill him. Even later, they started a fire at his feet and heaped more kindling upon it. Hugh had shouted at them to no avail and had used up his tears early. Now he just watched as his friend writhed within the consuming flames. He tried not to, but his gaze kept returning to the spectacle. Soon it would be over. Then, of course, it would be his turn.

He remembered a small container of vermillion dye which he had borne with him from Galveston Island, as it had some commercial value and he'd hoped to sell it on reaching civilization. He hated to see it burned up, wasted; it would make fine body paint, a thing his captors seemed to favor. What the hell, he decided. Maybe it could do even more for him here.

He groped with bound hands at the place where he carried it at his belt. Painfully, he unfastened its ties. When it came free and he had a grip on it he raised himself.

Casting the bundle at the chief, he cried, "Here's a present for you! Hate to see it go to waste!"

The chief stared at the parcel, then extended a hand and picked it up. He removed it from the leather pouch and examined it closely, until he had discovered the manner in which the tin might be opened. When it had been uncovered his eyes widened. Tentatively, he touched the substance with a fingertip, raised it to study it, drew a line with it upon his forearm.

A pair of braves was already headed for Hugh by then, but the chief raised a hand and said something Hugh did not understand. The warriors halted.

The chief advanced then and addressed Hugh, but Hugh shook his head and said, "Present. It's a gift. I do not understand what you are saying."

The chief continued to speak, however, finally calling something back over his shoulder. Presently, a brave approached, drawing a knife as he advanced upon Hugh. Hugh gritted his teeth as the blade's point passed near his abdomen, but the man used it only to cut his bonds.

The brave helped him to his feet, and the chief came forward and assisted him. They guided him back to his quarters, where he sank upon his sleeping skins. The chief said something else then, smiling as he said it, and went away. The man who had freed him remained on guard outside.

He did not think he would sleep easily that night, yet he did. The evening's events returned in his dreams, and in the morning he recalled awakening several times to the sound of his own voice calling Tom's name. After a while a woman brought him breakfast, and he was surprised at his appetite. He finished everything and when she brought him more he ate that, too.

The day wore on and he waited. He was fed again at about noontime. No one approached him other than the woman with the food. He made no attempt to venture beyond his confines. He sat and thought, about Tom, about Lafitte, the Caribbean, ships, sailing on a bright day, Pennsylvania summers.

Later they came for him and escorted him back to the site of the previous night's feasting. He surveyed the area hastily, but this time there were no stakes in sight. He moved to settle into the position he had occupied before but was halted by his companion and taken forward, where it was indicated that he should sit beside the chief.

This dinner was different from the previous one in that it was preceded by a speech from the chief and a ritual of sorts where he placed his hands upon Hugh's shoulders and head several times, struck him lightly with bundles of twigs, bound his hair with a beaded cloth, and finally draped a small skin over his shoulders. Then the feasting proceeded in a jovial spirit with others of the tribe passing by to clasp Hugh or lay hands upon him. Gradually, he came to understand that the chief had adopted him, that he had become a member of the tribe, that he was now a Pawnee.

In the months that followed he learned the language, the customs, discovered that he had a knack for tracking, became a deadly marksman with bow and arrow, took him a Pawnee wife, became one of the tribe's better hunters. He learned, too, that the life of the trail appealed to him more than the life of the sea, with its cramped quarters. The plains held all the freedom of the vast and changing sea, without the confining drawbacks. He did not know exactly when he resolved to spend his days on the frontier. The realization grew in him slowly. Before the first winter had passed, however, he knew that he had finished forever with a sailor's life.

Yes, he had enjoyed it. But reflecting upon it now, as the Pawnees' less reputable relatives vanished into the west leaving a cloud of golden dust behind them, he saw that meanness again, on the night the Pawnee women had tortured Tom. True, they'd had grievances against the whites, but a bullet in the brain or a quick knife-thrust would as easily satisfy a need for a death. It was nothing special against the Pawnees, though, who had been good to him during his stay in their midst. Rather, he felt, they had their cussedness because they were members of the same race as all the other tribes of the earth.

He rubbed dust from his eyes then, and licked his lips. Time to crawl down and get himself a drink, see what he could find to eat.

Slowly, he descended and made his way to the river, where he drank and washed his face, hands, and neck. The area about him was too trampled to retain edible roots or berries. He crawled then to the carcass where he had fed the previous evening. It had been picked clean, however, its bones cracked and scattered or carried off.

Back in the direction of the bluff where he had spent the night, beyond the trees, Hugh saw a movement. He lay perfectly still and watched. Some final straggler of the migrant Rees.

He crawled ahead then, among the trees, through the brush, shortcutting a bend in the trail to bring him to a waiting place ahead of the shuffling figure.

An old woman clad in buckskins moved carefully along, bearing her small bundle of possessions. He licked his lips and checked behind and ahead. No one else had come into sight to the rear, and the rest of the tribe was gone from view, far ahead. There was sure to be some food in her pack, and the others would hardly soon miss someone they hadn't even bothered to wait for. Flint, steel, a knife. . . . Even in his condition it would be no problem to take them from her. Her cries would not be heard above the noise of the vanguard.

He watched her move. She shuffled nearer, and he wondered at her life. How many babies had she carried? How many were living now? Just an old woman. . . . He watched as she passed, remained still till she was out of sight beyond a clump of trees.

"Fool!" he muttered, to have let her go by, mother of Rees. It was not the same as when he'd refused to kill a helpless seaman. This was the enemy. He shook his head. "Fool," he said softly. Sometimes he was a fool.

Growling, he turned away, heading back toward the river.

He followed the water's course, down along the trail

the Rees had come. It was easy traveling, though the dirt irritated his nose, and he halted to wash his face several times. Berry bushes beside the trail had been stripped, as had the lower branches of fruit trees he passed. He dug a few roots when he was beside the river, washed them, broke his fast with them.

Before long all of the fog had burned away, and the dust had settled. During the next hour he made good progress. The sun spilled some warmth through the yellow and green of the tree-limbs, and there was a fresh strength in him today.

Topping a small rise, he halted and sniffed the air.

Smoke. The breeze brought him a hint of smoke. Beginning of a brushfire, or its residuum? Or might someone be camping nearby?

The breeze shifted and the smell vanished. Had it really been there, to begin with?

He crawled forward again, sniffing the air regularly. Nothing now. Still. . . .

It was several minutes before it came again. It was still faint, and a breeze's vagary took it away once more. But now he was certain. He had smelled woodsmoke. It was impossible to determine its direction, so he continued along the trail.

Another hundred feet and it came to him clearly. The trail, then, did seem the proper course. He wondered again at what it might represent. Aid? Or an enemy?

He moved off the trail and continued to advance, with more difficulty now, among the trees, brush, and rocks which paralleled its course. It seemed prudent to have a look at any campers without being seen himself.

The campfire smell grew stronger. He slowed when he felt he was nearing its vicinity. Finally, he halted and lay still for a long while, listening for voices. There were none, though he thought he heard the growling of one or more dogs. Finally, he began to move again, deliberately, soundlessly.

After a time, he drew near the periphery of a cleared area. He parted the stems of a shrub and peered through at it. It had obviously been used as a campsite recently. There were no people in sight, but several dogs prowled it now, whining, scavenging.

Studying the grounds, where a great number of people had probably passed the night, he realized that this must have been the Rees' latest encampment. They had proceeded from here past his aerie. He watched a little longer, until he was satisfied that the place had been completely abandoned.

He moved forward then and entered the area. No telling what might have been lost or left behind by a fleeing tribe. Their fires were normally extinguished completely, but with the Sioux at their heels they were moving fast. It would be worth a quick survey. He shouted at the dogs in Pawnee and they slunk away from him.

He advanced upon the one fire which still smouldered, then halted and lay staring at it. How long had it been since he had seen a fire, sign of humanity? How long since he had been able to kindle one himself? He thought of many he had sat beside—campfires, hearthfires—and he suddenly felt that he had indeed come a great distance, that he had come back to something. He chuckled in realizing that he lay prostrate before it. His life was wilderness, yet many things set him apart from the beasts. No bear could feel exactly as he did in returning to such a sign of a former existence. He patted the earth beside it, then moved on.

His tracker's eye caught all of the camp signs clearly— the places where the campers had eaten, the places where they had slept, their trails to water and latrine. Even without having seen them go by, he could roughly estimate their number, could separate the tracks of the aged and the children from those in between. The dogs studied him as he explored but seemed afraid to draw near this man-scented thing of low profile and bestial movement.

With a stick, he stirred the ashes of their fires, where all of their trash seemed to have found its place. All of these others were cold now, and while some of the trash—bits of cloth, leather, wood—had not been completely incinerated, it seemed that nothing of any value lay within. Until the fifth. . . .

Poking within the soft gray heap at the center of a circle of stones, he almost missed the tiny flash. But he did not even pause as it registered. Immediately, he moved the stick again, to knock free its outline and clear its surface. A slim, worn length of whetted steel, its point broken off, haft charred, lay before him in the dust.

He dropped the stick and snatched it up. Steel, serviceable steel. . . .

He wiped it on his pantleg, held it up for closer scrutiny. He tested its edge. A bit dull, but easily honed. And he could wrap the handle with some cloth torn from his shirt. Then, turn up a piece of flint and he could strike a fire whenever he needed it. He smiled.

He could carve a crutch. The hip and leg were feeling somewhat better. It was possible, had he something to lean on, that he might be able to hobble along in an upright position now.

He studied the rocks that ringed the burned-out fires, seeming to recall a small, flat one that just might serve as a whet stone. Yes. Over to the right. . . .

He fetched the stone and began honing the blade. He found himself wanting to whistle as he did it, but refrained.

Later, with a satisfactory edge upon the blade and the jagged point somewhat blunted, he cast about among the trees for a limb suitable for his crutch.

It was the better part of an hour, spent crawling among trees, before he located an appropriate branch, at a height to which he could drag himself by holding first to the trunk then grasping a lower limb, the knife clasped in his teeth. After notching it and whittling it free, it took him another hour—sitting, back to the tree trunk—to trim it properly, find and adjust to the right length through repeated testing, and to carve a comfortable armrest upon it.

He held it across his lap and regarded it. A knife and a crutch in one morning. . . . If he could use the latter as well as the former this was a very important day.

Hand against the tree trunk, pulling, left leg straightening, he drew himself up to his full height and then leaned as he fitted the rest to his right armpit. Still holding to the tree with his left hand, he shifted weight onto the crutch. It bore him. He allowed his right foot to touch lightly upon the ground.

He took a step with his left foot, shifted his weight, moved the crutch a small distance, shifted again. He let his left hand fall from the tree. Another step with the left foot. Shift. Move the crutch. Shift.

To be upright again—albeit with aid—not to be crawling—yes, it was an important day. He smiled. He made his way about the campsite. The dogs watched him, but kept their distance, tails sinking when he turned his attention upon them. He thought of killing one for food, but they were wary of him. Yes, he really was human, they must have decided. And a stranger, and odd.

Now. Now, then. Now. Time to search out a piece of flint.

A canvassing of the immediate area did not turn up a chunk of that stone. So he decided to continue on his way, scanning all rocky deposits as he went.

Upright. It did not take long to get into the rhythm of the trail with his new gait. He sprawled periodically to rest his left leg, and his right shoulder. It was difficult to determine whether he was covering ground more rapidly in this fashion or when crawling at his best. Yet he was certain that with increasing familiarity, usage, and strength, this means of progress would soon outstrip the earlier.

He swung along his way into the afternoon till thirst drove him from the trail down among the cottonwoods by the river. And it was there he found his flint. Almost singing, he made his way to the water's edge. When his shadow fell upon it, he saw a darting of forms. Fish had been browsing in the shallows.

After he drank his fill, he used his blade to fashion a spear from a straight stick. Waiting then in such a position that his shadow did not impinge upon his chosen stretch of water, he tried for half an hour before obtaining two catfish.

With some threads from his sleeve and a pile of wood-shavings, he was able to start a fire with his new tools. He fed it slowly, and while it strengthened to the consumption of larger sticks, he cleaned his fish on a flat rock and washed them in the river. He grilled them on willow wands, trying the while to calculate how long it had been since he had eaten food that had been cooked. He had to give up, however, as he soon realized he had lost track of the days during his crawl.

After he had eaten he stripped and bathed in the river, remembering that bitter pool near the beginning of his journey. Here, he could tilt his head and drink whenever he wished. And amid his buoyancy and movements he felt that he was coming back together again.

He washed his tattered garments then and donned them wet. He was tempted to loaf the day away, letting them dry on a bush, but he felt uncomfortable this near the Rees. He doubted any would be doubling back to check after pursuit, but it was possible, if the Sioux had indeed pursued them for a time. And though it seemed unlikely there would be any stragglers this far back, some mishap might have slowed someone who was even now hurrying to catch up. So he remained alert as he swung along, ready to depart the trail in an instant at the first sign of humanity.

The afternoon wore on, however, with only the sounds of the birds and a few splashes from the sunken river to keep company to the small thumps of his crutch. A few yellowed leaves came loose and dropped about him. His armpit and shoulder grew sore, but his leg was feeling better, even when he touched it down in occasional testing. His scalp, forehead, and nose were feeling better, also, some of the scabbing having come away as he had bathed. He could not recall when the headaches had ceased.

There were no fruits or berries to be had along his way. The Rees had stripped the bushes and trees as they had gone by. Hugh decided that it would be fish again for his dinner, if they were to be had. He stumped along, realizing, for the first time in a long while, that he was enjoying the day.

He thought back as he hiked, to the time he had spent with the Pawnees, his earlier reverie having breathed fresh life into those memories. He recalled their leader's decision to journey to St. Louis where a meeting involving large-scale trapping was to be held. It had been decided that it might be a good thing to send a peace mission, to let the fur company know that the Pawnees were a dependable, friendly people, who might be counted upon to provide guides, messengers, labor, in their enterprise. It might benefit the tribe by promoting a preferred status when it came to trading, particularly for metal goods, firearms, ammunition, horses. It certainly seemed worth the effort.

It felt strange, entering the city, being there, back among his own kind—or were they? He had changed, he realized then. It only took a few days, in rooms and on busy streets, before a feeling of confinement came over him. Reading a newspaper was a pleasure he had all but forgotten, though, over a morning cup of coffee. It was there that he saw an ad, in the *Missouri Republican,* which tied in with the Pawnees' journey, and which got him to thinking again of things that had passed through his mind more casually during the past couple of days. The Rocky Mountain Fur Company was looking for men to supplement this year-old trapping company's crew at its Fort Henry trading post. Major Andrew Henry, after whom the post was named, needed hunters as well as trappers, and especially people with knowledge of Indian languages and ways. He was later to learn that the fort, near the mouth of the Yellowstone River, had lost both horses and men to raiding Assiniboine and Blackfoot warriors.

Yes, it sounded like the sort of enterprise which might meet his fancy, and for which he doubtless was qualified. He had grown tired of the tribal life of the Pawnees. But this— All that movement, and new lands to see. . . . He smiled as he finished his coffee. He would have to go for an interview and learn all of the details.

So he had gone, talked, and been offered employment. His experiences seemed to impress the interviewer strongly, and he had signed him on for the work.

In the days that remained in St. Louis, Hugh met a number of men who had lived in the wilderness—some of them attracted by the fur company's hiring, others just passing through, in both directions. One of these had been that strange man, John Colter, who had actually traveled to the far ocean with Lewis and Clark. There was an odd light in his eye, which Hugh at first took as a touch of lunacy but later decided was . . . something else—something like the look of a medicine man who had been long in the dreamtime. Colter did not recite his tales with the braggadocio of the seasoned yarner but with a conviction Hugh found vaguely unsettling. He came away from their talks of travels and adventures with a belief in the man's absolute sincerity, and he was to wonder about him for years afterwards. . . .

• • • Later, as the evening came on, he caught his fish, grilled them, and dined. Then he washed up, massaged his leg, shoulder, and arm for a time, and removed himself a good distance from the trail to make his camp. He fell to sleep with a feeling of satisfaction.

In the morning he dined on berries and water from the river. A few days of steady travel and he'd be accustomed to swinging along with the crutch, he felt. There was a rhythm to it which he was beginning to pick up, and he knew that he was making better time upright, and with less effort.

Each stride took him farther from the Rees and nearer to Sioux country. They called them Dakotas up here. Same thing, though. They'd trust him all right. Henry's boys had always gotten on well with the Sioux. The closer he got to the Cheyenne River and the farther from the Moreau the better he felt. Hard to judge how many days it would take to really be into their country. If it were a few weeks later, with less foliage on the trees, he'd have a better view westward. Could catch a glimpse of the Black Hills then, to know better where he was. At least he knew where he was headed. He'd come a good distance toward Fort Kiowa, and while it was still a long way off he'd come into a much more congenial piece of countryside. And his strength was beginning to return. Already, long stretches of his inchworm progress had taken on the fragmented quality of dreaming. . . .

He tried to think about meanness—from Lafitte and

the Pawnee women to Jamie—but his spirits were too high. So he just set his mind to rising and falling with the swells like a ship at anchor, and the day passed through, along with pieces of Pennsylvania, the West Indies, and the mountains, most of them involving days such as this.

He slept deeply that night and did not remember any dreams. In the morning, though, as he headed to the river to bathe and seek after berries and roots he found a succession of stripped berry bushes, bear tracks and bear-scat about the area. This upset him for a long while. That night, after a good day's travel, he dreamed again of the bear, crushing him, breathing into him, with a certain feeling of urgency, as if it were trying to pull him back, to that time, that place, to do it all again, this time not to let him get away. He awoke sweating and shaking. He sought the shadows and sniffed the air, but he was alone in the night. Later, he slept again.

There was no bear sign the next day, and several times it rained, causing him to take refuge among the trees. The going was slower because of the mud this produced, and his fear of falling. He was unable to take any fish and dined entirely on roots.

The following day the land began to rise about him, assuming rougher, more hilly features. Eventually, he moved among bluffs and the river was inconveniently low to his left. Still, he crossed the streams and creeks which fed it, and he speared fish, bathed, and drank from these. It seemed to his recollection that this terrain marked the edges of the valley of the Cheyenne. A day or so here and it would be an easy, downhill walk into the safety of that place.

... And the pain in his hip was better than it had been since the bear. Even the leg was beginning to feel a little stronger. Every time he had inadvertently put weight on it there had been twinges, but none of the terrible pains of a break. Even these had eased during the past few days, so that he began to wonder whether it might have healed to the point where it could bear his weight for a few paces. Gingerly, he began to experiment. A little weight. . . . Not bad. A little more. Still all right. Bit of a twinge there. Try again.

The next morning, as he took his way down a slope, he heard the sound of horses. Immediately, he swung toward the nearer, right-hand side of the trail, heading for cover. Late, maybe too late, he decided, as he hurried. The sounds had been muffled by that huge outcrop of rock, only reaching him just as the riders were about to round the bend. He dug in with the crutch, gave himself a great swing, ignored the pang as his right foot came down hard. He thrust the crutch forward again.

Two mounted Indians rounded the bend and, from an exclamation one of them uttered, he knew that he had been seen. A moment later, two pack horses made the turn, and it sounded as if more were coming behind them. Hugh halted and turned as the foremost reached for his rifle.

He faced them, raising his left hand, open palm facing them, and his right as high as he could under the circumstances. Two more riders rounded the bend, also leading horses loaded with baskets and bags. These riders also reached for their weapons.

As they approached, Hugh grew certain that they were Sioux, even guessing that their baskets might contain a harvest from the gardens of the vanquished Rees.

Thinking again of human cussedness, he waited until they drew near and halted, rifles still upon him.

Then he said, "Hugh Glass," and added "friend" in their language.

COLTER

The hawk soared.

GLASS

• • • **A**nd, growling, the bear raised himself onto his hind legs.

SEVENTEEN

COLTER

He came out of the mountains and staggered into the sea of grass that led to Fort Manuel Lisa. He limped as he walked with the sun hot on his neck. There were no more mountains to climb, no more bluffs or buttes, no more raging waterways. What was left, the wind-driven grass of the great prairie country, was the route a blind man might take to the Fort. Colter knew the grasslands like the back of his hand, having crossed it with Lewis and Lisa, and by himself. He'd been through it in the loud winds of winter and in the softness of a summer breeze, but he had never been through it when his bones ached and creaked and his head swam with fever. Now he could not tell if the grass was water, or if the water was grass; he could not tell if he was moving and the grass was still, or if the grass was moving and he was still.

He contented himself with the dream of flight. Overhead the tremulous sky burned white hot and the dust-motes that speckled it were birds, his brothers. Yet he could not join them any longer. His breath came in stagnant, wheat-leavened gasps. A hobbling, hopping, stranded thing, he flew no more. The shuffling uncertainty of his fate—being drowned in sheaves of grass—frightened him more than the pursuit of his foes, the Blackfeet.

He traveled now with the temper of a wounded hawk. He had seen the bird that he was once before: sun-spent, the great red-shouldered had landed on a dead limb only to be shot by Cruzat. Felled, the hawk floundered in the wet morning grass. He remembered the embered eyes, the unrepentant talons, the hobbling hop as the great, hurt hawk tried to gain the air.

The men had laughed. No one made a move to put it out of its misery. Not even, he was ashamed to recall, himself. They threw the hawk pieces of fresh-killed rabbit, watched it turn its baleful eyes in disdain for meat not downed by claw alone. Next morning Colter saw it limp the headland hill, the sharp, darting head, the wound-weighted wing. It held off the coyotes at dusk and warned away the polecats at night, but there was no pity in the man that shot it, nor the men that watched its slow suffering. Pity them, Colter thought now, not the brave thing nature wrought. Well he remembered the hawk's last hour, the broken, bird-foot gait, until, backed against the cliff, it could do nothing but cast a scornful eye on the fate that had brought it down. Finally, Colter put it to rest with a clean shot through the eye.

And now he wished that someone, or something, moved by his own pathetic crawling, might offer him a similar kindness. For, at intervals, he stopped and plucked the blood-ticks from his skin, twisting them counter-clockwise, popping them between his fingernails. Sometimes he'd drop down, double up, snapping at them, or, head in armpit, he'd wildly bite at them, drawing his own blood.

On he crawled through the maze of grass. Kick and

crawl, heave and sprawl, every few yards falling in a heap and gasping for breath.

The ticks weren't the only pests that plagued him. Grasshoppers with sawblades for legs sprang up into his eyes, stinging him with pain. The knife-edged grass carved his chest and chin, slashed his legs; bluebottle flies and wasps hammered his head.

He imagined himself coming out of the grassland that first time with Lewis. He envisioned himself on a knoll, looking down at the sea of grass. They were finally out of it and the two of them were laughing with relief. And it was there on that Olympian butte that the trouble had first begun: this, the proving ground between Lewis and Clark's men and the Blackfoot tribe.

"Let me tell you how I remember it," Meriwether Lewis said.

"Where do you come from, man?" Colter asked, shaking his head.

Lewis gave him a grand smile.

"Where we all must go, of course."

"Which is?"

"Where you're headed yourself."

The grass was blowing at Colter's ears. He wasn't sure he was hearing right.

"Where I sent the red-shouldered hawk?"

"Where hawks and all other hellions collect and disperse. . . . May I, with your permission, go on?"

"To that place?"

Lewis frowned with displeasure.

"May I, dear John, continue with what I was going to say on the matter of the Indian conflict?"

Colter gave him a tired nod.

"Now, then . . . we were assembled on a rise overlooking a vast expanse of grass so like this, when, on impulse, I put glass to eye and observed at the distance of a mile, an assemblage of about thirty horses. On an eminence just above them I espied their owners, Blackfeet, as many as there were horses.

"I made ready to make the best of our situation, resolving to present ourselves in a friendly manner. I directed J. Fields to display the flag that I had brought for that purpose, and advanced slowly toward them. So, what do you suppose they did, John Colter?"

"I don't hardly suppose—I was there."

"Yet, if you do remember, you cannot, due to your taciturn nature, speak of it in a pretty way. Therefore, I shall tell. What they did was to hold back, perhaps not seeing us in the entire. I calculated their number being equal, or close to, the number of their horses and, there being nothing else to do, I decided we should advance upon them."

"Instead of just meeting up with them."

"Now, as we proceeded apace, one of their members, when we were a quarter of a mile off, mounted and rode at us full speed. I then alighted from my horse and waited him out. Yet when he was a hundred paces off, he examined our party, as if looking for things unseen."

"That one was the scout, giving us the once-over."

"The whole time he was there, I beckoned him to approach."

"He didn't take kindly to the overture, did he?"

Lewis ignored Colter and went on with his summary.

"Now he returned to his assemblage and the group of them made their way toward us, when—"

"—There was eight men in all, I counted them."

Lewis curled his lip, flicked the air with a wand of grass.

"I believed there were others well-hidden, in reserve, since I had observed their leaving behind a goodly number of their horses."

"What was they supposed to do, bring on the whole lot?"

Lewis looked askance, shook his head in disbelief.

"Look here, is this story to be mine or yours?"

"Depends on whether you're in a mood to tell the truth," Colter commented laconically.

Once again Lewis chose to ignore him.

"I expected, as commander, that we would have some difficulty with them. This was only natural, their being Indians."

"And they," Colter cut in, "had bought the same bit of goods."

"But as I reflect on it, we were most correct in our dealing with them. When we were all assembled and had alighted from our horses, they asked that we share a smoke with them. I said, 'Our man with the pipe is off a ways, so we should have to wait a while.' This way, I could size them up a little better."

"I have to butt my head in again, Commander. How do we rightly know whether they was asking you to share your pipe, or whether they was asking us to share theirs? Could be our interpreter got it wrong. Wouldn't be the first time; in any case, the delay was kind of insulting."

"Had to be my pipe, my tobacco," Lewis announced. "After all, we were making the gesture, you remember. Therefore, I gave to one a Jefferson medal; to another a flag; to a third a handkerchief. And they appeared, all of them, well satisfied."

"To your eye."

"Towards evening, I proposed that we should encamp together, which they agreed to do wholeheartedly. They took the lead and showed us a peaceful place beside a river near three large trees in front of which they put up some dressed buffalo skins in a semicircle; here we bedded down for the night. I told these people that I had come a great way from the east up the great river, which runs towards the rising sun; that I had been to the great waters where the sun sets and had seen a great many nations, all of whom I had invited to come and trade with me on the rivers this side of the mountains. I further reported to them that I found most of them at war with their neighbors and that it was I who had succeeded in restoring peace among them. I took the first watch, until half after eleven; by that time the Indians were all asleep. Then I roused up R. Fields and laid down myself. I directed Fields to watch the Indians most carefully, and that if any of them were to move—"

"—In their sleep—"

"—That if they were to move, threateningly, as I apprehended they might, he should wake me straight away. At daybreak one of the Indians to whom I had given the Jefferson medal slipped behind Fields and took his gun—"

"—Wouldn't be hard to do."

"While another took that of his brother—"

"—Easier still."

"At the same instant two others advanced and seized the guns of Drewer and myself—"

"—Easiest of all."

"J. Fields turned around and saw the Indian running off with his gun and his brother's, whom he called to action. The two of them went after the Indians whom they overtook at fifty or sixty paces—"

"—'Cause the Indians let 'em."

"R. Fields, as he seized his gun, stabbed the Indian to the heart with his knife. The fellow ran about fifteen paces and fell dead. After we recovered the rest of our guns, they tried to run off our horses, and—"

"One dead Indian. . . ."

"I can assure you we killed some more as they were attempting to steal our horses."

"One dead Indian. . . ."

"We left him where he lay, with the medal round his neck. We took four of the Blackfoot ponies as compensation for the raid; I shot a man through the belly and after he crawled off into the rocks, I burned four shields and two bows and quivers in the campfire, these with a good many other personal effects. Naturally, I retook the flag."

"Naturally."

"That night when we rested ourselves, you, Colter, shot a buffalo cow and we ate a small quantity of the meat, which was quite good. Before us stretched a plain as level as a bowling green, with only a few prickly pear. Under heavy thunderclouds, we traveled by moonlight. All around us the immense herds of buffalo walked, as if in a dream, moonstruck they looked to be. And we, to these great shaggy beasts, must have seemed ragged ghosts indeed. My Indian horse carried me along very well: in short, much better than my own would've done, which leaves me with but little reason to complain of the robbery."

"Little reason," Colter repeated.

Then the face and form of Meriwether Lewis in his moonstruck jacket-skin vanished, and Colter knew that he was alone. The day was, once again, night. The star children were out again, dancing. He watched them from his blanket of gathered grass. The star children were singing some strange songs.

"Will you let me live a little longer?" Colter asked them.

"Little reason," came their song, "little reason."

"Dance your damn heads off," Colter sighed, "for I don't much care if I live or die."

He couldn't recall when he'd eaten last. Some bitter bread-root tubers back by the riverbottom, chokecherry bark somewhere, old fallen-over morels, some seeds the prairie dogs had left, some bullsnake eggs . . . for water he'd had rainfall, lying on his back and opening his mouth.

What did it matter?

Eating and drinking were for those who wanted to live. He was a ragged thing, come hundreds of miles, a creature that crawled, couldn't walk.

When something in the cold grassy ground growled near his face, he asked it politely what it was. Who goes there? he asked the badger making its evening rounds.

The badger would not identify itself.

Nor did it growl a second time, sensing in the man something beyond the measure of its concern. It went by

him, turning its nose away, heading somewhere else, hunting.

The night got dread cold.

So cold, the star children shivered.

Somewhere, along the margin of the forest and the plain,
an old man and a youth, sitting on a hill in the moonlight,
blanketed and still, thought about a person. The person
they had once called Seekheedha. Now they did not call
him that. He had passed beyond such a name, had entered
the simple world of things unknown.

"Once," the old man told the youth, "there was a man
whose body was found in a swamp. Long had the man
been dead, yet in his face you could clearly see who he
was, what he had once been. The man was a great warrior,
many hands taller than the tallest member of our tribe. And
his skin was of a different color: neither very dark nor very
light, but some color between."

"How long had the man been in the swamp?" the
youth asked.

"A long time," the old man replied, "longer than the
memory of the oldest storyteller of our tribe."

"And he was still a man?"

"He looked just like a man."

"Was he one of the First People?"

The old man answered, "we thought so. But then, after
a while, the wisest man among us said that it could not be
so. For if he were a person of the First World, then his magic
was gone because we had looked at him, face to face."

"What did you do, Grandfather?"

"We gave him a proper burial. After that we forgot about him. He has not, to my knowledge, been mentioned since that time."

"Then why have you spoken of him to me?"

"Because we shall soon forget about Seekheedha. We shall forget the white man who ran better than the best of our tribe. We shall forget him."

"I understand, Grandfather."

Lewis?" Colter called, as he started out of his sleep.

It was the time before the dawn when the two times merge, when the bright and the dark are confused, and the air is shrouded in mystery, and the mist comes out of the grass like the ghosts of ancient rabbits.

"Lewis?" Colter said again, sitting up in the grass.

The shadow said not a word, but lay at his feet a small firebrand of sweet, smoking sage, tied in the Indian manner with a string of red thong.

He knew the youth from the soft slope of his shoulders. There was a familiar presence about him, something that harkened back to the crossing of the great mountains, something about Charbonneau and that Snake woman of his, what was her name?

Sahcahgagweah.

She and this youth had the same swiftness, sure and clear like a stream that comes out of the rocks. No white person that he'd ever met moved like that, except, maybe, Charbonneau and some of the French river-runners he'd met in St. Louis, those men who'd gone red. For some reason, he saw Sahcahgagweah again the morning she was about to give birth to the child. Her own medicine required she eat some of the bone-tail of the rattlesnake. This, according to her tribe, the Snakes, ensured good birth.

Then he was back in the grass country.

Dawn wind, attended by a pricking of rain. Colter trembled. A dark cloud passed overhead. He drew the gathered grass around him like a robe. The youth did the same.

"I've gone and forgot your name, lad," Colter grumbled.

The youth made two circles with his forefinger and thumb, and pressed them to his eyes.

Colter shrugged.

The youth put his hand behind him.

"Ringtail Boy," Colter said.

The boy smiled, said something in his own tongue.

Colter smiled: the same word in Crow, Raccoon's Brother.

The youth was holding a chunk of rock, looking at it admiringly.

"I carved that," Colter told him, "that's my sign. Never learned to read or write, but I can make my sign pretty good. My totem," Colter chuckled, tapping the stone with the nail of his right forefinger.

The youth chuckled, his long straight locks hanging down, shielding his face. He motioned with the stone, handed it back to Colter.

"No, you keep it," Colter said, "it belongs to your tribe. Give it to the man who wanted my liver. Tell him I burned another one in a tree back in the devils' pit; and there's one in a big open meadow under the Teat Mountains. There's others, but—"

Slowly, the youth's face burned away in the morning sun; the mist of the grassland lifted. Colter saw another face superimpose over the Indian's; this one was white, a young man of about the same age. Standing next to him a barmaid was scratching numbers on the surface of a slate. Colter could not read the numbers, but he retrieved his penknife and made his own sign on the slate. The barmaid gave him a dark look, demanded he pay up. Across from him the youth reached out with a coin. The fatigue of Colter's whole life seemed to rise in his throat. He believed that he was going to vomit.

The young man's face was just in front of him, now. Colter saw someone who looked for all the world like a young saloon tramp, fresh from the farm. But there was something willful about him, a tiny-eyed, bearlike look, a shambling grace, a cunningness.

Colter fought for air, pushed back the stale, steely taste rising in his throat.

Who was this person who pretended to know him, that he almost seemed to know himself?

The nausea passed like a wave, on its way to elsewhere. He looked the lad in the eye once again. Big and glad and just off the farm: an animal warmth about him, someone the flies would cling to.

"Who the devil are you, lad?"

Then the young face disappeared in the thick barroom smoke.

Colter sighed.

"Will there be no end to this facing-off?"

He groaned, dreamed, vomited brutally in the grass. His guts came up in dry heaves. A threesome of crows coughed in the clouds overhead. The wind spun in the golden grass of noon.

"How long must I wait for death?" Colter cried at the crows.

Then he seemed to rise and fly across the wide river that the Minataree had named Scolding River. He was swimming, flying, swimming, landing, trying to land, his armwings beating the grass, the rain, the river, the grass, as he flew out of himself to meet the shadows behind the feathered heads.

EIGHTEEN

GLASS

The foremost rider narrowed his eyes slightly, then said, slowly, in English, "What happened to you?"

"Got in a fight with a grizzly bear," Hugh said, "some time back." Then he repeated it as best he could in Sioux.

"Grizzly bear?" the man said. "He did that to you?"

"Yes," Hugh said.

"Where?"

"Up near the fork of the Grand."

"How'd you get here?"

"Crawled, mostly."

"What became of the bear?"

"He's dead."

"What were you doing, up that way?"

"I was hunting, for Major Henry."

"We fought with Major Henry against the Ree. Just finished some more fighting with them." He gestured at the baskets on the nearest pack horse. "Their village burns. We bring home their corn, pumpkins, and squash."

Hugh nodded.

"Saw them heading west," he said. "I was with the major, against the Ree."

"Why aren't you with him now?"

"Got left for dead. Guess I looked it. Maybe I still do."
He chuckled dryly.

"Grizzlies are pretty tough people."

"Can't argue with that."

"You seem to be, too. Come home with us. We will
feed you and our women will treat your wounds."

"I accept your hospitality," Hugh said.

The first man gave an order in Sioux, lowering his rifle
as he did so. Immediately, the others put away their weapons and dismounted. They moved to the pack horses and
began unburdening them and redistributing their loads.

Shortly, they had freed one horse for riding, and Hugh
was invited to mount it. With considerable assistance, he
was lifted into a riding position upon its back. His legs so
spread, his weight resting upon his buttocks and the base of
his spine, he discovered fresh aches radiating from his right
hip into his leg and lower back. He sat for a time, adjusting
to the feeling, Then, when the leader signaled they move
on, it was at an easy pace.

Still, bareback after all this time. . . . Hugh felt every
hoof-fall at the center of his pain, and his teeth were
clenched for much of the ride.

He clung to his mount and allowed himself to be dis-
tracted by any unusual trail feature—anything, to keep his
attention outside himself. When they took a turn westward
from the way he had followed, this became easier, if only
because he always made note of trails. And though he desired the knowledge, he refrained from asking the distance
to the Sioux encampment, knowing this could be taken as
a sign of weakness.

They halted to rest several times along the way, and Hugh was certain that some of these pauses were for his benefit rather than the horses'. The leader, Dancing Buffalo, asked him as they went for more and more details concerning the bear. Hugh replied at length, even mentioning some of his dreams—knowing the stock they placed in the dreamworld—for the bear was feared, respected, sacred. From the many questions he answered, he began to realize that they respected him, too, for having lived through the encounter. And the more he thought of it, the more he began to wonder at the event himself. Strange that he was here at all. Not just because of the bear, though, but considering his whole life. . . .

The day was cool and bright, with a few leaves turning color, and they rode on into afternoon. Hugh was beginning to wonder why they hadn't stopped for a meal when it occurred to him that they might be nearing the camp.

A little later he smelled smoke. Then he heard the barking of dogs. Shortly after that there came the sound of a child's shout in the distance. Before too long, they came into sight of the village. It stood in a clearing beside a stream, several dozen tipis, people and dogs moving among them. The dogs set up a chorus of barking, children stared, and shouted greetings were exchanged among several of the men.

They rode into the encampment, where Dancing Buffalo dismounted and gave orders for the sharing out of the food his party had brought back. Then he helped Hugh to dismount and led him toward one of the hide-covered dwellings.

Inside, he helped him to a sitting position on a buffalo

robe, where he joined him. There were several women about—Dancing Buffalo's wives, Hugh assumed, save for the older woman who was engaged in making a pair of moccasins and was probably a mother-in-law. His host asked the women to bring food for himself and his guest.

While a stew was being prepared several of the other warriors who had accompanied them entered the tent, speaking greetings, and were invited to join them on the robe. As they spoke, Dancing Buffalo took up a long pipe and began filling it. Shortly after, he lit the pipe, raised it skyward, lowered it earthward, and offered it to each of the four great directions.

Then he drew upon the pipe, exhaled a slow, thin stream of smoke, and passed it to Hugh. Hugh did the same, then gave it to the man next to him. A feeling of contentment he had not known in a long while filled him as the pipe went around.

. . . And smells of cooking mingled with the aroma of tobacco. The stew involved, Hugh could see, venison, corn, squash and other vegetables.

Hugh enjoyed the smoke and the company, and particularly the pleasure of being off of that horse. His hip and buttocks still ached, but the feeling was already changing to a dull, warm thing. To follow it all with cooked food. . . . He went into a small reverie recalling reveries past during his crawl, when he had catalogued meals and their tastes and smells.

Dancing Buffalo's wives gave them all wooden bowls, and they made their ways to the pot, where they ladled out the warm meat and vegetables. Back on the buffalo robe they ate with their fingers, licking them clean afterwards.

Surreptitiously, Hugh swallowed several mouthfuls of air, so as to manage a loud and appreciative belch when he had done.

Afterwards, the others departed. Dancing Buffalo asked Hugh to disrobe, so that his wives might mend his garments and treat his injuries. Hugh stripped, then lay prone on the buffalo robe as the women directed.

After bathing him, they applied some hot, pungent liniment to his right leg, hip, and shoulder. They rubbed it in; at first, gently, then with increased vigor. It was almost too hot, almost too vigorous. But it never quite went over the line. It felt warm, it felt relaxing. . . . Hugh's eyes closed as he enjoyed the sensation. Soon he slept.

It was not until the following morning that he awoke. That day they fed him well, and the women massaged him and plied him with medicines between meals. He took his first tentative steps without the crutch that evening, though he held it in his hand ready to catch himself should he stumble.

The following day he walked farther. The pain continued to ebb. All of the scabbing had been washed from his wounds. He managed ten short steps before leaning on the crutch and panting. A little later he took twelve steps. That afternoon he did twice as many. The break in his thigh had knit, he felt, though it was hard telling whether the healing was complete, whether his present pains were from muscles which hadn't been used in this fashion in a long while. He walked again that evening, over thirty paces, and he could have gone farther. He felt that tomorrow he would be stronger, though, and decided to wait. He surrendered himself again to the women's ministrations and continued to partake of the meals they provided. Soon, he felt. Soon his spirit would find him again. His strength would return. He would be on his way. In the meantime, he savored what remained of the day. Waiting was not difficult in these surroundings, not when things seemed to be improving so rapidly. He swung his great limbs and worked the muscles in his back and shoulders. Better, better. . . .

And the next day he walked. He rose that morning without the crutch, and he did not take it up again. He rested often as he went about his business, but he walked all day and that night he slept well.

The following morning, Dancing Buffalo's wives brought him a new shirt, breeches, and moccasins of buckskin. He drew them on and they fit him well. He strutted in them and they did not bind. He felt better than he had since before the bear, and he headed off into the wood and sought the game trails, as it had been a long time since he had been able to do so.

Hours later, he returned to the camp where he borrowed a bow and arrows. There had been sign he wished to follow. Armed now, he limped back into the wood, returning to the trail. There he took up its course, an old exhilaration returning to him as the signs flowed clear and he commenced his slow pursuit. He would would soon be into the mind of his quarry, anticipating its movements.

The leaves were patched with yellow, and a bright autumn sunlight was filtered among them. A few lay on the ground, too damp to crunch as he trod them. A cool breeze brought him the scent of earth and decomposing wood. A squirrel chattered at him from overhead, and birdsong came from a distance. From time to time he paused, stood absolutely still, and listened to these and every other sound—the cracking of a twig, the rustle of a branch, sound of some fruit or cone striking the forest floor. He heard the passage of the place's other denizens about him and above.

It was browsing, he could tell, alert, but not suspicious. Though it wandered, it seemed to be bearing in a general northeasterly direction. He followed a little farther to confirm this.

When he was certain, he speculated as to its pace as well as its course. Then, turning to his left, he cut a chord across its arc. When he reached what he presumed a likely spot for its passage, he sought about for cover.

A small thicket straight ahead seemed a good candidate. He made his way to it and settled into a kneeling position. He readied his bow then, took up an arrow.

"Deer," he whispered then, "I'm sorry I got to kill you, but folks got to eat, and these folks have been good to me. I owe them a little payback, and I want it to be you. I hope there's no hard feelings here. I don't mean it personal-like, and I want you to know we'll try not to waste nothing you give us."

Then he was still and let his mind get big and quiet, only watching.

It was perhaps half an hour before it came into sight, a buck, three years upon it. He waited till it came into the clearing. Drew back his bow then, released the arrow.

It flew true to its target, forward on the body, piercing a lung and presumably the heart. The creature started, stumbled, dropped to its front knees, blood appearing at its mouth. It tried to rise, failed, fell, and lay panting. It exhaled a red trail upon the ground.

Hugh rose and went to it. He commenced skinning it, then butchered it and hung it from a tree-limb, using strips of the hide to tie it. Then, cleaning his hands and knife-blade with fistfuls of leaves, he headed back to the camp.

On his return, he told Dancing Buffalo of his present, and they fetched it back together on a pack horse. That night there would be a feast, and he would thank them formally for their care.

That night he did, though he did not tell them of his intention to move on in the morning, to continue on his way to Fort Kiowa. He slept well.

He woke before daybreak, and when he reached for his clothing he discovered that Dancing Buffalo had laid the bow he had used and a supply of arrows atop his garments, a parting gift. He dressed and moved soundlessly, departing the tipi and heading to the camp's nearest perimeter, where he passed on into the woods. A silence lay upon the camp, and the birds still slept in their trees. He'd left the crutch behind, and it pleased him to swing along in a relatively normal fashion again.

He took his way back in the direction of the river, though he struck a southeasterly course rather than the one he had ridden in on. The way seemed easy, and it would save him a little time. And there was always something to be said for walking a new path.

Daybreak found him well away from the camp. Later, he killed a squirrel for lunch. Afternoon brought him back to the river. There he drank deeply and ate fistfuls of berries. The Missouri was low, flowing silent, masses of driftwood along its banks. The leaves of willows and cottonwoods flashed within it. Dark birds followed it southward.

Later he passed a deer partway out in the shallow water, drinking. His fingers twitched, but he declined to use the bow. Too much meat there. Most of it would go to waste. He'd stay with small game and trail food the rest of the way down to Kiowa. He trekked on. More berries and roots that afternoon. A canoe passed and he hid himself from it. Most likely Sioux, here in their country. Still. . . . He was out of danger now, and there was no sense courting more.

Leaves fell about him as he walked. Every gust brought a few more drifting down. They crunched pleasantly beneath his moccasins. So good to be able to cross them in this fashion. . . .

He began wondering how many days it would take him to reach the fort. Once he'd made it he would get outfitted again. He supposed that Henry would be back at his post on the Yellowstone by now. So he'd have to head upriver then and look in there if he wanted to find Jamie.

Fine. He was beginning to feel up to the confrontation. It would be good to settle up soon, to clean the slate. More birds passed, heading south.

Hugh fingered his scars as he rested. He watched antelope moving atop a bluff. The sun passed behind a cloud and a chill wind rose up out of the north. He realized he'd crossed a turning point in the year. Soon one would not be able to count upon the weather's clemency.

The chill remained with him throughout the day. That night the temperature dropped even more. In the morning he started early, for the heat of exertion to warm him.

He was well into the valley of the Cheyenne, and he hoped to come into sight of that river today. The chill persisted and the skies were gray.

At twilight he caught a glimpse of what might be that distant river, or of some haze above it. Either way, he bedded down in high spirits despite the cold. From memory, he retraced the route from beyond the river to the fort.

After he'd crossed the Cheyenne and continued for a time he would come to the place where the Missouri entered a big bend, curving to the northwest then down to the southeast, for a thirty-mile stretch before it swept past Kiowa. He would leave the river at the beginning of the bend, heading cross-country, shortcutting the loop, for a much faster passage to the French Fur Company's outpost. Then he could tell his tale, vent his spleen, rest a day or so, and sign for new equipment. Yes. Soon.

The following day he brought down a migrant goose for lunch and picked it clean. His leg had almost stopped bothering him. Good not to be crawling with the weather changing, he reflected later, when a cold rain caught him in the open.

He slept before a campfire that night, awakening regularly to feed it the branches he'd gathered. After grilling his fish for dinner he'd decided to keep the fire going for warmth. Be good to have a blanket again, and, later, a buffalo robe.

The next day was foggy, with a drizzle which accompanied him until he gave up and sought shelter in a shallow cave. He sat for hours, watching the shifting fog, watching small puddles grow larger, watching streamlets flow by. There was nothing dry with which to build a fire.

He slept fitfully, and the dampness brought twinges to his leg and hip. His dreams came in pieces. Riding with Jamie, hunting. . . . Bears, campfires, Indians. . . . Crawling through a cloudburst. . . . Hoofbeats. . . . A long procession passing below him—Tom, Lafitte, Dancing Buffalo, Major Henry, Jamie, an old woman of the Ree. . . . Thunder, and lightning, nearby. And the steady sound of rain. He was walking through a cave, deep underground, and they were all painted upon the walls. . . . Blackness, and then the bear again. Now it was walking away from him through the cave, and there came a sense of desertion, abandonment, as when his friends had left him on the plain. He wanted the bear to turn back, and he tried calling to it but no words came. It lumbered, growling, down the dark way, and suddenly he found himself weeping.

He woke with tears on his face, and the storm still filled the night. He wiped his eyes and squirmed into a more comfortable position. After a while, he slept again, dreamt again, wept again, though this time the dreams were far more chaotic and fled even as he tried to recall them.

In the morning a slow drizzle still descended through the fog. He pushed himself up into a seated position, back against the rock and stared out into it. Dry now, should he move on and be drenched again? But he was cold, and the exercise would warm him. Still, when he halted the chill would be waiting in his garments. He knew he would feel hunger shortly, yet it was unlikely he would come across much that was edible under the circumstances. He wanted to move on, make it to the fort, be about his business. Yet, what did one day more this way or that matter? He had already established that he had lost track of time since his mishap. He drew his knees up and clasped his arms about them. For how long he watched the gray screen of mist, he could not say. Hours, perhaps. When the rain finally let up and he moved on, though, he could not recall what his thoughts had been during that time.

The cotton-wrapped day had a way of muffling sounds, and he walked in silence, tree-limb and stony outcrop suddenly growing into his quiet, pale world, pieces of a special order of reality. He thought of the time he had crossed the divide. It had been like this then, too, a world which existed in its own right between a pair of worlds through which he was passing.

A bird flashed past him, was gone again. From overhead, he heard the cry of a hawk. It had passed too quickly for him to identify, to know whether the bird he had seen was the same one he now heard.

Then, in the fog, he saw the outline of a man, walking the trail ahead of him. Startled, he almost called out. Instead, he paced him, attempting to ascertain whether he was accompanied. But no. He seemed to be alone. Big, hulking, moving with a limp. The image fled off to the side, was interrupted by branches, returned.

The limp. . . . The synchronization of the stride, of the swinging of the arms. . . . He smiled.

He halted and threw up his arms. The figure before him did the same. He lowered his left arm. The act was repeated ahead. Then he commenced walking again, and his double imitated him, sliding into and out of existence as the fog grew patchy.

He thought of Indian tales as he hiked, of the need to pause and let one's spirit catch up after a long journey. This seemed just the opposite—as if, near his journey's end, he was rushing to catch up with his spirit. Soon the mist began to fade, though, and his shadow fled with it.

By midday, it had burned off fully, and though the sky remained overcast, it did not rain again. The trees had lost even more of their green, and the trail was covered with yellow and gold leaves, damp now, glued to the earth. He climbed another low hill. At its top he halted. The dull gray ribbon of the Cheyenne River lay below him in the distance. He looked westward along it, deciding on the point of his crossing—there, where it narrowed near a bend.

He noted the point ahead where he would leave the trail to strike off for the crossing. Finally, the end of his journey was beginning to seem real. He headed on down the hill.

The temperature declined about him as he passed through the open area, and when he came to the riverbank the air felt as cold as the water. He passed along the shore, testing its depth, and decided to spend the rest of the day, if necessary, in hunting his dinner, cooking it, and eating it, camp in a partly sheltered area he had found, and cross in the morning.

It took him a half-hour to locate a rabbit-run, and a twenty-minute wait before a rabbit passed along it. His shot was soundless and quick. Ten minutes later he took another. He returned then to the riverside and cleaned them.

Sitting beside his fire, he roasted the coneys slowly with herbs he had gathered. He ate slowly, his appetite at last returned to normal, and he finished both. Afterwards, he buried the remains and drank long from the river. He erected a stone backwall to the fire, heaped on kindling, and curled up before it. He awoke periodically throughout the night to feed more sticks to the flames.

In the morning he covered the ashes and made his

way to the riverside. With a small curse for the weather, he stripped, bundled his possessions, and tied them with leather thongs to a piece of driftwood he had set aside the previous evening. Then he waded into the water, teeth clenched, and began kicking his way to the other side, bow jutting, one sleeve flapping from his parcel.

He emerged downstream some minutes later, shivering under gray skies, with a cold wind passing.

Garbing himself hastily, he set off at a brisk pace, hoping to warm himself quickly. Blue cracks appeared in the cloud cover as he hiked, but the chill remained in the air.

For the better part of an hour he hastened, coming into and out of places of trees, climbing, descending. Finally, he achieved the top of a low hill, and there he halted. The river was again in sight, and on its bank stood the French Fur Company's post. He had come upon it from the rear, its huge gate facing the river to the east. The stockade wall stood at over three times his height and ran for perhaps one hundred fifty feet in either direction. The blockhouse was on the river side, to the south, while the nearest internal structure was a rifle tower. A pair of riflemen manned the high walk within, and when Hugh started down the hill the nearer one halted and stared in his direction.

"Good afternoon!" he hollered to the man. "I'm Hugh Glass."

"Hugh?" came the response. "Thought you were with Major Henry."

"Was," Hugh replied, moving nearer and seeing it to be Bob Terry, an old-timer who'd slowed down and pretty much stopped trapping for work around the fort. "Got hurt, got separated, need supplies. Tell someone to let me in, will you, Bob?"

"Sure thing, Hugh," the man called back. "Was it the Ree?"

"Nope," Hugh answered as he reached the corner and started along the northern wall. "Bear. Tell you about it later."

He made his way to the wall facing the river and turned right. Shortly, he reached the big gate, and a moment later one side of it opened before him.

Entering, he spied Young Cayewa's cabin across the parade ground. The bourgeois—Joseph Brazeau, who'd built the fort—had been called Young Cayewa to distinguish him from his uncle—another Joseph Brazeau—the founder of the French Fur Company, who had borne the nickname Old Cayewa, after setting up most of their trade with the Sioux. The Columbia Fur Company had a post a couple of hundred miles farther north, in Mandan country, but it was much smaller than Kiowa and nowhere near as well-provisioned.

The clerk's home and office were farther to the right. Hugh headed that way. The storehouses beside it should still be loaded with surplus from the Ree campaign, left when General Ashley had moved on, and Hugh wanted to place his order for reoutfitting before he did anything else.

From beside the stables to his rear, he heard the sounds of hammering from the smith's shop. Lew—stocky, red-haired, one of the riverboatmen—greeted him as he headed for the clerk's office.

"Hugh!" the man hailed. "Thought you was with Henry up on Yellowstone."

"Fixin' to be," he responded. "Got separated and lost some equipment, though."

"Your face is kind of messed up. That come of it?"

Hugh nodded.

"Got hurt. I'm all right now."

The man gestured to the stockade wall opposite the stables.

"Come by my place 'fore you go," he said. "Third cabin off the left there. I want to hear your story."

"I'll do that, Lew," Hugh said. "See you later."

He crossed the compound and rapped on Brazeau's door.

"Yes? Who is there?" came the familiar voice from within.

"Hugh Glass," he replied. "Need some supplies."

He heard footsteps, and moments later the door was opened.

"Hugh!" the shorter, dark-haired man exclaimed. "It really is you. Why aren't you up on the Yellowstone?"

"Kinda long story," Hugh said.

"Then you'll need a glass of brandy while you tell it," Young Cayewa suggested. "I want to hear the whole thing."

Hugh nodded and seated himself in the chair to which the other gestured. Moments later, he accepted a glass. Soon he was talking.

It took him several glasses before he finished, and Brazeau had simply listened, hypnotized.

". . . So if you'll outfit me," Hugh concluded, "I can head north for the Yellowstone, to catch up with Henry and settle my business."

" 'Course we'll get you outfitted," Brazeau said. "But

you got me wonderin' about your unfinished business with some of the others up that way."

Hugh nodded.

"There's some of that waitin', I'll grant you. All I can say is it's personal and I've always been a pretty fair man. Let it ride."

"As you say, Hugh. Why don't you go next door to the storehouse and have Percy fix you out from Ashley's gear? You can stay across the way in the second cabin— it's empty right now. You will be stayin' a while, won't you?"

"Tonight," Hugh said, nodding. "Maybe two nights."

". . . And you'll dine with me tonight, a little after sundown?"

"With pleasure," Hugh said, rising. "Thanks for the drinks."

He shook his hand again and departed, limping off toward the storeroom.

By evening he was outfitted and settled into the cabin. He had drawn a new rifle, powderhorn, powder, and bullets, as well as shirt, cloak, robe, cap, and a new knife. He also drew tea and coffee, salt and tobacco, cooking utensils, trading goods.

He bathed and trimmed his beard and donned a new shirt that evening. He sorted the gear for packing before heading back to Young Cayewa's.

Partway through the meal, Brazeau said, "I hope you'll come by for dinner tomorrow night, too. You've got too much story there for one sitting."

"To tell the truth," Hugh said, "I was thinking of moving on tomorrow."

"That's damn silly," Brazeau responded, "when I'm going to send a party up the river on Thursday to do some trading with the Mandans before the weather gets too bad. You can ride in the boat. I could use a good hunter to go along."

"What day's today?" Hugh asked.

"Monday."

He grunted. Then he nodded.

"It would save me time. All right," he agreed.

Brazeau grinned.

"That way you get to sleep in a real bed for a few extra nights."

Hugh shrugged.

"S'pose so."

"Give you a chance to rest up. There must be a few people here you'd like to pass some time with."

"S'pose so," Hugh said.

"Ain't so many of us out this way but that we mostly know each other."

Hugh nodded.

"True," he said.

"Ain't a whole lot of justice either, like back east. Courts and all."

Hugh nodded again.

"Not that we really need 'em," he said. "It's been my experience that most people take care of their own."

"Mine, too," Brazeau said. "Done it myself. Will again. Most have."

"Please pass the salt," Hugh said. "Thanks."

"Wouldn't ever do to ask a man if he's thinkin' on killin' another man," Brazeau remarked. "If he says yes and then somethin' happens to that fella, it's almost like there's a witness."

"You're right," Hugh said.

". . . And if he says no, you still don't know."

"So don't bother."

"But a real good Christian should try to talk him out of it."

Hugh grinned.

"Know any?" he asked. Then he added, "And if he doesn't say one way or the other, the real good Christian just won't know what to do, will he?"

"Guess not," Brazeau said, taking a drink.

"Then if it were me, I wouldn't say," Hugh observed. "Pass the bread, please."

"Here you are. I want to hear more about your journey now."

"Sometimes feels a lot like a dream," Hugh said.

It felt that way when he talked to Lew about it later, too, over more drinks. He returned to his cabin past midnight, near-overwhelmed with human society, but with a light feeling, too, that persisted in the morning despite a mild hangover. It took him a time to realize that he was happier than he had been in a long while. All this time till they departed. . . . He was going to be hard put, he decided, finding ways to spend it. He walked outside to visit a few acquaintances. . . .

Amazing how quickly the time had passed, he reflected, as he loaded his gear into the big flatboat. Just the opposite of when he was crawling and the minutes seemed sometimes like hours.

It was a damp, foggy morning, foliage red and gold within it and stirred by a small wind. A half-dozen of them would be heading upriver on this trading expedition—rowing most of the way, unless some unseasonable winds permitted use of the sail. The trip was prompted by Brazeau's desire to be sure that the Rees had indeed departed and to learn what the Mandans' feelings were over the raids on the Rees—much more than from a sudden desire to trade this late in the season. Hugh appreciated his curiosity and approved of the venture. He touched his new rifle, there amid his other gear, vowing to see the party well-fed.

Later that day, as they rowed the mackinaw upstream, the cold wind blew against them. The fogs blew off the river but the sky remained overcast. Flotillas of bright leaves raced past them to the south. Geese passed, honking. Hugh watched the sandbars, the bluffs, the trails along both banks, noting the movements of game. He talked about the Rees with Brazeau's man Langevin, who was in charge of the expedition. They practiced the tongue together much of the afternoon.

Well before sundown they put ashore, and while the men made camp Hugh hunted with his new flintlock. He fired a single round within the first fifteen minutes he was out, bringing down an antelope. It was turning above a fire before night came on.

That night, warm in his buffalo robe, he dreamed himself back to the plains. This time he crawled in pursuit of a bear. But it stayed ahead of him, vanishing into the distance and the dawn. Fingers scrabbling in the earth, he awoke, feeling cheated. From somewhere, he heard a coyote howl.

Funny feeling, later in the day, being on a boat again for a long period of time. Listening to the splashing of the oars, feeling that steady rocking. Dampness in the air. . . . Cold here, with all the signs and smells of autumn, yet somehow reminiscent of certain Caribbean mornings. . . . This near to shore there would be a steady buzzing of insects from the jungle, the shriek of a parrot. . . . Suddenly he was in a tropical inn celebrating a successful raid. Lafitte was calling for another roast pig and more grog. As he raised his arm, Hugh noted the streak of dried blood on his shirtsleeve.

He laughed, causing Langevin to look his way.

"What are you laughing at, *mon ami?*" the other inquired.

"The absence of parrots," Hugh said.

A few snowflakes swirled by that afternoon. The river remained slate-gray, and the fall made no mark upon it. After perhaps an hour, however, the air grew white. Soon brown leaves and bare branches bore pale accent and outline. Hugh held out his hand, watched flakes accumulate on its back, licked them off. It felt like something a shaman might do, or one of those *obeah* men from the Islands, if they'd ever had any snow to taste. It was as if he'd taken power over the season, as the bear had once taken him. He stretched and yawned and the wind no longer seemed cold. Then he laughed.

"What now, *mon ami?* The parrots?"

"The flavor of winter," he said.

And he thought again of Pennsylvania winters as he hunted through the afternoon's blizzard. Raising his rifle to take aim at the buck where it stood beneath a cottonwood tree, he hesitated. For a moment, it was an old Ree woman that he saw, gray, head held low. He pulled the trigger and the scene was brightened.

That night, dreaming again, he tracked the bear into a cave and followed it deep within the earth, where all of life was held within the cave walls like a vast mural. He followed it past the giant lizards and back into the place before flowers and the insect-people, watching all of life shrink and vanish into the sea. Then he hunted and the bear wailed and they embraced each other without animosity. . . .

They rowed past sandbars, beaver slides, high bluffs. Hugh saw small bands of buffalo on occasion. Deer were plentiful enough, and there was sometimes an elk.

They passed the Teton River and the Cheyenne. Looking to his left, Hugh could trace his route in reverse. There was a place where he had speared two fish. . . . He had been stumping along on the crutch. It was back before he'd met the Indians. The pain had been worse along through here, though his hopes had risen. . . .

It was a peculiar feeling, traveling back in time this way. The oars creaked and the cold winds blew, and he was glad that he had not met the bear a few weeks later in the year. He watched a small band of antelopes drink from the river. . . . A low rumble of thunder reached him from out of the west.

The days, like the weather, were smeared in their uniformity into a gray expanse of damp cold filled with the sounds of wind and the creaking of oars. The Moreau River came almost as a surprise. Yes, he was passing near to the beginning of things. The place of the bear was inland to the left, the place of the Rees farther ahead.

A snowfall later they passed the mouth of the Grand. A few miles after that, they came to the place of the deserted Ree villages. The charred dwellings stood stark against the whiteness. A few dogs wandered the ruin. There were no people anywhere in sight. He watched until it was gone about the bend.

"Wonder where the survivors got off to?" Langevin asked.

"Crossed the river," Hugh replied. "Headed off west. Fixin' to throw in with the Pawnees, I'd reckon, them bein' kin and all."

And he saw the old woman again, shuffling by him. He'd felt small pity for her painful gait, not even being able to rise and shuffle himself. Yet, it was as if he'd seen her life and that of her entire people gasping past him into the west, knowing that the end was near, and he would not touch those final hours all would like to have for the settling of their affairs.

The snow alternated with rain during the next several days, leaving the land muddy under barren trees. Mornings, it sparkled with frost. Later, it seemed to steam under November's skies, and only dark birds remained to pass the winter here. The grasses had all turned brown. The winds were always with them now, here in the land of the Upper Missouri. Soon they came to the mouth of the Cannonball and passed it.

Snows came and went, and after they'd passed the Heart River another small accumulation occurred. Old Charbonneau, along with his Shoshone wife Sahcahgagweah, who had accompanied Lewis and Clark in 1805, had them put him ashore the day before they were to reach the

Mandan village, saying he wanted to walk the final distance. This troubled Hugh, who tended to trust old-timers' instincts, and, now he was becoming an old-timer himself, he noted that he felt unnaturally wary.

The next day, though, Hugh requested that they put him ashore a few miles below the village, permitting him to hunt his way northward and hopefully arrive with a gift of meat. Langevin agreed, and Hugh headed off among the trees. Working his way northward, he heard the sound of a distant warcry, followed by musket fire. It came from the direction of the river. Even though he and the others had speculated about the Mandans' attitude toward the traders following the recent campaign, the thing that came to mind was a Ree ambush. Not Mandan. Certainly not Sioux. He guessed that a band of warriors had disagreed with the recent retreat into the west, had stayed behind for—something like this. The screams continued. There was another shot.

He turned, cursing, and began to backtrack. Obviously, his friends in the boat were under attack. If the attacking band were small enough that his killing a few might complete a rout. . . . He hurried.

As soon as he reached the shore he slowed and worked his way through a thicket. Shortly, he came in sight of over a dozen Ree warriors. They were still laughing and calling as they looted the mackinaw, transferring the goods to their own boats.

Hugh lowered his rifle and backed away slowly. His companions were nowhere in sight, and several of the Ree bore fresh scalps. It was already too late to help anyone but himself.

As soon as he'd removed himself from the thicket he headed north, keeping to cover as he went. He wondered at the Mandans' relationship with the Rees he had just seen—if there was one. It was possible, he supposed, that the Rees could have been en route downriver when they spotted his party. Best not to assume anything, however.

A couple of miles later he heard women's voices and he dropped to his belly and crawled forward. They were working in a garden outside a village of dirt lodges. The language they were speaking was Ree. There were Ree warriors outside the lodges. Hugh studied the disposition of the village. Then, as carefully as he had come, he withdrew.

Working his way slowly, he passed about the village. Never having visited the Mandans, he speculated wildly for a moment that the Ree had wiped them out and moved into their village. If this were the case, he would simply keep going, on his course up to the Yellowstone. But there were no signs of such a takeover, and they were definitely Ree lodges he had just skirted.

He moved more quickly once the village was behind him. He located several trails in regular use by moccasinned feet and unshod hoofs. He stayed to the woods.

After traveling for perhaps twenty minutes he came into sight of another village. He spent twice as long studying it, moving nearer, spying on its inhabitants, listening for people to speak to be certain their language was not Ree. Satisfied, finally, that this was indeed the Mandan village he rose and entered slowly, hands empty and in plain sight.

An older man emerged from a lodge and approached him. Hugh greeted him in both English and Ree. The man thought a moment and decided that Ree would be easier.

His name was Dreams of Two Antelopes, he told Hugh, and yes, he agreed that the Ree were sons of bitches. (Hugh had lapsed into English here, for want of a good Ree equivalent.) His people had let them settle nearby when the other Ree had departed, in return for a promise to keep the peace with the whites. Hugh's friends were not the first they had slain since then, however.

Dreams of Two Antelopes took him into the lodge and offered him food and drink, which Hugh accepted. Hugh gave more details on the ambush, and asked about Charbonneau. Dreams of Two Antelopes told him that the man had arrived safely earlier and was being entertained in a nearby lodge. He would take Hugh to see him when he had finished eating.

Later when Charbonneau had heard the story of the slaughter, Dreams of Two Antelopes mentioned nearby Tilson's Fort, belonging to the Columbia Fur Company. He offered to take them to it if they wished to confer with other white men.

"How many folks over there?" Hugh asked.

"Four."

"How long's it been there?"

"They built it in the autumn," Dreams of Two Antelopes told him. "There were more of them then."

"What happened to the others?"

"The Ree killed them. The Ree are the reason they built the place."

"Think they might stake me to a few supplies?" Hugh asked.

"Probably so. They must have more than they need, now some of them are dead."

"I guess we'd better go and visit."

Charbonneau nodded. "I should get to know them if I'm planning on spending the winter.

"Why would you want to do that?" Hugh asked. "I'm planning on moving out myself as soon as I pick up the supplies. The more distance between me and the Rees the better."

"Probably be more dangerous for me going back than staying," Charbonneau said. "I can blend right in here. If they do hear about a white man in camp they'll think it was you. We'll let it be known you headed on out, too. I can wait till spring to head on back to Kiowa."

"All right," Hugh said. "My business can wait for another day. I'll get to leave that much sooner."

"What business?" Charbonneau asked.

"I figure they owe me four heads of hair, for the folks I was with. I'll settle up later."

Dreams of Two Antelopes said, "The older men—the ones who made the promises when we told them they could settle here—they are not without honor. But it is hard for them always to control the younger warriors. It is the same way among our people, and I have heard it is sometimes that way with whites, too."

Hugh nodded.

"... And a son of a bitch is a son of a bitch, no matter what his tribe or race. He's just got an extra measure of human cussedness. Let's go see those folks at the fort."

Four hours later, under a moonless sky, Dreams of Two Antelopes and a younger brave ferried Hugh across the Missouri to its west bank. Between the Columbia Fur Company and the Mandans, Hugh was completely outfitted again, with fresh blankets, ammunition, tea, salt, pemmican. All of these in a backpack, he commenced hiking northward as soon as the Mandans struck out again for the eastern shore.

He made his way along the litter of the bank, climbing to higher ground the first chance he had. It was good to be back on the trail and upright again, despite the cold wind, despite those frosty flakes that had just now blown against his face. And the river was an old friend.

He trudged on steadily, through the higher land among the bluffs now. The temperature continued to drop, and he knew that he would be moving all night—for purposes of keeping warm as well as putting distance between himself and the Rees. It was about three hundred miles, he judged, to Henry's post, where the Yellowstone flowed into the Missouri.

By morning, he figured he had traveled ten or twelve miles. The sky was the color of slate, and night's cold wind remained. He ate pemmican and looked about for a place to camp. He decided on a hollow between the roots of a tree, wrapped himself in his blanket and reclined there, his hand upon his rifle. His eyes were shaded from the sun. He did not linger long over thoughts of the day and the night.

He woke late in the afternoon, drank from the river, and decided against wasting a shot on a squirrel. Pemmican would do until larger game came his way. He commenced the northward trek again.

He doubted there were Rees in the vicinity, though it was possible, and he reflected on the other Indians he might encounter on his way to Fort Henry. The Blackfeet were the most dangerous by far. The Assiniboins could be nasty, as might the Minatarees. But they could be dealt with, whereas the Blackfeet had that extra measure of cussedness which made people dangerous.

This day and night seemed colder than the previous. It was sure to be a bleak, snow-filled winter when he arrived a few weeks hence, he reflected. He was pleased that the cold was not affecting his former injuries. He'd been fearing his hip and leg would ache when the winter came on. But the coldest thing about him was his nose, and it always got that way, winters. He watched the stars through steaming breath, resolving to take to cover at sound of voice or hoofbeat.

But none occurred. The days followed each other with a monotonous similarity and he continued his steady, ground-eating pace, making ten or twelve miles' progress between sleeps. The first time he fired his rifle, to bring down a deer, he wondered what attention it might draw. He butchered it quickly, carrying off as much as he could, not halting until several miles later to build a fire and dine. But the fire attracted no unwelcome visitors either. He removed all traces of it and of himself when he had done and continued on quickly, keeping the song that rose to his lips internal.

Each night seemed just a little colder, each successive day held just a little less heat than the previous. Snow squalls came and went. More and more of the snow remained after each of these. So far, there was not enough of it to slow a hiker.

It took him a little over two weeks to come into sight of the confluence of the Yellowstone and the Missouri. Staring into the distance, he could see the palisades of Henry's post on the point between the two rivers.

He sighed a great sigh and started for it immediately. It was difficult to believe he was finally so close. Soon. . . . Just a matter now of getting over to the north shore.

Standing on the bank of the Yellowstone, he tried to estimate how far upriver he would have to begin, paddling a log raft, to make it across before getting swept into the Missouri. Better to be conservative, he decided, as he began hiking.

By the time he'd finished lashing the raft together it was too dark to use it. He ate a cold meal and slept in a gully. The morning was sunny but frigid, and he was half-soaked before he'd completed the crossing. Still, his estimate had been correct. He made his landing perhaps a hundred yards west of the fort.

He unloaded his gear, then advanced upon the stockade. Something was wrong.

The gates stood open. There were no sounds from within. Holding his rifle at hip level, he entered. There were no signs of violence, but Major Henry and the others were gone. It would seem a permanent move, too, since they had taken everything worth looting with them. A few minutes later he came upon the message. It was written on a board and nailed to the door of the largest cabin: *Gone up the Yellowstone. The new fort will be past the fork in the Little Bighorn.*

When he had done with a few oaths he left the fort and began walking, making ten miles before sundown. Day after day, he maintained this pace. Three weeks later he spent Christmas Eve in a gully beneath a hastily assembled lean-to, eating rabbit stew and wondering how much farther it might be to the new Fort Henry. The snow fell heavy and fast, seeming to deepen from moment to moment about his campsite. The wind screamed like some beast in pain. At least, he was out of the Blackfeet's country now. He wondered whether they might have had anything to do with the move. More likely, the trapping was better down this way, he decided. Though he must be nearing Crow country, and they were a lot easier folks to get along with than the Blackfeet. He cleaned out his cup, melted snow in it and drank it. He took a sip of whiskey from the small medicinal flask he carried, and wondered how Major Henry and the men were spending their Christmas. Had they a fine meal underway? Was Jamie singing a carol? Jamie. . . . How much farther to the new fort, where they might even now be singing of love and goodwill? He felt a pang in his breast. What if he'd missed it? He'd come a long way. Could he possibly have taken a wrong turning, be heading away from the fort now?

For a moment he was certain that he had, and black despair washed over him. Immediately, observations to the contrary occurred. He had seen no evidence of local trapping activity, nor trail signs indicating the presence of whites. No, he had not yet traveled far enough, though he was certain that he had already come farther from the old Fort Henry than he had from Kiowa up to Henry in the first place. Not that it mattered. Not now. He yawned and closed his eyes. Time was not all that important outside of cities.

The next day he made snowshoes and trudged on. There were three bad blizzards that week and perhaps a half-dozen rabbits—and one beaver taken more by accident than by stealth. The following week he spent two days in a cave, staring at a wall of rippling whiteness. New Year's Day had come and gone. It had caused him to think again of the major's crew, feasting, singing, Jamie among them. Had his name been spoken then, he wondered?

Three days later he webbed his way through a wood, having crossed three frozen tributaries of the Yellowstone. The wind howled like some forlorn spirit, and the snow swirled faster and more heavily as he advanced. He felt what seemed a change in the pressure, not unlike the night of his crawl before the storm broke on the plain. Through the snow every shadow seemed part of several other things in its shifting; trees emerged suddenly, as if gone rootless and roving in this half-world, so like the dreamworld of the sleep of the plains when he had found his way into the valley.

It stood before him. The great tree trunk the sourceless light had limned out of shadows was suddenly before him, near enough to reach out and touch. Only, its slow movements were not respondent to the direction of the wind. It raised its snout high and squinted myopically through the rushing flakes. Hugh stood stock-still, stomach tightening painfully. It was not a grizzly, unless it was a very young one. He could not tell its true color, for it was covered with driven snow. Probably, snow masked his own beard right now. It swayed, paws testing the air. It was slightly taller than him, and this one's breath did not smell like his grizzly's. All that he smelled now was wet fur.

His rifle was cold in his hand. He carried it loaded, ready for any chance encounter with game. He knew that he could raise it and fire a shot into the bear, placing it any-where. Of course, if it were not instantly fatal he would be face to face with an injured and very angry bear. So he stood and stared, remembering the last time.

"I know you, bear," he said, "and maybe we owe each other and maybe we don't. I'm for saying good-bye and going our ways. How about you?"

Eyes squinted, the bear twitched its nose several times, then dropped to the ground, turning to its left as it de-scended. It lumbered off then and Hugh stood for some time regarding its absence. "Well," he sighed finally. "Well." Then he turned to his left and made his way through a stand of trees. That night he dreamed of the bear in its whiteness, departing.

Three days later he stood upon a small rise at evening, regarding the stockade that stood at the confluence of the Little Bighorn and the Bighorn. He watched the smoke rise above it, sniffed its fragrance. To have found the place at last. . . . His palms were suddenly sweating despite the cold.

He made his way forward, mechanically, mind empty now. Something deeper than thought would control, once he was inside. A pale owl swooped low before him. Snow flurries swirled in a small wind out of the northeast.

When he came to the gate he kicked it and hammered upon it with the butt of his rifle. Over a minute passed before a voice called out, "Who's there?"

"Hugh Glass," he replied, "and it's damned cold out here."

"Hugh Glass," the voice repeated, after a long pause.

"That's right, Martin. It's been a long hunt."

"Heard you were dead, Hugh. Killed by a bear."

"It ain't as if the bear didn't try, Martin. Who told you about it?"

"Jamie, and Le Bon. Hell, I seen you myself, layin' there, near the end."

"I imagine you did, along with a lot of others. Now, you going to let me in? Or you think I'm a haunt?"

There followed another silence. Then, "No, if you was a haunt, you wouldn't need anyone to open the gate for you. You'd just walk on through—wouldn't you?"

"That's right. Now open the damn hatch."

A minute later the gate swung inward and Hugh entered. Martin, a short, wiry trapper with a smoke-shot beard, hesitated only a moment before clasping his hand.

"Sure enough," he commented. "You're real."

Hugh nodded and looked away from him, for he saw Major Henry and two others approaching from the blockhouse. Martin swung the gate shut and secured it.

"Damn it, Hugh! You're alive!" the Major said, coming up and taking his hand and clasping his shoulder. "What happened? We thought you were feeding worms. How'd you get here?"

"Crawled to Kiowa."

"Crawled?"

"I was kinda broken up. Was walking by the time I got there, though. Took a boat up to the Mandan village. There's still some Rees about there, by the way. Walked to your old post. Followed the river to this one."

"I think you've got quite a story to tell, and we want to feed you and hear it," Major Henry said. "Let's go inside and get warm and get you settled and do that."

"All right," Hugh said. "By the way, is Jamie here?"

"No, he's been away some time now. We'd a message he fell ill and the Crow took him in. That's upriver of here a good piece."

Hugh groaned. "What about Le Bon?" he asked.

"He up and left sometime back. Said he was thinking of joining the Army."

Hugh lowered the butt of his rifle to the ground and leaned on the weapon.

"What's the matter with Jamie?" he said.

"Feverish and weak and croupy is all the Crow told us. Could be the typhus."

"Could," Hugh agreed. "Guess I will be staying for dinner."

"Come on. Let's get you into a sleeping place where you can leave your gear. Get you settled and warmed up and a glass of firewater inside you."

"Could use a noggin of grog," Hugh said. "Yes. Let's go inside."

Later, over a rabbit stew heavy on vegetables, Major Henry observed, "Good thing you're back, Hugh. I can see us eating a lot better. Think you might hunt us up a nice fat buck tomorrow?"

"Like to," Hugh said. "But I really do want to find Jamie first. How about giving me directions to that Crow village?"

Major Henry leaned back in his chair and stared into the fire for several moments.

"Exactly what is it you've a mind to do when you find the boy?" he asked.

"With all respect, that'll be between him and me."

"I see. Well, I don't know that I care to tell you exactly where the place is."

Hugh shrugged.

"I'd be a pretty poor tracker if I couldn't find it on my own."

"True," Major Henry said, nodding. "So I think I'll let you do that. That way, if anything happens to Jamie I won't feel I had a hand in it."

"Fair enough," Hugh told him, taking a drink of his whiskey. "I'll be leaving in the morning."

"Why not stay a little longer, Hugh? Get rested some."

Hugh shook his head.

"Hate to have him die on me," he aid. "Hate to miss him by just a little after all this wait. Hate to do that."

"He was doing hunting for us, you know," Major Henry said. "He was pretty good at it. You taught him well, Hugh."

"Glad he learned something from me," Hugh said.

"When he and Le Bon were keeping deathwatch for you, they thought there were signs of Ree in the area. Fact, they were pretty sure about it. That's what scared them off right before the end—so to speak."

"Do tell. Didn't see any myself—nor any sign of 'em— after I came around. Not while I was crawling neither."

"I'm just saying that old thing about there being two sides to every story, Hugh."

Hugh sighed.

"Guess you're right," he said. "Maybe it's even good you're right. I suppose the Crow are to the south."

"I suppose so."

"I might backtrack a little to the Rosebud and work my way down. They must be near the water."

"Guess they would."

Hugh belched lightly.

"Well, thankee for the meal. Guess I'll be turning in since I want to leave early. Probably won't see you then so I'll say my good-bye now."

"You'll stop here—later?"

"Hard to say." Hugh rose. " 'Night, Major."

" 'Night, Hugh."

Hugh headed back to his quarters and slept a long dreamless while.

W alking. He webbed his way through the predawn light, along the western bank of the Rosebud. Ill. He thought of it now. Not by choice. It was just that he could think of nothing else. Ill. Jamie lying there, God knows how sick. Just like that kid. Getting sick at the most inopportune time. Probably his own fault, too. Probably got wet feet and didn't take the time to dry them. Probably not eating right, or drinking too much. Damn fool kid. It was almost as if he'd done it out of spite. He'd wanted a bright, alert, healthy, sassy, don't-give-a-damn Jamie for their confrontation. Now this—

Hugh cursed. Just like Jamie to make things difficult again.

He trekked steadily southward, coming upon occasional signs of human passage. Good, he was headed in the right direction. Perhaps tomorrow, or the next day—

Ill. He wondered just how serious it was. He flinched at the thought of the awful irony of arriving to discover that the lad had passed on, to be cheated so by death itself.

Hugh began to curse in time with his walking—a word for each step—to see how far he could travel before exhausting his vocabulary of profanity. After a goodly distance he had used up all his words, and he started in again. Again. . . . To his startlement, he realized some time later, the litany had changed. He found himself in the midst of unconscious prayer.

". . . And don't take him yet, Lord, please. Not after all I been through on his account. I want to talk to him. I got a right to talk to him, if anybody does. It just wouldn't be fair—"

Then he cursed again and grew still.

He slogged along in silence after that, breath pluming before him, crystals in his beard. A rabbit broke from cover and cut across his path. He let it go. No need. Not yet.

It lightened only gradually as the world worked its way into day. A cold wind pursued him. There was a prestorm feeling to the air, and he hurried to cover as much distance as he could.

The snow began perhaps an hour later, a few small flurries at first, quickly changing to a heavier fall. The wind, fortunately, still pushed at him from the rear, and the flakes rushed by him. Trees were plastered and the world grew white as bone.

Ill? It could well be that he was trekking into the south to view a corpse, pay his respects, say good-bye, he reflected again. He saw Jamie then on the dappled mare, riding over the plain, yellow hair blowing in the wind, faster, faster, into a sudden evening where owls flew.

"Jamie!" he called, but the boy did not hear him as he vanished into the twilight. Hugh gnashed his teeth and was alone in a white world.

It grew icy that afternoon, and he was jolted several

times from dreamlike reveries where Jamie was his ship-board mate through blood, gunfire, and looting, swimming beside him in the cold, dark waters of Galveston Bay, partly skinned by the squaws, tied to a pole, burning, screaming for him to come and kill him, as he fell and rose from the ice, fell again, and finally began crawling—snowshoes long lost—crawling through the long grasses, lying on his back, mouth open, as the storm raged above him, mounting to the pass of the divide, watching the buffalo go by, and the Rees, the old, tottering squaw who the slightest push might take from her path to darkness, and hearing Lafitte's voice say, "Deal with him," and he raised his pistol, and it was Jamie who stood before him, and he began to scream for him to kill him. . . .

Hugh woke with a start, teeth chattering, there in the lee of rock and evergreen where he had gotten himself somehow, wrapped in his blanket, against a profound darkness through which the whiteness fell. And he brushed the snow from his face and beard, rolled onto his other side, and slept.

When he woke again he was buried. He did not move but thought of the grave beside which he had awakened—when? And so this was it, the feeling of interment he had raged against that bright day. Let it be, he decided. 'Tis a warm and snug place. A man would be a fool to rise up out of it and go forth from its certainty into the cold unknown. He shared it with Jamie, perhaps that other mound where the rocks had lain. They lay now, again and forever, in the place where the hates and loves—how small a commerce with the cold!—could never come into the deep warm earth of which they were a part.

And yet there had been things to be said and done which had never been spoken or executed. He had refused the earth before because of them. And if the other mound were but a portent rather than an actuality—and he now knew this to be true, as the dreamtime retreated like a lumbering bear—he knew that he must rise, though now he desired the sleep. Stretching, he broke the crust, sat up, and brushed himself off. He rose, and, shaking out the blanket, folded it, rolled it, added it to his pack. He ate of his rations with several hardpacked snowballs, relieved himself, and went on.

The snow continued to swirl about him. He did not swear or pray as he went now, but let his mind drift over the entire expanse amid white trees, seeing graves he had long forgotten and the faces and forms of men and women long dead. He thought of the sea, which had claimed others he had known, and how it was like this whiteness full of swells and like the prairie through which he had crawled.

That afternoon the snow ceased, and before he retired that evening he had come upon fresh tracks leading into the south. Near, he decided. I must be getting near to their village.

His dreams were a jumble of the last days' thoughts and reveries, and he woke convinced that if he were not too late he was close to it. Jamie might be drawing his near to last breath at that very moment. In seconds, he was on his feet, about his simple ablutions, breaking camp. . . .

He ate as he walked, his mind far ahead. After a time, a few flakes began to fall. They came and went throughout the morning.

Sometime in the early afternoon as he mounted to the

top of a hill and rounded a bend in the trail he saw it, far off in the distance: a tiny wisp of smoke. Or thought he did. The winds whipped it apart so quickly that he could not be certain. And then the snow came again and there was no confirmation to be had in observation.

He slogged downhill, wondering. How far off had it been? Was it the village or some lone traveler's fire? Was this trail even taking him in the proper direction?

It seemed he might be going the right way, if there were another bend farther along. He continued walking as the snowfall grew more heavy. There was no real choice.

He worked his way to a lower level, then followed a rugged course. Its twisting disoriented him with respect to the spume he had seen. He could only continue along the trail and hope that they had followed a practice of locating their encampment near a watercourse.

As he passed through the curtains of white he thought again of death, of his own nearness to it this past month, of Jamie's now. The wind began to gust from his left—likely, the southeast. He drew his cap farther down and lowered his head.

It buffeted him, dashing crystals into his face. He raised a hand to shield against it. After a short time the ground began to rise again. The wind was worse as he mounted. He fell once, scrabbled about, rose again. Leaning, he continued on.

It was a gale by the time he reached the top, and later it followed him downhill. His face felt raw beneath its lashing. And it sang a terrible song as it passed. It was as if he could feel it reaching after Jamie, seeking to tear his spirit from his body. A killer wind. The kind of wind to whisk a man from his deathbed.

Even now, it was likely stealing the boy, a piece at a time, taking him away, out of his reach. Hugh increased his pace. Soon he was jogging, hunched against it, lurching occasionally. His foot struck a stone and he fell again. He rose and continued his rush. No time. The wind was eating time.

Faster, he decided, when he reached a level area. I can go faster here.

He increased his pace, running now as if he were pursued. And it seemed that way. The wind sang and tore at him, and at his back some dark presence followed, matching his pace. Was it the bear, which had seemed with him since that day, coming and going, in his life and his dreams, or some other dark thing?

He raced it, falling again—how many times, he lost count—scraping and bruising himself, picking himself up, running again. The wind sang in the treetops, blew their snows down upon him. Or was it Jamie's soul? So cold, so cold!

How far might it be? Just ahead, about the next bend? Or some great distance down the river? He pushed himself, the cold air burning its way into his lungs, the thing at his back seeming to gain slightly upon him so that now he heard its breathing within his own.

His heart hammered in his chest. A small cramp began in his left side.

As he picked himself up again, he growled back at whatever pursued.

"You can't have him," he said. "If the wind ain't already got him, he's not yours."

The air was alive in its whiteness. It was as if he ran under water, and then it was as if he ran through nothingness, a vast void. Even the constant howl became a special sort of silence now. A kind of numbness came over him, so that he no longer felt the cold.

And this was life, empty at the heart of its fullness, filled at the center of its vacuity, raging and still about him, accepting whatever he put into it—and he had crawled to this place across a lifetime, to stand here and give it or not give it what he would.

"Jamie!" he called in words that he could not hear. "Hang on! I'm coming!"

And he was running as he could not recall having run before, and there seemed to be no motion to it. It occurred to him then that he need never return to the world he had known, that he could stay in this still white place and know a kind of peace forever, that this was one of the spirit lands of which the Indians sometimes spoke.

Then he heard the words he had called, "Jamie . . . I'm coming!" and suddenly he ran on snow again, and it was cold through his moccasins and the wind cut at him again and there was a stand of trees before him and along this way cutting through them he glimpsed a winter tipi, saw smoke above it. Two men—Indians—were staring along the trail in his direction, watching, watching his approach.

He kept running, somehow maintaining his balance, through the trees and out again, extending his arms at the last, looking about for something to catch hold of, failing to find it, falling at last, there in the camp, before them. He lay gasping, covered with sweat, twitching from his exertions. Then he felt their hands, raising him gently.

They were speaking to him, though he could not make out the words at first. He realized without looking behind him that there was no longer anything at his back. Swaying, he blinked his eyes, rubbed them.

"Jamie," he said. "Is Jamie here? The boy?"

"Jamie. Yes, Jamie is here," answered one of the men, still holding him by the arm. He looked past Hugh, back down the trail. "Running, and there is blood on your face and your hand. Are you pursued by enemies?"

"Yes. No," he said, looking back. "Not now. Not any more. Take me to Jamie."

The other man moved to his other side, helping to support him. They led him among the tipis.

"Then—he is still—alive?" Hugh asked.

"Maybe," said the one to his left. "He still was, last I heard. He is your son?"

"No."

"A friend?"

"He was."

Near to the middle of the camp they slowed, halting before a tipi.

"In here?" Hugh asked.

"Yes. Though he may be asleep. Better not to wake him if he is."

"No, I won't. I'll wait."

"Come inside."

They took him into the tipi where a small central fire burned, its smoke rising to escape through the overhead opening. He stood blinking against the gloom for several seconds, his eyes still full of the white.

Then he saw the face, above the form covered with

robes. Thin and pale. . . . Almost, it seemed, the face of another. But then it overlay memory like a mask, and he saw. . . .

Sleeping now, but bearing the marks of illness even in rest, Jamie was with him by firelight once again. Hugh dropped his pack and his rifle near the doorway, advanced, and rounded the fire. He hunkered at the boy's side. So still, so still he lay. He extended his hand, held it before the boy's face until he felt a faint breath. Then he lowered himself into a seated position.

"I'll wait here with him."

"Would you like something to eat?"

"No thanks. Not now. I'll just sit here."

The men departed silently.

Hugh stared at Jamie's face. So changed, yet so similar.

"How'd you come down with that, Jamie?" he asked. "Some kind of fever from drinking bad water? Should of boiled it. Or not keeping yourself warm and dry? Damn you, Jamie, you always were careless about yourself. Tried to teach you better. You never listened, though. Think you'd value your own life, anyway."

He snorted then, leaned forward and lay his hand upon the covered chest. He nodded at the slow rise and fall, then lay the back of his hand against the boy's forehead.

"Cold. You're cold and clammy, Jamie. Like death," he said. "It's nothing to be practicing for, boy. Wish you wouldn't do that." He tucked the robe more closely about the sleeping form. "You get yourself warm again. Come back and join the living so we can talk."

Jamie made a small sound.

"What's that? What'd you say, lad?" Hugh asked.

Jamie moaned then, and his eyelids flickered but remained closed.

"Can you hear me, Jamie?" he asked. "It's me, old Hugh."

Jamie's brow twitched, his mouth tightened.

"Hugh," Hugh repeated. "I found you and I'm waiting here."

"Hugh?" Jamie whispered.

"That's right. I'm here with you."

Jamie opened his eyes. He blinked several times, then stared.

"I'm dead, ain't I?" he said.

"No," Hugh told him. "You're not dead."

"But you are, so I must be, too."

"I ain't dead, Jamie. I lived, after you and that other fellow left me."

"Oh damn, Hugh! I didn't know! I—"

Hugh shook his head and, leaning forward, placed a finger over Jamie's lips.

"Hush! Wouldn't do to get yourself all stirred up. It's all right. I'm all right. I'm going to take care of you now."

"Hugh, it must have been—"

"Wasn't all that bad. You rest. Go back to sleep now. You're going to be all right, too."

The boy nodded, closed his eyes, and sighed. Hugh did the same.

NINETEEN

COLTER/GLASS

St. Louis, 1812

The years had flowed along and Colter, easing himself into the slow current of life on a midwest farm, had drifted with them. The walk, run, crawl was behind him, way behind him. He found himself a Missouri bride, a Sally in a land of Sallys, settled on a piece of black riverbottom dirt, farmed, called himself lucky to be alive. From his cabin porch in Sullens Spring, a short distance above the junction of the Little Boeuf and the Big Boeuf on the south bank of the Missouri, he could watch the keelboats come and go. He wished them luck, no regrets. The years of drafty tipi life among the Crows had taken its toll. Colter wanted, finally, a modicum of comfort, got it with a wife, a simple backwater on a bluff farm; sired a son, Hiram. Old Daniel Boone, another great wayfarer, was a neighbor upriver, the two smoked and talked of an evening, both detested lies, liars, especially when their own names were called into the telling of a tall tale.

John Colter sat at the very back of Dutchman's Bar. Hunkered down, his woolen coat buttoned up, as if, at any moment, he intended to leave, he looked pretty much like the others, except that his clothes were made of cloth hand-sewn by his wife while the loud men gathered in the bar wore leathers and fringes, jerkins and dusters, richly beaded and quilled, long greased from wear around the campfire. These were not townies, they were mountain men, the last of the breed.

It was the second time in the past four years that he had made the trip to St. Louis, each time to try and secure money for the farm and his family. He did not like having to raise money and he liked being in a tavern less. For one thing he seldom drank, for another, ever since Meriwether Lewis had been murdered in a tavern along the Natchez Trace, he had reason not to like such places. To make matters worse, Lewis had gone to his grave penniless, still owing Colter the balance on their old exploratory account. Back wages on the expedition that was now world famous came to $377.60 and Colter knew he would never see it.

It was early spring, the ebullient time when rivermen and mountain men would meet and talk of things that only they knew of—stash and cache, purse and plew. The good old days of beaver plunder were gone, but the tales of these men lived on. Many of them were still fairly young, but they had ruffianed off their best years and were now preparing for their worst. They looked, most of them, old and bedraggled. Lives of constant danger had steeled their nerves, silvered their hair, creased their faces. Many had but one arm, one leg, some only a single eye. A few had lost their scalps, the forehead and facial skin loose, jowly, held up by the headband of a felt hat. They shared, these roughened men, a common thing they called "mountain misery." Now, beyond the sting of arrowpoint and bullet, the burn of summer snow and winter rain, they sat in tavern warmth, shoulder to shoulder, a funny lot of feathered, furred, creased, crushed, wrinkled, beaten, black and red and blue-faced old rascals who liked nothing better than to talk tall. . . .

Colter had no use for ale or whiskey, but the drinks came on; he drank, was soon drunk. He'd come to town for one reason: to square a promissory note for $45.00, in favor of William Clark. Sick of late, he saw himself, fleetingly, in the tavern glass, and though it was fogged with ropes of smoke from the old men's briars, Colter saw his image all too well. Though younger, he looked older than the rest, and so, took his seat in a dim and darkened corner. Momentarily free of the difficulties of burning out stumps, growing corn and tending stock, he should've felt easy in his bones. But he didn't. He drank the foamy brew, mug after mug, to counter his uneasiness. The shock at seeing his early-old face knocked him off balance.

How old was he, really?

He didn't rightly know.

He guessed: not past forty.

And yet his eyes, the so-called whites of them, were sour yellow; dull, dispirited, nearly lifeless.

Something was in him that wouldn't let go. He wondered if it was the wilderness.

His skin was sallow, pale. Itched as if fire-ants were living in it. Those tiny Mandan devils? He'd been warned not to put his hand into their hole, but that's just what he'd gone and done. His whole life had been lived that way, in defiance of danger.

Above the hubbub, he heard a name spoken: Colter, someone said. His head jerked up and he saw a man making elaborate hand gestures. He knew this, had seen it before. The man was telling a story about the legendary John Colter.

". . . Why, the man's got a collection of scalps that number no less than a hunderd-an-one!"

Colter felt the old fever. His head reeled from the strong ale; he felt suddenly chilled. Scratching his hands, he slunk back into shadow.

". . . heard tell his buffler-mocs was blood-full and still he ran on, a-gurgling and a-bubbling!"

Colter flipped up his eight-inch drover's collar, sunk down into the safety of the dark.

". . . naked as a jaybird, he outrun them savages, all they ever saw was his bouncing butt!"

Sinking ever deeper into the recesses of the coat, Colter's face became birdlike, the mask of a hawk, the sharp nose protruding, the rest of the face in shadow, with the tall collar rising up in back like a hawk's hood.

". . . thems what knows, and I am one, says he left his redskin victims sitting up, like they was sipping tea, 'twas the mark of the man, you know, his signature, kind of like."

Colter had slipped out of sight, but the headless coat had a hand that held a mug of ale.

". . . five hundred mile he run 'em thet day and his feet, when he made it to the fort, looked like buffler hoof!"

Colter shut his eyes to the noise, saw the bear rise up as it charged him, paw falling on his face, smashing his nose, tearing through the skin of his brow. Then its great forelimbs came about him. The last thing he remembered, as the blood ran into his eyes, was the awful breath of the thing, fetid of ripe flesh, overlaid with a sweetness of berries and honey that made him think of a perfumed corpse.

He opened his eyes to back-thumping and guffawing, the crash of ale mugs met in the fisted air. He peered out of his collar, saw an old man get to his feet.

"Fools!" the old man hollered, "every pisspot one of you. Yarn spinning's one thing, lying's another. Not one cuss among you has the right to speak up or down about John Colter because none of you polecats ever met the man."

He adjusted his wild, white hair, patting it down with his palm. Glared balefully at the mountain men, daring them to look him in the eye.

"I tell you, I find so much deceit and selfish foolery going on in this room, it's enough to make a man wish he was dead and buried. The old arrowhead in my shoulder hurts some, but no worse than your lies."

He scanned the lot of them, the fire rising in his craw.

"Whiskey I can't drink, bread and salt I don't care for, lies from the likes of you I can't abide. Where does that leave me? Think I'll go again amongst the Indians. At least the bragging they do is done in private."

His voice trailed off; he'd lost the resolve to say any more. Dropping a chewed-up beaver hat on his head, he turned upon his heel and headed out of the tavern.

Colter smiled weakly. He knew the man, or thought he did. Old Richardson, once a trapper, now a dirt farmer like himself. Trueblood he was, no blarney in him, just an Arikara arrowhead.

He, Colter, got up to leave, follow the old-timer out the door, but a stout barmaid appeared, handed him a grey-blue slate with his total scratched on it.

Squinting at the thing, unable to read the hieroglyphic of it, he beckoned her to give it to him, whereupon he took it and drawing forth his penknife, scratched his sign, J.C., with the ragged cross underneath the initials.

Then the young man who had been sitting across the table from him stood up. He quickly glanced at the mark on the slate, recognized it, took from his pocket a small, roundish, amber-glazed burl of wood, and presented it to Colter.

"Man from Stuart's Draft, Virginia gave this here medallion to my Pa," the young man said cheerfully. Then, seriously: "Matches yours, John Colter, sir."

"What's this palaver got to do with the tally on my slate?" the barmaid said crossly. "As if anybody cared who the likes of you was!"

Immediately the young man spanked a heavy round coin on top of her open palm; the coin jumped off, rang on the cobble floor. The barmaid, a hefty woman, shot down like a pike, snatched the coin. Then she took the slate and marched off, mumbling oaths about mountain men.

Colter smiled thinly.

"If you've a head on your shoulders," he said dryly, "you'll keep it where it belongs. My advice is to stay in St. Louis where you belong."

"I've a mind," Hugh Glass answered, "to see what's back of beyond. Head or no head, I got to see it for myself. Take my chances, sir, just like you."

Colter's eyes narrowed as he measured the boy into

the man he would soon become. His were not boasting words, they were fresh as a spring is fresh.

He nodded.

"By God," he whispered, "I believe you'll outcrawl the likes of me," and he stiffly got up from the table. Then, without looking back, he left the tavern and walked slowly out into the night.

The following year, John Colter died of jaundice and was buried on a knoll overlooking his farm.

Walking, of course, away from it all,
the run and the crawl.
Walking as we must
beyond talesend, the dark,
the light, and the grey, past
reefs of bleached buffalo bone,
the seasons, the years,
the opened graves and closed,
the burnt villages and blackened plain
where time the river flows,
we look for real endings, finding none,
and graves that come and go.

John Colter died leaving

> *2 beds, 4 chairs, one glass tumbler,*
> *1 dish and 5 puter plates,*
> *1 plow, 1 hoe, one Dutch oven,*
> *2 tie pans, 3 puter basins,*
> *1 coffey pot, 1 little spinning wheel,*
> *2 bottles, 4 tin cups,*
> *knives, forks and spoons,*
> *1 piggan, 1 pane of cotton cards,*
> *1 flat iron, 3 books,*
> *1 mare, 1 colt, one heffer,*
> *1 cow and calf.*

His estate, settled December 10, 1813,
was valued at $233.76-¾
after his debts had been paid,
and, in an unmarked grave on Tunnel Hill,

outside St. Louis was he laid, later forgotten,
and used as landfill,
becoming part of the track bed
of the Missouri Pacific Railway.

None knows where Old Hugh
came to rest, though Jamie Bridger'd
a Wyoming fort to bear his name.

Walking then away from it all
down endless caverns,
through citied futures,
one finds, as at the end of every trail,
a skull. Whose, is hardly important,
but that into the coming together place
where time crosses the world, it held
the act of continual passion,
granting meaning to the bright moment
of its execution, beneath sun, sky, stars,
where lives and futures fuse,
turning courses away from the greater darkness,
signing the earth with the long pressure of its gaze.

Walking, you see them painted now
in ancient halls of the Earth;
walking, you see them all painted,
deep, on the walls of the cave.